The Case of the Clerical Cadaver

The Case of the Clerical Cadaver

Being yet more

Chronicles of Brother Hermitage

By

Howard of Warwick

The Funny Book Company

Published by The Funny Book Company

Dalton House, 60 Windsor Ave, London SW19 2RR

www.funnybookcompany.com

Cover design by Double Dagger.

ISBN 978-1-913383-11-4

Howard of Warwick's Middle Ages crisis: History-ish.
The Domesday Book (No, Not That One.)
The Domesday Book (Still Not That One.)
The Magna Carta (Or Is It?)

Explore the whole sorry business and join the mailing list
at
Howardofwarwick.com

Another funny book from The Funny Book Company
Greedy *by Ainsworth Pennington*

The Case of the Clerical Cadaver

Caput I

Telling the Time Will be the Death of You

𝕿he monks were in turmoil. It was as much as Brother Egbert could do to stop them running howling into the night; apart, obviously, from the normal suspects who were taking such a close interest in the body that they had to be moved on quite firmly.

As the doors of the monastery were sealed there was no question of anyone actually getting out, but the sight of the man lying there like that? Well, it was enough to give even Egbert pause. And he hadn't paused at much in his long life.

He had been with old King Edward's forces in Scotland when they killed some total loon called Macbeth who kept going about daggers and spots before his eyes and how much trouble his wife was going to be in when he got home. He had seen some pretty revolting things up there. He'd then been forced to give his blessing and pardon for them on threat of some of the revolting things being done to him. But he'd never seen anything like this. He acknowledged that he was relatively new to this particular community but couldn't believe that this sort of thing was a regular occurrence.

A barked order from the abbot brought silence to the chaotic scene. As usual, the man had simply appeared in the midst of his flock without anyone having a chance to shout a warning.

'What is the meaning of this?' the great man demanded as he took in the scene.

The skeletal countenance of the abbot, rumoured to be as

old as the monastery itself, had its usual impact. Everyone found something else to look at and the normal suspects made themselves scarce.

Egbert stepped forward and bowed his head. 'A great cry was heard, father,' he explained. 'Many of the brothers were roused from their sleep and came to find out what was happening.'

The abbot looked horrified at this news. 'Sleep?' his outrage was clear.

'I mean study and prayer, father,' Egbert corrected himself.

The assembled brothers mumbled about what a shame it was that their post-midnight study and prayer had been disturbed by this event. Several of them even yawned with disappointment.

The abbot cast his awful stare around his community. The community looked away.

'And what is that brother doing lounging there?' The abbot pointed a withering finger at the corpse in the middle of the small courtyard.

The cloister of this place was as common as any monastery. A simple square walkway, covered by a roof of stone held up by plain pillars circumnavigated a square courtyard of grass. As in a thousand monasteries, monks would wander their cloister in thought and discussion, or just to keep out of the rain. In this place there were stone seats built into the back wall, upon which the monks were not allowed to sit. From the cloister a monk could be in virtually any monastery in Christendom, such was the regularity of design.

Except, of course, this one had a dead body in its courtyard.

The strong moon, hanging in the sky and dropping its pale light onto the monastery could do nothing but make the scene even more gruesome.

'Erm,' Egbert was puzzled by the question. 'He's dead father.'

'Dead?'

'Well, yes.' Egbert knew that the abbot frequently missed the concerns of the ordinary man, but a corpse in your courtyard?

'He cannot be dead,' the Abbot said simply.

Egbert's overwhelming urge was to say that the abbot had better go and tell the body that. He knew better.

'We have no weaklings or disease in this place,' the abbot stated loudly as if his voice alone was enough to banish both. 'Why is he dead?'

Egbert frowned. He held an arm out towards the body. Surely he didn't have to explain this. 'He's been impaled on the sundial father,' he pointed out.

The Abbot took half a step forward and peered as if examining some piece of illumination presented for his inspection in the scriptorium. A rather poor piece by the look on his face.

'I see.' The abbot seemed to reluctantly accept that a monk with a large sundial sticking through him was entitled to be dead.

In fact, not only was the sundial passing through the deceased, but it was raised on a pedestal and it looked like a bit of that had gone in as well. The unfortunate man must have hit the device with some considerable speed and force.

Or been pushed.

The abbot glared at his monks once more. 'Back to your study,' he commanded, with a wave.

The monks departed gratefully, but with many a backward glance at the body. Most of them would rather spend the night with a dead monk that five minutes with their abbot.

'Well then?' The abbot turned his countenance on Egbert.

'Well then, what, father?'

'Move him.' The instruction was impatient. 'How are we going to read the sundial with a monk lying all over it?'

Egbert looked around and made sure that the last of the brothers had left the scene. The clatter of closing cell doors assured him they were alone.

'I think there may be more of a problem than telling the time,' he said significantly.

'Why?' the abbot snapped. 'It's not the cook, is it?' He sounded as if he suspected the cook. Just the sort of thing that idle waster would do, lounge about in the courtyard being dead when he should be working.

'No father,' Egbert explained wearily. 'It is not the cook. It is Father Ignatius.'

'Ignatius?' That had taken the abbot back. '*The* Father Ignatius?'

Egbert rolled his eyes, 'We only have the one,' he sighed. He knew the abbot was a greater leader of men and a devout and pious soul. He had that energy and internal confidence that just made people do as he directed. Egbert just wished the man wasn't quite so stupid.

He knew that he was a simple soul himself, he had no great understanding of the ideas of the world or the finer points of theology. Or any of the points, really. He had been a plain friar in service of the king's army. He went where he was told and did what was wanted. He never needed to apply much thought to anything.

In his quieter moments though, reflecting on his wide experiences of the world and those who seemed to be in charge, he sometimes wondered why leadership and stupidity seemed to be such frequent companions. And why people leapt to follow those who were plainly wrong. People who instructed them to do the impossible and then berated them for doing exactly what they'd been told, when they knew it was never going to work in the first place.

This abbot was a prime example. The man could turn from friendly confident to fire-breathing demon at the drop of a sandal. Most of the brothers kept their distance to avoid being caught in the back of the head by one of the violent mood swings. Egbert suspected a touch of madness lurked just under the abbot's surface, occasionally sticking its nose out to see if the world was ready for it yet. How the man had been put in charge of anything was a mystery.

Egbert had frequently been told he needed to address this problem with authority that he seemed to have.

'Just so,' the abbot confirmed, thoughtfully. 'Father Ignatius.' The disappointment at everyone and everything that habitually camped on his face was disturbed by a veil of worry. His eyes seemed to be moving about of their own accord and his regular frown had transformed to something deep enough to echo.

Egbert thought this might indicate that the abbot was thinking. He had no idea what the outcome of that was likely to be. Nothing good, he suspected. 'And I think he may have been put there by someone.'

'Put there? On the sundial? Why would anyone put a dead body on a sundial?'

Egbert now went so far as to wipe a hand over his face

and look to the sky.   'I suspect he was put there while he was still alive, and then he died.'

'Death by sundial?' the abbot made the connection.

'Indeed.'

'Who would do such a thing?'

That, thought Egbert, is a very good question. In fact, it is *the* very good question. Not that the abbot would realise that of course. 'I think we need to find that out, Father. Before it happens again.'

The abbot frowned even more. 'We haven't got another sundial,' he said, to which Egbert could not even manage a sigh.

'I mean before someone else is murdered.'

'Murder?' The abbot was shocked at the word.

'When someone makes someone else dead? It is the usual term. Unless you're just a very bad physick. But I doubt even the worst physick in the world would prescribe impaling on a sundial for anything.'

The abbot actually bit his lip. Egbert had never seen him so disturbed. He was disturbed in many ways but this time events were doing it to him. He looked at risk of losing control. That could only be very bad indeed.

'Father Ignatius. Murdered?'

'It would seem so.'

The abbot took a cautious step into the courtyard and approached the bizarre scene.

Father Ignatius was on his back, spread-eagled in mid-air, the spike of the sundial emerging from his front like the mast of some dread ship. The morbidly minded might still be able to tell the time by the position of the sun's shadow on the various bits of Ignatius's anatomy, after all, he wasn't using them anymore. half-past Terce was going to be a bit embarrassing.

Egbert joined the abbot at the side of the dear departed. Not that anyone would have conceived of the word "dear" in any description of Ignatius. This situation constituted the sunniest disposition the man had ever had.

The priest was the opposite of the abbot in many ways, or rather, he had been. He was frighteningly intelligent, being able to pierce either a complex text or the schemes of brothers intent on avoiding their duties. As a leader of men though, his personal qualities were such that people wouldn't have followed him out of a burning building. Even young novices were prepared to mutter about the man within his earshot. They wouldn't have even allowed such thoughts about the abbot into their heads. After all, the abbot was in their heads with them.

Ignatius's very particular role in the monastery made this situation complicated. Granted, an ordinary monk, done to death on the monastery time-piece would be trouble enough, but that might be put down to some personal conflict, or piece of brotherly revenge.

Ignatius though. The Sacerdos Arcanorum, priest of the mysteries, was separate from the rest of the place. His duties and rituals were known only to him. Egbert immediately suspected that it was the Sacerdos Arcanorum that had been murdered. It was just unfortunate for Ignatius that he happened to be in the job at the time.

Which in turn meant the murder was probably for a very specific reason. What that reason might be, Egbert had not a clue. He had no idea what the Sacerdos Arcanorum did. Nobody had. Or, perhaps the abbot? If anyone in this place would know, surely it would be its leader.

'The Sacerdos Arcanorum,' Egbert said, hopefully

prompting a revelation of some sort.

'Great Lord,' the abbot cried out.

That scared Egbert more than being in a sealed monastery where people were impaled on the furniture. 'What?' he shrieked.

The abbot's trembling finger pointed to Ignatius.

Egbert couldn't see any new surprises that hadn't been visible from a distance.

'Look where he's pointing, man.'

Pointing? Egbert moved so that he could see Ignatius's left hand. It did look like it was pointing, but that could just be the result of his recent experience with the sundial. Three fingers were clenched tightly, the remaining one sticking out like a sign. He moved again at looked at the priest's right hand. This was more normal. It was thrown wide open, which Egbert imagined would be the natural reaction to events.

He followed the line of the pointing finger. And drew a sharp breath.

It was too much of a coincidence. Surely a man speared on a sundial would not go to the trouble of pointing as his life departed. Much less would he point straight at the small, dirty and unused door set in the wall of the monastery; the door that was the subject of so much speculation.

Newcomers asked questions about what lay behind the door, but they were never answered. Nobody knew. The natural result of this was that the contents of the room behind the door were reliably and positively known to contain any one, or combination of the following;

The abbot's private collection of tapestries by Wat the Weaver. The ones that showed all the details of human anatomy, from the outside.

The body of the previous abbot.

The current abbot's wife and children.

The abbot's mother - an impossible prospect but apparently eternal life was a certainty for any who got through the door.

Great treasure.

Even greater treasure.

The relics of a saint.

A saint in person.

A huge supply of food and drink.

Virtually all the tableware from the last supper.

Joseph of Arimathea - having given up his own tomb.

King Arthur, several knights and a table of some sort.

A dragon, or at least a dragon's egg. Or a chicken, whichever came first.

Another door which led back to the first door again which was then slightly smaller. (This was the firm conviction of Brother Daly, but Brother Daly had a lot of very strange ideas.)

And, of course, the Holy Grail. The Holy Grail was hidden in virtually every hidey-hole in Christendom. If every Holy Grail that everyone absolutely positively knew the location of was gathered together in one spot there would be enough to give the five thousand a drink to wash down the loaves and fishes.

Perhaps now was the moment Egbert was going to find out. Surely the abbot carried the secret.

'The door, father?' Egbert asked. 'What does it mean?' He looked back at the pointing finger.

The abbot sighed heavily, some new weight pressing down on him. 'We must send word.'

'Send word? Who to?'

'The king.' The abbot said it simply but it sent a shock through Egbert.

'The king?' What on earth was going on that the king needed to be told of this?

The abbot faced Egbert and his gaze was terrible. That was normal, but this time it carried an added intensity. The man even laid a hand on Egbert's shoulder. It had all the substance of a light breeze from yesterday, but it was clear Egbert was being given a great confidence.

'Ignatius points at the king's door,' the abbot intoned.

Egbert checked the door again to see if it looked at all regal. It didn't. 'The king's door?' he said in amazement. 'That's the famous king's door?' He couldn't believe that this humble slab of wood was the actual king's door.

'It belongs to the king,' the abbot snapped, his old familiar persona returning quickly.

'And what's behind it?' Egbert couldn't help but ask.

The abbot looked very thoughtful - for the abbot - and was clearly considering whether to go further.

'Only the king and the Sacerdos Arcanorum know.'

Well, that was a disappointment after all this time.

He hesitated to make the next suggestion. Not for long though. 'Perhaps we should open it?'

The abbot found a whole new catalogue of facial expressions to express his opinion of the very idea.

'All right,' Egbert got the message very quickly. 'We don't open it.'

'Only the king and the Sacerdos Arcanorum may open it.'

It sounded like the king and the Sacerdos had a lot on their plate.

'Why would he be pointing at the door?' Egbert speculated. 'Especially when he's just been given the time in such a pointed manner.'

Speculation was something the abbot seldom tolerated or was capable of.

'Was he trying to tell us to take the responsibility from him? A sort of dying instruction as it were?'

The abbot looked rather blank.

'Or mayhap he was telling us to look there for some clue to his fate?'

No, the abbot was now as lost as a lamb in a butcher's garden.

Egbert took a breath. Back to basics then. 'So we send for the king who comes here to open the door and see what all the fuss is about?' he asked.

The abbot looked more comfortable now, 'Hardly,' he scoffed at Egbert's stupidity. 'The king will have people who deal with this sort of thing.'

So secret doors in monasteries which were pointed at by corpses on sundials was "this sort of thing" was it?

'Really?'

'Of course. King Harold will know the significance of this more than you or I.'

'Harold?' Egbert was taken aback.

'Yes,' the abbot growled. 'The king.'

Egbert couldn't think of a subtle way to deal with this. 'King Harold is dead,' he announced.

The abbot looked suitably shocked. 'When did this happen?' he demanded, obviously offended that no one had told him.

'Two years ago,' Egbert said with disbelief. He knew the abbot was a solitary individual in this solitary place but news did travel. You'd think he'd at least find out when kings died.

'So who's the king now?'

'Fellow called William, apparently,' Egbert explained. He thought about adding that William probably didn't even know he had a door, and when he found out he would likely just burn it to the ground, if the stories were true.

The abbot mused, 'Funny name for a king.'

'A Norman.'

'Is he?' The abbot shook his head in sympathy for the poor man.

'From Normandy,' Egbert explained.

'Aha.' The abbot clearly had not the first clue where Normandy was. 'Well, we shall send word to this William.'

'Must we?' Egbert enquired. 'King William won't even know he's got a door. And I have heard that he is a fearsome fellow, more likely to wreak havoc than resolve the mystery of a locked door.'

'Of course we must.' The abbot waved away the objection. 'It is a sacred duty. We dare not interfere, it is for the rightly crowned king alone to command.'

Egbert wondered if explaining that the rightly crowned king had become so by killing the previous incumbent. No. Not worth the effort.

'And how do we do send word?' Egbert asked. It was a good question. They were a closed community with outside contact limited to that which passed through the hatch in the main gate. It was rumoured that things could get through that hatch that were simply unbelievable, but there was never any proof.

What these brothers did not do was go traipsing around the country passing word.

'We shall send Brody,' the abbot announced.

Egbert caught his breath, 'Are you sure about that?'

Brody was their servant and go-between with the outside world but he was the most awful gossip. The man couldn't keep secrets that he didn't even know in the first place. If there was a sure-fire way of getting a piece of information in circulation it was to give it to Brody with strict instructions not to tell anyone.

The abbot cast a beady eye at Egbert, 'I have not been an abbot so long that I cannot cast the fear of God into such as Brody.'

Egbert could believe that.

'And the king will not come in person. He will have someone appointed to tasks like this.'

'The bishop?' Egbert suggested.

'The bishop,' the abbot coughed his scorn. 'I don't think we'll be letting the bishop near another dead body. Not after all that unpleasantness the last time.' The old man pondered the problem, 'Perhaps one of his trackers. One who seeks out information on his behalf.'

'A *vestigare?*' Egbert suggested, considering the Latin root.

'Someone who tracks, perhaps *investigator*,' the abbot mused. 'A King's Investigator,' he announced.

King's Investigator? Sounded like a perfectly stupid idea to Egbert, but he didn't like to say.

Caput II

King's Investigator

The King's Investigator was hiding under his bed.

'Hermitage,' Cwen called from her perch on the top of the straw mattress, 'you've got to come out sometime.'

Brother Hermitage poked his head out and peered cautiously at the young woman who looked down at him kindly.

'Have they gone?' Hermitage asked. He was a few years older than Cwen's teenage years but he lagged her by a country mile when it came to confidence in the face of adversity. Cwen could stare adversity straight in that pitiless face, probably just before she slapped it and sent it on its way.

Hermitage couldn't do adversity. He'd seen a lot of it but it always gave him the shakes. He would admit he was not a courageous man but then he wasn't supposed to be. He was a monk; a monk who would rather be on his own in a scriptorium fretting over some fine point of interpretation. Apart from the occasional parchment cut, the scriptorium was seldom adverse.

'Yes, they've gone,' Cwen assured him. 'And they weren't looking for you anyway. It was only some more of Wat's old customers asking if he'd done anything new recently.'

That took Hermitage's mind off his main concern. Being appointed King's Investigator still felt like it was just some huge mistake. King William hadn't known what he was doing. Hermitage had just been the wrong monk in the wrong place at the wrong time.

But still William kept sending him investigations to be

done. Him and that awful Le Pedvin, the only Norman Hermitage knew who made William look quite nice.

He had decided that when people came to call he would simply not be available. That way no one could ask him to investigate some hideous murder ever again. If it meant hiding under the bed whenever there was a knock on the door, so be it.

But people asking about Wat's disgraceful tapestries had to be dealt with. Well, it was more the case that Wat had to be dealt with. Hermitage did not want any temptations falling into Wat the weaver's ears that might persuade him to go back to making tapestries that were, well, rude. Hermitage knew that other people had much better words to describe the sort of tapestry Wat could make, but he was a monk and wouldn't use those words in any circumstances.

'Has Wat sent them on their way?' he asked, climbing out from under the bed.

'He has,' Cwen placated him. 'He wouldn't really go back to the old trade.'

'He might when the money runs out,' Hermitage observed, sagely.

'We'll all be dead before the money runs out,' Cwen said with confidence. 'Do you know how much he got paid for the last in the bath-house series?'

'No, I do not. And I do not want to know.' He brushed down his habit and ran a hand through his tonsure, flattening once more the tuft that refused to lie down. 'I don't know who carries the most sin. The man who made it, the man who paid, or the man who looks at it.'

'What makes you think they're all men?' Cwen asked, nonchalantly, reminding Hermitage of her own history in the production of revelatory tapestry.

Hermitage had no answer to that.

He left his room and headed for the upstairs chamber where Wat usually received guests and visitors. As ever, he was conscious that his comfortable surroundings and the food and drink that made his life so much more bearable than being in an actual monastery, all sprang from Wat's disgraceful trade. And as usual he didn't let that stop him berating Wat.

Neither did it seem to stop Wat berating Hermitage about the fact that they weren't making money any more. The new, decent and occasionally devout works were a lot less outrageous and a lot less popular.

He found Wat on his hands and knees in the large, open space of the upper floor of the workshop, chalk in his hand, lines and shading spreading in all directions. His mop of unkempt black hair flopped about as if he could use it to clean the boards.

'Are you still doing that?' Hermitage asked.

Wat looked up as Hermitage and Cwen stepped around the edge of the room.

'Of course,' Wat squinted at one chalk line, erased it with the palm of his hand and then drew it again. 'Be good money in this one.'

He stood now and took a step back to take in the large image he had been drawing. He was the oldest of them, but not by much. It always puzzled Hermitage how the weaver had managed to squeeze so much into his young years. Much of it questionable if not downright sinful.

'And you still think they'll pay?' Hermitage asked.

'They ordered it,' Wat said as if there could be no question.

The fact that Wat and Cwen were making a

commemorative tapestry of the death of Gilder of Shrewsbury brought that awful experience back to life.[1] Hermitage was not convinced that the moot of that town would ever want to hear from any of them again.

And the tapestry Wat was proposing commemorated the event in what Hermitage considered to be revolting detail. Surely something of this nature should take the best of the deceased's life and celebrate it through a heroic representation. It certainly shouldn't take the actual, detailed events of a very grizzly death and recreate them in wool. Hermitage thought that even the sheep would be ashamed.

'I'm not allowed to make the old tapestries anymore,' Wat complained. 'Which, after all only showed men and women as they were in the Garden of Eden.'

Hermitage raised his eyebrows at this. That could hardly be used as theological support for Wat's works, and it was unlike the weaver to refer to biblical authority at all. 'I think you'll find Adam and Eve at least used a fig leaf,' he pointed out.

Wat ignored the remark. 'Perhaps I'll move into blood and guts,' he held his arms out to illustrate his great work. 'Much more wholesome.'

Hermitage frowned.

'And still a good market I'm sure.' Wat was full of enthusiasm at this new idea. 'All those Normans wanting something to hang on the wall to remind them of the good old days. The cut and thrust of cutting and thrusting.

---

[1] You too can have an awful experience by reading *Hermitage, Wat and Some Nuns* wherein the whole Gilder-Shrewsbury situation is explained in unnecessary detail.

Heads lopped off, limbs cracked and insides spilling. Something for the whole family to admire. You can't complain about that.'

Hermitage felt he should, but couldn't think how just at the moment.

'I could do one of William's victory battle near Hastings. He'd like that.'

Hermitage did have something to say on this. 'I heard there's one already being done. Some nuns in Kent making a history of the whole thing.'

Wat shrugged, 'Mine will be shorter,' he said. 'Get it out first, take the money and move on.'

Hermitage tutted.

'I could get the apprentices working on a dozen copies, sell them all to leading Norman nobles.'

'Get them all taken from under your nose,' Cwen snorted her contempt for the new king and all his compatriots; and his family, friends and animals.

This was familiar territory. Many of their evenings were filled with discussion about how the country would be under the new ruler.

Wat saw opportunities for trade and profit, Cwen saw nothing but gloom and despair which, when pressed, sounded very much like the gloom and despair she had felt under King Harold. Hermitage always pointed out that his faith and role as a monk meant that his world was steady and predictable. He usually ended up urging them to take their duties to God and the church more seriously. Or to take them at all.

Wat usually ended up urging Hermitage to go back to the monastery at De'Ath's Dingle if he felt that strongly about it.

Hermitage never felt that strongly about it. The more time he spent in the company of Wat and Cwen the more he came to realise what a truly awful time he had had at that monastery. And he had thought it was pretty awful when he was there.

Nobody changed their position but Hermitage felt he was at least doing his bit by arguing the case.

A new knock at the downstairs door caused him no alarm at all. It was probably the last visitors coming back to have another go at Wat. Many days had now passed without him being bothered by the king's business. It was only when he was feeling particularly nervous that he took to hiding.

Wat looked at Cwen to go and answer the door. And Cwen looked at Wat.

'Mrs Grod will get it,' Cwen said, making it quite clear she was not Wat's door opener.

'Then you better get down there,' Wat instructed. 'Make sure Mrs Grod doesn't think it's a delivery for her pot and thicken up the stew with a visitor or two.'

'I'll go,' Hermitage said, weary at their bickering but not entirely confident that Wat's cook, Mrs Grod, might not do something unspeakable if the new arrival was caught unaware.

He stepped down the rude wooden stairs, careful of the third step, which wobbled. And the fifth which was slippery-smooth. And the seventh which wasn't there at all.

Approaching the main door to the weaver's workshop, a great slab of oak planking scattered with bolts and hinges as if they'd been shot at it, he did feel a shiver of anticipation. This new encounter could be trouble. But then Hermitage thought that of all his encounters.

The door was not bolted and he pulled its weight back to

19

reveal a slight young man, no more than Cwen's age. Even as he stood on the step it was clear the boy had a questing and inquisitive nature. His eyes darted about and his head craned so that he could see past Hermitage into the workshop beyond.

He was dressed well enough, not wealthy but not poor either, and his clothes had a travelled look about them as if his journey had been long and rather troublesome. A simple pack on his back and a staff in his hand completed his possessions.

The boy beamed at Hermitage as if they were already the closest of confidantes. 'Have I found the workshop of Wat the Weaver?' he asked, brightly.

Hermitage looked at him and shook his head in disappointment. 'Not one so young, surely?'

The boy grinned at the question which seemed to mean absolutely nothing to him.

'I'm Brody,' the boy introduced himself as if Hermitage was expected to remember this for future occasions. 'This is Wat's workshop? They said in the town that it was up here.'

'Yes,' Hermitage confirmed.   'This is Wat's workshop, they told you right.'

The workshop was away from the town for several good reasons, the main one being that the townsfolk preferred it that way.

'Excellent,' Brody clapped his hands. 'Can I come in then?' He peered again around Hermitage as if the monk was hiding something very exciting.

'Wat has no tapestries of that nature anymore,' Hermitage explained. 'He now does only wholesome and decorative works. There's nothing for you to see.' He was used to turning away idle visitors. Wat could spot them on the path, the ones who had no money who just wanted to come and gawp. The ones who had money, he dealt with personally.

'Oh, shame,' Brody said. 'I've heard all about the bath house series.'

'I'm sure you have,' Hermitage replied. It seemed the whole world had heard about the bath house series. And Hermitage had had the misfortune of actually seeing one of them in the flesh - as it were. He was going to do his best to make sure as few people as possible did the same. Especially one as young as this Brody.

'It's all right though,' the young man went on. 'I've not come to see the tapestries, I've got a message.'

'A message?' Hermitage asked, suspiciously. People had used a variety of fabrications to try and gain access to the workshop. 'Who from?' he narrowed his eyes.

Brody stuck his chest out and struck a pose of rigid importance, 'From the king,' he announced.

Cwen and Wat came running down the stairs at the sound of Hermitage's shriek.

Caput III

News; Not the Good Sort

'What did I say?' Brody asked.

They were gathered in the kitchen, Hermitage trying to gather his wits on a chair by Mrs Grod's cauldron. The cook herself was regarding them all with suspicion. Strangers in her kitchen usually meant trouble. Frequently for the strangers.

'You tell us,' Cwen replied, putting a hand on the shaking shoulder of Hermitage.

'I only said I'd come here with a message from the king.' Brody still leant importance to the word "king" but it was more nervous now, as it had caused a very strange reaction in the monk.

'There you are then,' Cwen scolded. 'What did you say a thing like that for?'

Brody's eyes started to look worried that he was trapped in a small kitchen with these people. 'Because it's true. I really do have a message from the king. What's the problem with having a message from the king?'

'Brother Hermitage here has a thing about messages from the king,' Wat explained. 'They usually mean trouble.'

'They usually mean death and disaster,' Hermitage whimpered.

'Oh,' Brody said admiringly. 'He's right there.'

This did nothing for Hermitage's constitution which took another downward spiral, twittering its distress as it went.

'You'd better tell us then,' Wat said with heavy resignation. 'What's the message? What were our dear king's words this time?'

'His words?' Brody asked. 'You want to know his actual words?'

'Well, yes,' Wat replied, frowning slightly. 'That's usually how messages work.'

'Please yourself.' Brody settled himself on his short stool, 'They're only his words though,' he pointed out, 'not mine. Don't blame the messenger.'

Wat waved him to get on with it.

Brody cleared his throat and narrowed his eyes to bring the memory into focus. 'The king's words were; "get up to some God-forsaken rat hole called Derby and tell that idiot monk and his disgusting weaver friend that they can bloody well sort this out. I'll be buggered if I know what the devil you're talking about, I care even less and if you don't get out of my sight in the next one minute my friend Le Pedvin here will split you open and use you as a purse."'

He stopped and let the silence hold sway.

'Definitely the king then,' Wat confirmed.

'And of course,' Brody was proud of his knowledge, 'there was only one disgusting weaver in Derby worthy of the name, so here I am.'

Hermitage's impersonation of a small, scared animal was so lifelike Mrs Grod started to give him an entirely different look.

'And what is it we're supposed to bloody well sort out?' Cwen asked.

'A murder,' Hermitage muttered, weakly. 'It's bound to be a murder.'

Brody's eyes widened, 'How did he know that?'

'Ha,' Hermitage managed to get out from the depths of his despair.

'Who's dead?' Wat asked.

Brody leant in close, perhaps so that Mrs Grod would not hear the great secret. 'Father Ignatius,' he hissed.

Hermitage, Wat and Cwen exchanged looks of blank ignorance.

'Who?' Wat asked.

'Father Ignatius,' Brody insisted as if everyone should know who father Ignatius is. Or was.

'Hermitage?' Wat asked.

Hermitage shook his head. 'I heard of an Ignatius in Lincoln, but he was an old man even then. Probably dead now anyway. And unlikely to be of interest to the King I'd have thought, being the chief confessor of cattle.'

'Chief confessor of?' Wat stopped himself going any further. 'Not him then.'

'Father Ignatius at the monastery,' Brody explained.

'Ah, the monastery,' Cwen said as if that made things perfectly clear. 'We all know there's only one monastery with an Ignatius in it.' She really looked like she wanted to smack this Brody on the back of the head until his words made sense.

Hermitage frowned at her. The country was strewn with monasteries and Ignatius was a common name. He saw that she was being sarcastic. He really must get the hang of that one of these days.

Brody cast a cautious eye at Mrs Grod stirring the contents of her cauldron as it bubbled on the fire. Every now and then she would bat some recalcitrant piece of the meal back into the pot from which it had been trying to escape.

'Is there somewhere we can talk?' Brody whispered.

Wat looked at Mrs Grod and shrugged, he beckoned

them out of the kitchen.

Hermitage followed, slouching along in his resignation. He didn't know why they were leaving the room as he wasn't convinced Mrs Grod understood anything that was said to her. Nothing made any difference to what went into or came out of her pot.

Wat led the way back to the upper chamber, making sure no one trod on his drawing, and settled them by the window.

There was no questioning the fact that the workshop was a grand place, probably the grandest for miles around and all of it the wages of sin as far as Hermitage was concerned.

What had started out as a simple timber-framed, single-story building, the same simple space as anyone of worth would have, had been extended as Wat's income had spread. He had even named some of the extra rooms after the tapestries that had paid for them. Hermitage put a stop to that.

A whole extra floor had been added when King Harold took an interest in the weaver's works. Wat may not have gone to the expenses of the very finest workmen, but they were capable. Nothing had actually collapsed or fallen off, as was common with some of the more rustic constructions.

As business had really blossomed an apprentice hall had been added on at the back. It was here that the bulk of the work was done, and here where the minds of young apprentice weavers were corrupted by Wat's trade. Hermitage had managed to move them on to much more worthwhile and wholesome works. About which they complained continuously; those who hadn't actually left to start their own definitively less wholesome businesses.

He suspected some of the remainder were making their

own works under the table, but he had never managed to catch any of them at it. He had though discovered some preliminary sketches under a floorboard. They had gone straight on the fire.

Settled by a very expensive window that looked out over the front of the building, Wat addressed Brody. The three of them were sat on the simple window seat, which was padded with a nice tapestry covered cushion. Nice in all senses of the word. Brody was before them on a hard wooden stool.

'Now,' Wat said. 'In simple words explain exactly who you are, where you've come from, who's dead and what on earth it's got to do with us.'

Brody looked around the room to check no one could overhear. 'Father Ignatius is dead.'

'Yes, we know that.' Cwen was impatient.

'And we think he was murdered.' Brody ignored her.

'What makes you think that?' Wat asked.

'He had a sundial in him.'

'A sundial?' Hermitage's interest was roused. 'How could he have a sundial in him?'

'Well,' Brody explained, 'more sort of through him really. From his back to his front and out a bit. The big spiky bit did for him.'

'Gnomon,' Hermitage said.

'Was he? There you are then.'

'The gnomon is the part of the sundial that sticks up and casts the shadow,' Hermitage explained, wearily.

'Aha.' Brody nodded. 'It wasn't casting a shadow, it being night time and all, but it was certainly sticking up. Right through Ignatius.'

'Perhaps he slipped while telling the time,' Wat

suggested.

'I've only ever seen one brother try to use a sundial at night,' Hermitage observed. 'And that was young Londor, who also tried to use a cow as his substitute at Vespers. Even he had the sense to actually face the sundial.'

Wat shrugged.

'Anyway,' Brody went on, 'Egbert says to me that it looks like he was pushed.'

'Just a minute,' Cwen held up a hand. 'Who's Egbert?'

'Egbert's quite new but he's the abbot's second in command.'

'Claustral prior,' Hermitage corrected.

'What he said,' Brody nodded at Hermitage. 'Egbert says that there was so much of the sundial sticking through Ignatius that someone must have pushed him.'

'You haven't got to the bit about what this has to do with us,' Wat said. 'I'm sure your abbot can deal with it, or the local sheriff.'

'Oh, no,' Brody replied as if such a thing was unthinkable. 'You see Ignatius was pointing.' He gave this the most awful significance.

The others didn't see anything at all.

'He was pointing?' Cwen checked the fact. 'You went from your monastery to the king to here because some dead monk was pointing?'

'Priest,' Brody corrected. 'Father Ignatius was a priest.'

'Doesn't make much difference to the sundial,' Cwen observed.

'He was a special priest,' Brody went on, 'A, erm, what was the word. The abbot did tell me so I could tell the king. Once I had told the king it went right out my head.' He looked at the ceiling for inspiration. 'Sack of something?'

'Sack of what?' Wat asked with a snort.

'Not sack of, sack or. Sack or toss?'

They all looked at the idiot before them. Hermitage shook his head and thought that he shouldn't really be surprised. 'Sacerdos?' he suggested.

'That's the one.'

'It means priest,' Hermitage pointed out that this added nothing to the information.

'There you are,' Brody was triumphant. 'Ignatius was the Sacerdos Arcanorum. I remembered the other word.'

Wat and Cwen just exchanged looks that said they were getting very little out of this explanation. They looked at Hermitage and saw that he had gone very pale indeed.

'Are you all right, Hermitage?' Cwen asked.

In trembling voice Hermitage repeated the title, 'Did you say Sacerdos Arcanorum?'

'That's him. Or was him, I suppose.'

'You're sure of that?'

'Absolutely. The abbot was quite insistent I got it right.'

'Didn't stop you forgetting it,' Cwen pointed out.

'But it's back now. That was definitely it. Sacerdos Arcanorum, whatever it means.'

They all looked to Hermitage.

'It means the priest of the mysteries,' he informed them, taking a deep breath. 'And what is the name of this monastery where Ignatius was priest?' he asked Brody. 'The proper name. The one people use when they're writing it down or mentioning it in the orders of the day.'

'Well, we just call it,' Brody began.

'No,' Hermitage said urgently. 'Not the name you just call it. Its real name. Probably in Latin.'

'Oh, that one,' Brody beamed and winked. 'I'm not

supposed to tell.'

'You can tell us,' Hermitage pressed. 'After all, the king did tell you to come here.'

Brody gave this some thought and looked around the room once more. 'The abbot said he'd do horrible things to me if I told. And that when I died God would be waiting for me to do some more.'

'Sounds like an abbot,' Hermitage muttered. 'But you are instructed by the abbot to tell the king, and the king has instructed you to tell us.'

Brody took some time to assimilate this chain of events. Eventually his face brightened in the way a face does when it finds out something is not its fault after all. He beckoned them close. 'It's called the Monasterium Tenebrarii,' he hissed in a loud whisper.

Again, Wat and Cwen looked blank and turned to Hermitage for an explanation.

'Do you know the place?' Wat asked.

Hermitage was shaking his head in disbelieving worry. 'Oh, I know it,' he said, 'I know it very well indeed.'

They smiled at this.

'I know one thing about it for certain.'

'And that is?'

Hermitage took a deep and shaking breath, 'The Monasterium Tenebrarii doesn't exist.'

Caput IV

Out of The Tower

King William had forgotten the message about the Monasterium Tenebrarii almost as soon as the messenger had left his presence. He had a brief moan to Le Pedvin, his right-hand man and chief lopper-off of Saxon bits and pieces, but wanted to move on to other business - such as the best route to the north where he had some harrying to get on with. Why did people have to keep bothering him with these petty complaints and problems? Couldn't they sort things out for themselves? What was wrong with this country?

'You are king,' Le Pedvin pointed out. He may not have been the king's equal in majesty but was a very close runner when it came to contempt for the English. He shrugged his shoulders. These appendages, being in the place where the bone got closest to the skin, resembled nothing so much as naked sticks. If any physick wanted to consider the human anatomy he only had to look at Le Pedvin, there was no need for dissection at all. Holding a good, strong lamp behind the Norman would easily reveal what was going on inside.

The two Normans were in the building site that William insisted on calling the Tower of London. Built amongst and out of the ruins of the old Roman town, William had declared it his fortress, from which the whole of the country would be controlled.

There were some walls up, and some of them had bits of roof on, but there was no way it was a tower. Even the simple folk of London knew that a tower was supposed to be a tall thing. This place might be tall eventually, but only if they piled all the bits up that were scattered about the site.

William had pressed for at least one room to be made ready from which he could issue his edicts and instructions. When William pressed, things tended to happen. Or get flattened. Everyone told him that the thing was going to take years to build. To which his response was to ask why they weren't getting on with it then.

So it was that the first room of the Tower of London was made ready for the King - even though a couple of the walls were propped by timbers and there was no mortar at all.

Into the room had been put the King's long oak table and chairs, the absence of building material of any substance being neatly disguised by magnificent tapestries that hung the walls. The master-builder was just praying it didn't rain. Or if it did, that the tapestries were a lot stronger than they looked.

'Monks,' Le Pedvin spat from his seat at one end of the table.

'And this Ignatius?' William asked the question, taking another haunch of some animal or other from the wooden plate in front of him. 'How the devil am I supposed to know one priest in the whole country, let alone care less about whether he's dead or alive?'

'Let that investigator idiot deal with it,' Le Pedvin brushed the problem away. 'That's his job.'

'The king's door,' the king gave a hearty laugh, 'I really don't know where they get this nonsense.'

Before they could get on with looking at the very poor map which supposedly showed the way to the north, but which in fact gave a very direct route to Norfolk, a new figure entered the room.

It took a moment or two before they noticed, such was the discretion with which this arrival encroached on the space of the king.

'Good God it's you again.' Le Pedvin was startled from his comfort. 'Stop creeping about, will you.'

'I will sire,' the new figure bowed his obedience. Although in clerical garb, this was no priest or monk. A simple, humble servant, was the man's description of himself when he approached the Tower offering his services and his experience of building work.

Everything about the man seemed neutral. He was not too fat or thin and had no striking features, hobbles, squints or signs of disease. He was tall but seemed to stoop to reduce the impact of this. He had clearly led a comfortable life but it looked like that had been some time ago. Still only of middle years, he did look like a man of intent. Quiet, neutral but indefatigable intent. Probably to live comfortably again.

He didn't actually do any building himself he had hastily pointed out when William said that he might have a job for him, rather he organised those who did, and he made sure they stuck to the task. On further examination it became clear that he didn't even instruct those who did the building directly. He was many layers above the mere labouring craftsman.

Apparently, he held those to account who instructed the ones who gave the orders to the people who directed the supervisors of those who actually organised providing direction to the craftsmen who did the work; who in turn told their apprentices to do it. But he assured them he was very good at his job.

The man's main skill seemed to be to simper about the place, agreeing with the king and his court whenever the king and his court needed agreeing with. King William never tended to worry about whether people agreed with him or not.

Le Pedvin despised this new arrival, but finding fault in the man was like trying to make milk into butter with your bare hands. There was always a very good reason why this fellow should not have his guts torn out on the spot.

'What do you want?' Le Pedvin snarled.

The man bowed in that intensely annoying way he had, 'I merely wished to enquire if Your Majesty had any particular instructions for the messenger who has just departed? He seems intent on commencing his journey immediately and I did not know if that coincided with your expectations.'

Le Pedvin reached out a languorous hand and grabbed the newcomer firmly by his cloak. He dragged him close and pulled him down so they were face to face. He enunciated clearly and with several splatters of half-chewed meat. 'We don't care.'

'Excellent sire,' the man had enough humble for a pie. 'I shall see him on his way.' He turned from the royal presence and his expression turned from undeniable obedience to very high-grade contempt. The curl on his lip said that he was having to bite it very hard when dealing with the country's new rulers. The old one had been enough trouble and this William was showing no signs of being an improvement.

He marched from the king's chamber with a snort at the pretentiousness of the man and walked the short distance to his own hovel, propped against an old Roman wall, which was already earmarked for demolition. He had only got this by throwing out the previous residents on the strength of his service to the king - which hadn't even started at that time.

The messenger, Brody, had long since departed and so there was no chance of giving him any instructions, but that had never been the intent. The disappointment was that William and that awful Le Pedvin character hadn't revealed a hint more than was known already; known by eavesdropping on the King's private conversations, but then how was anyone supposed to find out anything in this place?

Le Pedvin reminded him of the old Bishop of Peterborough in many ways. Not in bulk, obviously, the Norman would barely make up one leg of the Bishop but their temperaments were the same; deeply unpleasant.

Snarling and grumbling, the man barged his way into his single room and cuffed his servant round the ear.

The servant said nothing. There had been a lot of cuffing since their fortunes fell with the Norman Conquest as people were starting to call it. The servant had considered leaving his master on many occasions, but he wasn't allowed to.

'Find the monk,' the master instructed.

The servant looked puzzled, but that was normal.

'Athan,' the man made the instruction clear. 'Find Brother Athan.'

'Prior Athan?' the servant questioned, having been corrected many times by the monk, who could cuff a darn site harder.

'He's not a prior any more,' his master said with a sneer. 'You have to have a monastery to be a prior. And being thrown out of the previous monastery by your own monks probably makes you a very poor candidate. We know the man is appalling but for a whole religious community to take against him like that must be unique.' A shape which was like the shadow of a smile briefly alighted on Nicodemus's face before leaving for somewhere more conducive.

'Tell him I have news. News that will cast a dark but satisfying shadow on his beleaguered soul.'

The servant looked blank.

'Just tell him to get here. And then we are preparing for a journey.'

'Yes, Nicodemus,' the servant replied, ducking from the hovel and wondering what preparation for travel would be required when they had no possessions.

. . .

'Hermitage,' prior/brother Athan said. 'Brother Hermitage.' The name was not said kindly, but then Brother Athan was not the type to say anything kindly.

He was an ugly man. There was no insult in this as it was Athan's description for himself. Whenever he found reason to challenge, castigate or threaten another he would point out that he was a very ugly man. Ugly to look at and ugly to deal with. He added that some very ugly things went on inside his head and if this other person didn't do what they were told, Athan would let some of them out.

He spent a lot of his time challenging, castigating and threatening. God had created the world to punish mankind and they weren't taking it seriously enough. Athan could help.

'Where is he?' he asked as if his hands could reach out and strangle Hermitage from here.

'Derby,' Nicodemus replied.

Athan scowled a disappointment that his arms weren't that long.

'With the weaver,' Nicodemus added.

If Athan had been on the verge of murderous temper at the mention of Hermitage's name he now climbed over the verge and was rooting about in the bushes. Such was the boiling temperature inside his head that his words of vitriol evaporated before they could escape to the clean air.

It was a good job they were sitting alone outside Nicodemus's hovel. If the servant had been within reach, or some supporting timber of the hovel within striking distance, the damage could have been significant. As it was, Nicodemus noted that Athan's grip on the Roman block on which they sat was starting to crumble the thousand-year-old masonry.

'So, we go to Derby,' Athan managed to get out.

'We do,' Nicodemus confirmed. 'We have unfinished business with Brother Hermitage and Wat the Weaver.'

'It won't take long to finish, I assure you.' Athan removed his hands from the stonework and used them to inflict pain on one another instead.

'There is more,' Nicodemus went on before Athan could stand and start walking to Derby this minute. 'We mustn't act too quickly. If what I have heard is true there could be a great treasure at stake.'

Athan's troubled mind seemed to change some sort of internal track.

'And the last time the wretched Hermitage and Wat were involved in anything it went well, did it?' Athan's attention was now firmly on Nicodemus. Even the strongest, most assured man crumbled when Athan's attention fell on them.

'The business at De'Ath's Dingle?' he reminded Nicodemus. As if either of them needed reminding.[2]

'That was entirely different.'

'It brought ruin on everyone and us to our current sorry state,' Athan pointed out. 'And it was all that monk and weaver's fault.'

'Exactly,' Nicodemus nodded encouragement. 'So we get to deal with both of them. But they are to be sent on a mission for the king. A very significant mission.'

'King!' Athan spat, 'bloody foreigner,' he summed up the new ruler.

'But a bloody foreigner who has been told the location of the Monasterium Tenbrarii,' Nicodemus said, simply.

Athan stopped. That internal track had fallen into a hole. 'Where is it?' he asked, it being a mark of his character that he would not engage in pointless chit-chat about not believing it, or it being a myth. Straight to the point with Athan. Preferably with something pointed.

'That was not revealed, but,' Nicodemus went on quickly so that Athan would not have the time to get angry again. Well, angrier. 'The messenger was from the Monasterium and the message was to do with an incident involving,' Nicodemus paused for effect. 'The king's door.'

Athan gaped. Athan. The man who would not blink an eye if he fell, face-down in a bank of nettles.

'And the king has instructed Brother Hermitage to investigate.'

'Why on earth would he do that?' Athan asked, still in wonder. 'Surely he'd go himself.'

---

[2] If you need reminding, or haven't a clue what's going on, you might try *The Heretics of De'Ath*. Now available in paper.

'Bloody foreigner,' Nicodemus explained. 'I imagine there was little time for a handover of important matters of state or the secrets of the kingdom when King Harold had his conversation with that arrow. It was pretty clear from what I heard that William had not the first idea what this messenger was talking about.'

'And you didn't enlighten him,' Athan pointed out.

Nicodemus held his hands out to demonstrate his innocence, 'I am but a humble servant. Far be it from me to inform the king of anything.'

'The king's door,' Athan repeated as if saying the words made the thing real. 'Do you believe it?'

Nicodemus was cautious, 'I believe the messenger believed it. He had been sent by the abbot of the Monasterium Tenebrarii to inform the king that someone called Ignatius had been killed and the king's door was involved. Hardly the sort of thing a liar would even know about.'

'If it's true,' Athan gave the idea breath.

'Treasure,' Nicodemus repeated. 'Secrets, knowledge, power.' The last of these words seemed to get him quite excited.

'No one knows what's there,' Athan came down to earth. 'The whole place is a myth and the king's door is a myth inside another one.' He waved a hand as if dismissing the whole suggestion. 'The king's door hides everything from the Holy Grail to God's own beard. It probably just hides the body of some dead king. If it's there at all.'

'But if it is,' Nicodemus went on, 'and we were the first to open it.' He let this thought dangle invitingly in the air.

'What?' Athan said, still down on the earth.

'The treasure, knowledge, secrets and power would be

ours,' Nicodemus explained, impatiently.

Athan didn't seem enthused.

'There might be new ideas of how to punish mankind for its sin,' Nicodemus suggested as if offering Athan a reward.

'Hm,' the monk grumbled.

'But never mind the door,' Nicodemus reminded him, 'or the monastery. We know who will be there when it's opened. Hermitage and Wat.'

Now Athan saw the advantages of believing in the king's door. If there was nothing behind it, he could at least take it off its hinges and batter Brother Hermitage to death with it.

'So we follow the messenger,' Athan declared.

'Not too closely,' Nicodemus smiled his normal smile this time, the insincere and vacant movement of his face in the right order, which wasn't very nice. 'We know Brother Hermitage and Wat are in Derby. We can simply go there. Don't want the messenger alerted to our presence. Then we observe carefully and follow them to the monastery. Can't have them seeing us before they reveal the location of the place. We particularly don't want Brother Hermitage catching sight of you. You know what effect you have on him.'

Now Athan smiled, which was even more unpleasant.

Athan questioned Nicodemus, 'Are you allowed to just walk away from this important building work for the king like that?' he asked. 'After all, you told me you were essential.'

'The art of the overseer?' Nicodemus reminded Athan of a conversation they had had several times.

'Ah, yes,' Athan nodded with some distaste. 'You don't actually do anything at all.'

'Exactly. And if people think I'm still here doing

something or other, but doing it in private, or I have gone off somewhere to get some very particular supplies, we might maintain the element of surprise over those we follow. Which could be very useful,' Nicodemus concluded.

The very nasty look on Athan's face said that he very much liked the element of surprise.

'Perhaps,' Nicodemus mused, 'I'd better take some of the king's coin with me. Just to make the whole thing more realistic.'

'The coin that doesn't belong to you.'

'That's the stuff.'

Caput V

Of Monasteries with Doors in Them

'It's a big place for somewhere that doesn't exist,' Brody said as he gulped his wine.

Cwen had fetched the drink to calm Hermitage, who was in an awful state. Content that he was now in a condition to deal with questions, Wat gently enquired, 'What do you mean, it doesn't exist? Clearly it does. Brody says he's come from there.'

'That simply cannot be,' Hermitage shook his head slowly. 'The place is a myth.'

Nobody said anything but the looks he was getting from Cwen and Wat were shouting their demand for more information.

Hermitage sighed heavily and explained. 'It goes back many years, to when the church was preparing for the imminent Judgement Day.'

'Was it?' Cwen couldn't help herself. 'When was that supposed to happen then?'

'The millennium,' Hermitage replied. 'When a thousand years had passed since the birth of our Lord, the world would be brought to an end and the souls of the living and the dead would be distributed according to their worth.'

'The millennium?' Cwen asked, obviously not quite following. 'You mean the year one thousand?'

'That's it,' Hermitage confirmed. 'Although there was some debate as to whether the one thousand years should actually be measured to the start of the year one thousand or the end. The year number one only being marked after that year had passed, you see? There were a lot of great

41

debates about the subject up and down the land.' He hoped he was explaining this complex issue carefully enough. 'People got terribly excited and I believe there were even suggestions of heresy when someone suggested we should measure from Christmas anyway.'

Cwen frowned and ignored all the careful detail. 'You mean the millennium that happened sixty-eight years ago? That one?'

'That's the one.'

'I know none of us was born,' Cwen said, thoughtfully. 'But I think someone would have told me that I'd missed Judgement Day.'

'Obviously it didn't happen,' Hermitage said, with some impatience.

'Good.'

'The point is that everyone thought it was going to. So there was preparation. There was much prayer and repentance and making ready for the event.'

'Most of which the church charged for, I imagine,' Wat commented.

'I wouldn't know,' Hermitage replied, dryly. 'One rumour was that all the secret knowledge and treasures of the church were gathered in one place. By that means any tests that awaited us upon entry to heaven would be easier to answer. If the church hierarchy knew where to put their hands on all those things that only the church knew about, they would be in a better position. And there was bound to be a lot of saints in heaven who would want their bones back, that sort of thing.'

'Get the church in a better position to get into heaven ahead of everyone else,' Wat snorted.

Hermitage ignored him. 'Of course, this was a huge

amount of information and a lot of bones, more than could simply be written down or put in a cupboard, so a special monastery was created to care for it all. A hidden, secret place, the unknown monastery, the Monasterium Tenebrarii.'

'So why do you think it's a myth?' Cwen asked.

'As you say, sixty-eight years have passed since then and no one has ever come across the place. You'd think, when judgement day didn't arrive, the monks would go back to their normal lives.'

'What if it was so secret no one could remember where they'd put it?' Wat asked, clearly not taking the subject seriously. 'Or all the people who knew where it was went inside and shut the door?'

'sixty-eight years later they'd all be dead,' Hermitage pointed out, with uncharacteristic sharpness. 'I think someone would notice a monastery full of dead monks, eventually.'

'Perhaps this place just calls itself the Monasterium Gene whatnot,' Cwen offered. 'As you say, it's not the real one, because that doesn't exist. It's just an ordinary place with ideas above itself?'

'I suppose that is possible as a lot of people would be aware of the idea,' Hermitage accepted thoughtfully. 'The story was in wide circulation among the learned of the church.'

'In fairly narrow circulation then,' Wat observed.

'And this Sacristy Amanuensis?' Cwen asked. 'Who's that then?'

'The Sacerdos Arcanorum,' Hermitage corrected. 'He was the priest of the monastery. The one person trusted with the most sacred and secret rituals. There would be an abbot and prior to maintain organisation and discipline and guard the material treasures. The Sacerdos was to guard the knowledge.'

'So, if this Sacerdos has just lost an argument with the pointy bit of a sundial,' Wat speculated. 'That's a lot of secret and sacred knowledge up in smoke.'

'I'm sure it wouldn't have been left to that,' Hermitage said. 'The Sacerdos would take precautions against his own illness or death. He would have a deputy or would hide the knowledge where others could find it if necessary. Probably cleverly disguised or buried or something.'

'Well.' Wat clapped his hands together. 'That's all absolutely fascinating. One dead priest in a secret monastery and all that knowledge lost. Great shame but there we are. These things happen.'

Brody looked very confused and worried, 'But,' he stuttered out, 'you have to come.'

Wat looked to the ceiling and appeared to be thinking deeply, 'Er,' he pondered the request. 'No, don't think we do.'

'But,' Brody tried again.

'Dead priest,' Wat pointed out. 'Not much we can do for him now, not with the sundial and all.'

'A murdered priest,' Brody pointed out. 'And the king's instruction.'

Cwen was thoughtful now. 'Did the king mention killing people and burning things to the ground at all?'

'Eh, what?' Brody was thoroughly confused. 'No, I don't think so.'

'Ah.' Cwen was full of confidence. 'When the king wants Hermitage to really do something he threatens to kill someone and burn things to the ground. If he hasn't done that it can't be important.'

'Not important?' Brody seemed completely lost now. 'Father Ignatius has been murdered by a sundial.'

'There you are then,' Wat said happily. 'Got your culprit. Hang the sundial.'

Brody looked to them all in turn, his most pleading expression was saved for Hermitage. 'What about the pointing?' he asked.

'Pointing?' Hermitage queried. 'What has the pointing got to do with anything?'

'Ignatius's pointing,' Brody explained. 'I did mention that.'

'We must have thought you were rambling,' Cwen observed rather sharply.

'People were pointing at Ignatius?' Hermitage asked. He thought it would be quite understandable for anyone to want to point at a priest impaled on a sundial; not the sort of thing you saw every day.

'No, no,' Brody corrected. 'It was Ignatius's pointing. At the king's door.'

Hermitage, who had been perched on the edge of the window seat so as not to be too comfortable, fell off it.

Cwen and Wat jumped up to grab him under the arms and haul him back to his feet.

'Hermitage, for goodness sake,' Wat said. 'What's the matter with you now? You're as jumpy as a frog on a hot rock.'

Hermitage helped them get him back on the seat. This was all too much. There would be very few people who could bring tales of the monastery and the priest, and this Brody did not seem the type to be well informed on the mysteries of the church. To bring the king's door into it as well was simply unbelievable. Yet here it was, happening. He had to believe it.

'The king's door,' he muttered, once he had got his wind back.

'The king has a door?' Cwen asked, with little surprise at such a revelation.

Hermitage sighed. Partly that he was going to have to explain this to his friends, who he knew would be mocking and difficult, but mostly because he knew this was going to lead to a whole heap of trouble. 'The Monasterium Tenebrarii is home to the secrets and the treasures,' he said.

'Yes,' Cwen said. 'And it doesn't exist.'

'And inside the monasterium,' Hermitage went on, in some sort of daze, 'is the king's door.'

'And behind the king's door is the king?' Cwen suggested.

'Hardly, as the old king is dead and the new one doesn't appear to care that he's got a door. The point is that the king, being anointed by God, is privy to the secrets of the monasterium. But even further than that he may open the king's door. The king's door is the means of securing the greatest treasures of all. The church thought that there was risk of someone deciding to take things for themselves, once all the treasures were gathered together. Probably some greedy or rapacious fellow.'

'Like a bishop,' Cwen suggested.

Hermitage snorted at this, but that was exactly what the thinking had been. None of the members of the church hierarchy trusted one another enough to leave them alone with a potato. A monastery full of treasure was too much temptation. It was quite enlightened that they made arrangements to deny access to everyone.

'Even the Sacerdos Arcanaorum may not open the king's

door alone.'

Cwen didn't seem at all impressed by any of this. 'What's inside exactly?'

Hermitage looked at her blankly. Surely that was clear from what he'd just said. 'Only the priest and the king may open the door. No one knows what's behind it.'

'No one?'

'Well, perhaps this Father Ignatius and King Harold, but I don't think either of them can help much now. And as neither of them was alive when the door was shut, I doubt even they know.'

Wat was silent, and when Hermitage looked at him to see if he was engaged with the depth of the problem, he appeared to have his mind elsewhere. 'What are you thinking? That this place might be real?'

'Oh,' Wat emerged from his reverie. 'I was just thinking that as this all seems so important perhaps we'd better go along and see if we can help.'

'What?' Cwen was surprised. 'A moment ago you said we didn't need to bother.'

'That was before we'd heard about this door that now belongs to William.'

'And you're suddenly worried about William's interests are you?' She folded her arms and stared at him, eyes narrowed and calculations running across her face.

'And there's a dead monk, sorry priest to consider,' Wat added, sounding unusually worried about clerical cadavers.

Cwen had reached a conclusion and smiled broadly, 'And a great treasure.'

'Treasure?' Wat asked as if he'd never come across the word before.

'King's treasure,' Cwen clarified. 'Behind the king's door.

The sort of quantity of treasure only kings have.'

Wat looked out of the window with studied disinterest, 'Hm,' he mused, 'could be. I suppose.'

. . .

Preparations for departure took no time at all. Wat even pressed some of the apprentices into getting his pack ready, and his instructions to Hartle, his apprentice-master, were short and to the point.

Hermitage was caught up in the whirlwind of it all and was most uncomfortable that he hadn't had time to think through this matter in the level of detail it required. Brody hadn't told them where the monastery was so they had no idea where they were going or how long it would take. They hadn't asked about the abbot of the place or the procedure for gaining access. He would prefer to go to the library in Lichfield where he could undertake some preliminary researches before deciding what the best course of action might be.

And then perhaps a letter of introduction should be sent, followed by an exchange of correspondence agreeing the purpose of the visit and the extent of the enquiries which Hermitage might be expected to undertake. The appropriate number of days could then be allocated and some support from the monastery population organised.

Hermitage could tell this was an urgent matter but proper planning and preparation would make its execution much more effective. If he was allowed to approach this in the proper manner, but really get a move on, he could be ready to depart in less than two months.

Wat was calling him from the front door. 'Come on Hermitage, where are you? We're ready to go.'

So much for planning and preparation.

With a sigh, he got up from his bed, wistfully thinking how nice it would be to sit in a quiet room planning and preparing things, without having to actually do any of them.

Brody and Cwen were at the door as well, Brody with his staff and pack and Cwen with her own small bundle for the journey.

'Aha,' Hermitage realised something.

'Aha?' Cwen asked, frowning at him. 'What's aha?'

Hermitage smiled and stumbled over his words, 'Just that here we are ready to go. Aha.'

Cwen's frown deepened but she shook her head at Hermitage's odd behaviour.

Hermitage's actual thought had been, "Aha, Cwen's here. I don't think they'll let a woman into the monastery." He didn't like to mention it as she always got terribly cross when things like that came up. Perhaps something would sort itself out when they got there. Or someone else could tell her.

'Right then Brody,' Wat addressed the young man. 'Which way?'

Brody looked at them all cautiously.

'Well?' Wat pressed.

'It's a secret,' Brody explained.

'I'm sure it is,' Wat acknowledged. 'But if we're going to actually get there we'll need to know where we're actually going?' He rolled his eyes at Hermitage and Cwen.

'The abbot instructed me never to tell anyone.' Brody seemed trapped in this dilemma.

'Just walk and we'll follow then,' Wat waved an arm in a random direction. 'That way you won't have told anyone but we'll still manage to arrive wherever it is we're supposed to be.'

Brody beamed happily at this suggestion and gave a confident nod. Adjusting the pack on his back, he strode purposefully away from the workshop.

'It's east then,' Wat observed, with a snigger at Brody's discomfort.

'Perhaps I could get you to wear blindfolds,' Brody suggested.

'You can try,' Cwen offered.

Brody looked at Cwen and forgot the blindfolds.

'We are on the king's business.' Hermitage tried to offer Brody some comfort. 'The king would know where the place was, so we should as well.'

Brody didn't seem convinced.

'How long till we get there?' Wat asked. 'You can at least tell us that.'

Brody gave this careful thought. He spoke very slowly as if each word was giving too much away. 'I should think about five or six days.'

'Hm,' Wat thought. 'Should put us about Sleaford if we keep in this direction.' He grinned at Brody, who said no more.

. . .

Two other pairs of ears caught the departing conversation and the faces in between those ears smiled at one another. Anyone seeing these smiles would have walked quickly away, probably to make sure the children were safe.

Nicodemus and Athan appeared around the corner of the workshop as soon as the party was out of sight. Athan seemed barely able to control his urge to run after them.

'We follow towards Sleaford,' Nicodemus urged, placing a cautionary hand on Athan's arm. 'If you do for them now we'll never find the monastery. That child, what did they call him? Brody? He won't even tell them where they're going. And they're the ones who need to know.'

'I could make him tell us,' Athan said, with disturbing glee.

'I'm sure you could. But then we'd have the trouble of getting in and finding what's hidden. The place is expecting Hermitage and the others. They're probably going to open the king's door as soon as they get there. We don't even know where it is or what it looks like.' Nicodemus was staring hard at Athan. 'If you let yourself get carried away again we'll have another London Bridge incident before we know it.'

Athan looked down and grumbled, 'London Bridge. How was I supposed to know he was a Norman?'

'You could have asked. And I don't think you should have done that to anyone, Norman or not. Never mind how sinful you thought he looked. I think getting you out of that one is the reason Le Pedvin hates me so much.'

'People hate you for a lot more reasons than that,' Athan noted, wryly.

Nicodemus waved him to silence. 'We wait until they're out of sight and head east. We know their direction.'

'I still think dealing with them here and now will save us a lot of trouble, and a lot of walking,' Athan grumbled.

Nicodemus sighed, 'Do you really have no interest, no curiosity to discover whether the great secrets and treasures of the church are hidden in some forgotten monastery? Is there not some spark of your religious calling that summons you to resolve one of the greatest mysteries of our time?'

Athan considered Nicodemus and answered him straight, 'Curiosity is an evil that can be beaten out of most people.'

'Most things can be beaten out of people according to you.' Nicodemus's face expressed his disappointment and disdain for Athan's approach.

'That's right,' Athan agreed, quite happy that all problems had their solution, and it was usually the same one.

Ducking back around the corner of the building, in case one of the travellers had forgotten something and turned back for it, Nicodemus sat on the ground to bide his time.

Athan stood.

Even he showed some spark of reaction when a new face appeared from the front of the workshop.

'Morning gentlemen,' Hartle, now in charge of the workshop after Wat's departure, greeted the men hiding behind the building with a rather friendly and familiar tone.

'Ah,' Nicodemus said, jumping to his feet and quickly trying to think what he was going to say next.

'Waited for the monk to leave I see,' Hartle even winked at them. 'He is a caution that Brother Hermitage. Keeps Wat on the straight and narrow though.' He paused for a broad smile, 'But then it's not the straight and narrow that you're looking for, I imagine.'

Nicodemus and Athan simply looked at one another.

'Come along then,' Hartle beckoned. 'Come along and see what we have to offer. There is a very private collection of Wat the Weaver in the outhouse. Only for the very discerning customer, if you take my meaning.' He beckoned them to follow him into the house.

Seeing that they had no alternative, hardly wanting to reveal what they actually wanted to do to Wat the Weaver and the monk, Nicodemus stepped out to follow.

As Hartle led the way, Nicodemus hissed into Athan's

ear. 'No matter what you see in there, no matter what they say or what they do. Do not hit anyone.'

Caput VI

The Way Through the Woods

The journey from Derby to wherever it was they were going would be perilous. Any journey these days was perilous. Stepping outside the front door without a goodly selection of weapons and a large man who knew how to use them was perilous. King William may have been crowned in Westminster Abbey but his arrival, as well as being a surprise to the Abbot of the Monasterium, was still to make an impact in many parts of the country.

Norman law could be what everyone swore by in Kent and Sussex, but elsewhere many still thought the Danes were in charge. And the worst of the lot were the ones who thought no one was in charge and so they could do what they liked.

The reputation of Wat the Weaver could be quite useful in dealing with people in a town or village where lodgings were sought, but protecting them from people who jumped out of ditches with large sticks was a different matter. The people in the ditches tended not to ask for introductions before they set to work.

Hermitage, being nervous when people knocked on the door, was understandably trembling at the thought of treading the open road. He had trod the open road many times and every occasion had been awful. Travelling alone, travelling with groups, even travelling with an army had done little to dissuade him from the conclusion that the open road was out to get him.

He would just make sure he stuck close to Wat and Cwen and let them take the lead in any ditch-related business they happened upon. 'Exactly how long is it going to take us to get there?' he asked Brody. 'You can at least tell us that.'

Brody frowned at him as if struggling to work out if this was a secret he was supposed to keep as well.

'We can't work out where a place is by how long it takes to get there,' Hermitage explained. 'It could be in any direction at all. Sleaford may be that far away but it depends if we turn off the road or not.'

Brody still wasn't convinced.

'Well,' Wat said. 'If we keep going in this direction for more than a couple of days we'll be getting our feet wet.'

'We have to be out of doors overnight?' Hermitage asked. He hadn't really thought about where they could get to in one afternoon, it already being past nones by the time they got away. He didn't know the local district very well, having done his very best not to go anywhere near it. Of course, the great and mysterious Monasterium Tenebrarii would not be just around the corner, but surely they would have safe lodgings along the way.

'We'll probably get to Nottingham today, easy,' Wat said. 'If not beyond.'

'Nottingham?' Hermitage was alarmed. 'What about the forest?'

'What about it?' Wat indicated with a wave of his arms that they were already walking through a wooded area. 'The whole country is one big forest.'

This was true of course. It was said that a man could walk from one end of the country to the other without ever coming out from the shade of the trees. It was also said that the trees hid some rather questionable men who stayed in the shade for very good reasons. And the trees around

Nottingham had a startling reputation for shady men.

Hermitage gave their situation careful thought. The thoroughfares in and around Nottingham must be thick with trade. After all, how could a place of such size survive if no one travelled safely through the forest? Of course, tales would be told of robbers and worse. That was what tales were about. No one would spin a yarn about a man who had no trouble whatsoever getting around and in which nothing happened. Who would listen to that, for goodness sake?

It was only reasonable that their journey would be uneventful and without incident.

Hermitage reached the sort of conclusion he always did when he carefully analysed a situation and saw that there was little reason for concern. 'We'll all be killed,' he wailed.

'Oh, don't be ridiculous,' Wat mocked him. 'I hear William has already laid claim to all the woodland in the country. There's probably foresters and all sorts about, keeping the place in order.'

'And we are on the king's business, I suppose.' Hermitage tried to convince himself.

'I wouldn't say that too loud,' Cwen cautioned. 'Anyway, Brody got here without incident.'

Hermitage took some comfort from that. It was true the young man had already made the journey once.

'Not entirely without incident,' Brody piped up.

'Really?' Hermitage asked, with dull dread.

'Nothing serious. Just had to climb a tree once, to avoid a sounder of boar.'

That was bad enough for Hermitage. Boar were nasty, dangerous things. Unless they were on a plate of course. But in that circumstance there were huntsmen and butchers between him and the boar.

'Boar won't bother four of us,' Cwen assured him.

'And I went off the path once and nearly trod on a viper's nest.'

'Vipers?' Hermitage squeaked. Everyone knew serpents could smell a man of the church from a mile away. They all remembered the Garden of Eden and wanted to get their own back.

'We won't go off the path,' Wat sighed.

'And the robbers of course,' Brody concluded his report.

Wat and Cwen growled at him for saying exactly the wrong thing again.

'But they weren't very good. Didn't seem to know what they were doing. Kept arguing with themselves most of the time, so I sneaked around without being spotted.'

'How do you know they were robbers then?' Wat asked.

'They were dividing up their spoils. That's what the argument was all about.'

'Robbers,' Hermitage quaked and quivered at the same time.

'Robbers only like robbing the helpless,' Wat said in an encouraging sort of manner.

Hermitage thought that summed him up quite neatly.

'All we have to do is stride along confidently and they'll leave us alone.'

Hermitage couldn't do confident striding. His legs weren't built for it and his habit kept getting tangled in his feet if he stepped too far.

'Anyway, Brody here will know what they look like.'

'What good will that do?'

Wat sighed, 'Robbers don't really jump out on people waving sticks you know.'

'Really?'

'No, of course not. You jump out on someone you make them twitchy and they're instantly ready for an attack.' Wat sounded like he knew what he was talking about. 'You frighten an old maid with a broom in her hand and the first thing she'll do is clout you on the head with it. Or startle a man with a bow and you'll be pulling arrows out of your chest before you can say "show me your quiver".

'If you're going to rob someone you either do it so they don't even notice 'till hours later; sneak something out of a pocket, or a pack or the like. Otherwise, you make them confident that robbery is the last thing on your mind.'

'I see.' Hermitage wasn't sure that this was a lesson he really wanted to learn.

'So you stroll up. Ask the time of day. Comment on what a fine horse they're riding, or what a lovely cart, or what strong legs they must have for such a journey. Then, when everyone's relaxed, bang.'

'Bang?'

'Hit 'em when they're least expecting it.'

'So not only rob people,' Hermitage said, with explicit criticism of the robbers and of Wat for knowing about all this. 'Be deceitful about it as well.'

'Robbers tend not to be the nicest people,' Cwen explained. 'They're hardly likely to ask politely if you'd mind being robbed.' She snorted. 'And if you say no thank you, perhaps they'd apologise for bothering you and ask for a more convenient time when they can come back and rob you.'

Hermitage shook his head slowly at the depths humanity could stoop to and at the worldliness of young Cwen, who should not know such things at her age. He still didn't know most of them at his age and he was older than her.

He hesitated to ask Brody the next question, fearing that the answer would only pile worry upon worry. His worry pile was getting quite precarious and he dreaded to think what would happen if it all came down on top of him. 'How many robbers were there?' He tried to sound light, disinterested and nonchalant but came out as squeaky, terrified and ready to run a mile.

'Two.'

'Two?' Wat's laugh burst from him. 'Two. Hardly a dangerous band to overcome us by force of numbers then.'

'I was only one,' Brody explained, taking offence that his robbers were being belittled.

'I think we can handle two,' Cwen added her contempt for the pathetic threat.

Hermitage was pretty sure she could handle two on her own.

'I was going to suggest that if we come across a band of travellers who appear to be friendly, we get our hands on our knives,' Wat said. 'Now I know there's only two, I think we can leave them to Hermitage.'

Hermitage's shock turned his face into a pale thing that looked like it was trying to drop off the front of his head. He was sure that there must be more than two robbers in the whole of the kingdom, and that the chances of them meeting the same ones as Brody was remote. That only meant there were more robbers probably queueing up to give him their attention.

'I'm only joking,' Wat reassured him. 'But sure as chickens lay eggs, two robbers are not going to bother us.'

Hermitage sighed his sigh.

'For goodness sake Hermitage,' Cwen complained. 'We

are going to find out about this great secret. The one the church has been hiding for years. That must be interesting at the very least. Anyone would think you want to be locked in a box and not have to come out at all.'

Hermitage thought that if the box was big enough and he had a book to read about the great secret that could be quite nice.

. . .

They walked on through the woods without incident for several hours. This gave Hermitage the chance to settle down from the shock of having walked out of the front door in the first place. He knew that he shouldn't be so nervous about things like this. Trouble never usually descended on him close to home. Most of the time he was quite a long way away before it spotted him.

Passing through regular clearings on the well-marked road, they did encounter other travellers but it was clear these were the genuine article. They said nothing, looked the other way and hoped the people they'd just seen would go away. Occasionally there was an exchange of eye contact, but it usually resolved in the mutual raising of eyebrows and drooping of heads that said how unfortunate they all were to live in times like these.

One old man on his own did hop out of the trees at one point, but as soon as he saw them he hopped back in again. Nobody wanted to enquire what he was up to in there.

As they emerged from one particularly dense part of the path, overhung with a roof of green summer and carpeted with a crisp layer of autumn, two men were seen sitting comfortably in the sun by the side of the path, their packs discarded at their sides and their tired feet bare to the air.

'Ho, fellow travellers,' one of them called brightly as they saw the band approach.

'Don't even think about it,' Wat responded across the distance between them. He turned and spoke softly to Brody. 'Is that them?'

Hermitage was disappointed that Wat had assumed the worst and only then gone on to check whether he was right or not. How was the world to reach a state of grace if people went on behaving like that?

'Yes,' Brody hissed back.

Hermitage thought he should perhaps take note of Wat constantly imploring him to think the worst first and so avoid most of the trouble he ended up in.

'Don't even think about what, friend?' the man on the ground called.

'I'm not your friend,' Wat replied. 'No, we are not going stop and join you in a comforting rest. We are not going to share tales of our journeys, or perhaps the bottle of ale you just happen to have. I am going to keep my hand on my knife as we walk past and leave you here.'

'Well, I say.' The man who seemed to be in charge of the talking sounded very disappointed. 'What a world do we find ourselves in that a simple traveller cannot exchange the time of day with those he meets upon the road?'

'A world where we all keep our own property and no one gets hurt,' Wat said as they drew close.

Cwen gave the two seated men one of her very best looks, the one that sometimes made even Mrs Grod look away.

The two men had the grace to stay seated and beckon that the group was free to pass along the path unhindered.

As they walked on, Cwen turned to walk backwards keeping a wary eye on the men for any sign of movement.

As they reached the safety of the trees on the far side of

the clearing, Hermitage was sure he heard one of the men talking in a loud whisper to the other.

'See,' he said, 'I told you we should have sticks and jump out on people.'

. . .

The next two travelling down the road, and doing so rather surreptitiously, had no idea about the change in strategy being adopted by the argumentative robbers. These two were not even keeping to the middle of the path, usually the safest spot as the people jumping out of the woods with sticks could be seen coming. They were walking, as quietly as possible along the border of the trees, looking very much as if they did not want to be seen. Like the robbers, they were engaged in their own dispute.

'Did you see?' Athan's sentences had been short and clipped since they left Wat's workshop.

'Yes, I saw,' Nicodemus replied. 'And quite honestly I am now very bored with your complaining and growling about the works of Wat the Weaver. We know very well what sort of thing he does, why does seeing them make it worse?'

'I never imagined,' Athan breathed.

'Lack of imagination will do that.'

'I don't know whether to deal with the monk or the weaver first.'

'Well, that gives you something to nice to think about,' Nicodemus called over his shoulder as he strode cautiously along.

'And why, oh why?' Athan raised his voice as much as he dared for someone who was trying not to be spotted. 'Oh why, oh why,' he went on, 'did we have to buy one of the disgusting things?'

'Why, oh why,' Nicodemus responded, 'do I have to keep explaining this to you? It would have looked very peculiar if we hadn't bought one. That Hartle fellow would have got very suspicious. He thought we were customers waiting for the right moment, not men with ill intent in mind for his master. He could have detained us.'

'He could have tried,' Athan grumbled.

'Or he could have sent word ahead to warn Hermitage and Wat that they were being followed. Then where would we be?' He tried to encourage Athan to think this through. He tried to encourage Athan to think a lot of things through. Even one thing would have been progress.

'It's all too clever by half for me,' Athan said.

'I know,' Nicodemus sighed.

'But all our money.' Athan complained.

'Our money?' Nicodemus queried.

'All right. All *the* money,' Athan corrected. 'Actually, all the king's money,' he pointed out with a heartless grin. 'The money we might need if we're going to have to follow this pair to the ends of the earth. I think the ends of the earth is where treasure is usually kept.'

'The tapestries are obviously expensive items,' Nicodemus tried to make this sound obvious but even he had been shocked at the original asking price for the modest work they had come away with. Modest in terms of size and complexity. Not modest in any other way whatsoever.

'It's no wonder the weaver's well dressed and always got plenty of coin. That much money for a piece of cloth and some wool.'

'But arranged in a rather unique pattern,' Nicodemus pointed out.

'A disgusting pattern.' Athan started again.

'Why don't you throw it away then,' Nicodemus asked, his patience running thin. 'Go on, throw it into the woods if you hate the thing so much. Some passer-by could pick it up and not believe their luck.'

Athan looked horrified. 'I'm not leaving something like this just lying about for anyone to see.'

'Burn it then.'

'Burn it?'

'Yes, burn it. That way no one will ever have to see it again. And you'll have rid the world of one more tapestry from Wat the weaver.'

'You do remember how much this thing cost?' Athan protested.

'Of the king's money,' Nicodemus replied. 'Which he doesn't know I took.'

The confusion was flitting around Athan's face like a moth round a candle, never coming to rest but never setting light to itself either.

'What are you suggesting we do with it then?' Nicodemus asked, quietly. 'You won't throw it away, you won't burn it. What are you going to do? Sell it?' Become a trader in the tapestries of Wat the Weaver?'

'Shut up,' Athan said. 'You're confusing me.'

'Happens a lot, doesn't it?' Nicodemus sighed again although this one came out through a small smile.

'Aha!' cried the man who jumped out of the woods in front of them, brandishing a stick.

'Ow,' the man said as Athan punched him firmly in the face and landed him on his backside.

'Idiot,' Athan commented.

'You hit me,' the man complained in a muffled voice as he clutched his nose.

'You're an idiot,' Athan explained. 'You deserved it.'

'But you're a monk,' the man moaned. 'You're not supposed to hit people.'

'I'm not that sort of monk.' Athan looked very ready to hit the man again if he tried to stand up. 'And I'll hit your idiot friend hiding behind that tree if he tries anything.'

The idiot friend emerged with his hands held out, a broad grin on his face. 'I am so sorry,' he apologised profusely. 'We thought you were robbers.'

'You thought *we* were robbers?' Nicodemus did not believe this for a moment.

'We've been followed for some time now,' the man went on. 'My companion here got carried away.'

'You'll have to carry him away in a minute,' Athan explained the next step in the process. He picked up the stout staff the man had been brandishing, gripped each end and snapped it in half. The man on the floor swallowed.

'Aha,' the second man tried to sound light and care-free but obviously wasn't. 'We can be on our way then, and disturb you no more.'

'Oh, I don't think so,' Athan sounded like he had a plan for these two. And they weren't going to enjoy it. 'I think it's my duty as a man of God to stop sinners like you causing any more trouble for innocent travellers like us.'

'Innocent?' the bleeding-nose man managed a hopeless laugh.

'Just a moment,' Nicodemus interrupted with a thoughtful tone. 'I imagine that these gentlemen have acquired a certain wealth from their activities on the road - if we were inclined to think the worst of them.'

'No, no, I assure you,' the man from the tree protested.

'Or we think the best and they are real merchant

travellers.'

'That's it exactly sir.' Much nodding from both of them this time.

'In which case,' Nicodemus beckoned Athan to open his pack. 'I imagine they would be interested in the opportunity to purchase a very rare object for a very reasonable price.'

'Oh sir, would that it were so. Trade is bad in these sorry times and we barely have enough to put food in our mouths every other day.'

Athan had retrieved Wat's tapestry from his pack and let it drop open in front of the men.

There was a long, profound silence which the man of the tree eventually broke. 'How much?' he asked with a very peculiar look on his face.

Caput VII

Goose vs. Leech

That night in Nottingham was a very comfortable one for Hermitage, Wat, Cwen and Brody. Once again, the weaver had used the outrageous profits from his disgusting tapestries to secure the very best accommodations. Once again Hermitage had fretted over the moral questions involved, but as he fell asleep very quickly after a magnificent meal, he didn't have to fret very long.

Cwen glowered and complained at the brand new, and very imposing wooden castle that William had put up. She moaned that he wasn't hanging around in his subjugation of the country. Wat pointed out that at least the soldiers in the castle were keeping the place in some sort of order. But apparently it wasn't the right sort of order for Cwen.

Nicodemus and Athan even had a reasonable time of it. They took good rooms very close to the Wat and Hermitage, although Athan expressed doubts that it was right to make profit by selling Wat's tapestry to the robbers. He would not have been pleased to hear that Hermitage suffered similar doubts.

Nicodemus didn't help by suggesting that Athan's sales methods had been more akin to extortion than negotiation. The dilemma dissolved nicely in some jugs of beer and a bowl of stew. A tavern boy was promised payment if he woke them when Wat and the others were leaving town and so they settled for the night.

. . .

The boy was true and honest to his word, although when he saw the coin he was offered by Nicodemus, his language was not that of anyone true or honest, let alone a boy. Athan tried to clip him round the ear but he was too quick and left promising that the whole of Nottingham would be warned not to assist the thieves who were as good as taking food from the mouths of children.

They observed from a safe and discreet distance as the party of Brother Hermitage left its lodgings. Such was the profit from this one stay that the landlord himself had come out to see them on their way and promised a warm welcome should they ever return.

The two groups headed off into the town, the first in the warm glow of approbation, the second watching their backs for any rotten fruit that might be coming their way.

They all wound through the streets of this busy place, which their landlord assured them had a population of over a thousand, a vast number which Hermitage found completely unbelievable. He also doubted anyone in the town was capable of counting to such a high number and so had little confidence in the figure. Such was their interest in the goings-on around them that they failed to notice the two figures behind, hopping from doorway to doorway in a blatant attempt not to be spotted.

The route Brody followed was clearly heading for the river. The Trent wound its way round the south of the town, heading generally east before it would turn north later on. This direction gave Hermitage concern for a number of reasons. If they were planning to use the river as a means of transport that would mean a boat. If the open road held terrors for him, the open river was where they came after dark to make his nightmares.

And if they were to cross the river that wasn't much better. The ferryman's journey may be a short one, but that only meant the robbery and murder had to proceed more quickly.

Perhaps they would simply come to the river and then turn along its bank to continue their journey on foot. Of course, that carried the risk of slipping off the bank and falling in to be carried away but one worry at a time. Well, maybe two.

Brody led on out of the safe surroundings of the town's buildings and down a well-trodden path until the river dominated their view.

'Ah,' cried Hermitage, in huge relief. 'A ford.'

The others gave him some very strange looks, clearly wondering why he found the presence of a ford so exciting. They hadn't been in his head with all the images of drowning.

This ford was obviously a major thoroughfare. It probably even explained the presence of the town itself, if this was the only place the river could be crossed with ease. Even at this early hour of the day, carts and people were coming and going through the shallow waters as they swirled over the rock below. The swirling looked a bit threatening to Hermitage but no one else seemed to be having any trouble. In the several minutes it took them to reach the water's edge, he saw not a single person dragged away to die a horrible death in the dark depths.

At least there was no queue to cross at this time of day and they were soon on the brink of stepping into what looked like a rather cold stream.

'Still heading east then?' Wat asked Brody, who did not reply. 'Or south, I suppose.'

'I think east,' Cwen concurred. 'The south road is a busy one. Nowhere to hide a secret monastery I'd say. Bound to be east. Off in the marshes where no one wants to go anyway.'

They looked at Brody who gave nothing away by acknowledging the speculation, but who was looking a bit put out.

'Cart for four sir?' a voice cried as a young man hopped in front of them, effectively blocking their entry to the river.

'A cart?' Hermitage asked, having somehow found himself at the front of his band.

'Oh yes sir,' the young man said, with enthusiasm. 'For a holy man like yourself, a fine merchant, the lady and your boy.'

Hermitage looked around for these people and realised it meant Wat, Cwen and Brody. He also saw that there was indeed a cart, stopped at the waterside. It was a simple affair with benches on its top to carry perhaps six or eight people at a time. The front was a single pole with a harness for a man rather than a beast, and another figure stood at the rear of the cart, obviously ready to push.

'I think we'll walk.' Hermitage knew that a cart across a ford was a luxury few but the wealthiest would indulge in. It was certainly not fitting transport for a monk.

'Well, of course you can walk,' the cartman acknowledged, 'although the river is particularly wet today.'

Hermitage just stopped himself looking at the water to see how wet it was. 'I'm sure we'll manage,' he tried to sound as if the decision to walk was made and no persistent cart man was going to persuade him otherwise.

'Good luck then, Brother,' the man smiled and nodded, stepping back to open the way to the river.

Hermitage took a step forward.

'I'm sure the leeches won't disturb the feet of a man of

God like yourself.'

'Leeches?' Hermitage stopped.

'Oh, yes Brother,' the man sounded very proud. 'Our river has leeches the size of puppies. Took a man's foot off completely the other day.'

Hermitage was about to express his horror at this when one's of Wat's lessons sprang into his head. "whatever anyone tells you" the weaver had instructed, "don't believe them." It was simple enough but a whole new world to Hermitage.

'And this is the truth in front of a man of God is it?' Hermitage was quite pleased with himself at this response, even if it did sound rather rude.

'Ah, well,' the cart man explained. 'Didn't see it myself, obviously. But I'm sure it's true. Everyone's been talking about it.'

'So how come the leeches don't take your feet?' Hermitage asked, in what he felt was a very rapid and pointed retort.

'It's the goose fat.'

'Is it?'

'Oh, yes. Common knowledge that the leech and the goose are mortal enemies.'

Hermitage looked around for some help with this. Wat and Cwen were simply watching with their arms folded. No help at all.

'Ever seen a leech on a goose?' the man demanded.

'Er, well, I suppose not.'

'There you are then. Slap of goose fat on the feet and the leeches keep their distance.' The man lifted one of his feet as if inviting Hermitage to check for the presence of goose fat.

'That's all very well.' Hermitage tried to get back to the

question before him. 'But we don't want to take the cart. We shall walk through the ford.' He looked at the traffic passing through the water. 'Like most of the people here.' He waved at several travellers who were splashing through the river without even looking down to see if leeches had taken their toes.

'Ah, well they're local and know all about the leeches and the geese, you see.'

Hermitage simply tried to look as if there was no way whatsoever that he was getting on a cart just to cross a ford.

'And it's only a penny for four,' the cart man sold his wares.

Hermitage took his courage in his hands, held the cart man's gaze and in clear, definite and unalterable terms said, 'We are going to walk.'

The man shrugged at this defeat and now beckoned that Hermitage should step into the water. He turned to invite the others to follow only to see that they were all sat in the cart.

'What?' he squeaked his dismay.

'I'm not getting my feet wet,' Wat explained, nodding towards his fine shoes as he flipped a coin to the cartman.

The man grinned and got into his harness. His companion set to pushing the back of the cart and they set off. Hermitage walked pointedly behind, the bottom of his habit soaking nicely in the water, and his attention focussed on any tickle of his feet that might indicate the arrival of the leeches.

As he crossed he saw a simple man coming the other way, driving half a dozen geese in front of him, doubtless on his way to market. They hissed as they waddled into the water. Perhaps it was at the leeches. Hermitage hurried his way out of the River Trent.

It wasn't long before the road from the ford came to the great old Roman highway leading from Lincoln to somewhere off in the far southwest - probably Spain. The highway was more old than great now, but it was still a major thoroughfare of the country. It was crowded as the day was advancing. Carts and people laden with their own loads travelled the path, many of them probably only going a short distance. There were even one or two riders on horses, but they naturally ignored the poor people who did nothing but get in their way.

The days of routine travel across the length and breadth of the land had long gone but this did not stop Cwen complaining that William had used the old roads to fasten his grip on the country. She said that this was completely unfair as he should have been made to build his own roads if he wanted to go anywhere. These were good Saxon roads and he had no right to set foot on them.

Pointing out that they were actually Roman roads and that the Saxons had probably used them for their own invasion, and that Harold had only been able to get to Hastings for the battle by using the roads, only made her cross.

Brody stopped them at the road and looked left and right for a gap in the stream of travellers so that they could cross.

'Certainly east now,' Wat observed.

'All right,' Brody snapped. 'So it's east. There's a lot to the east.'

Wat gave this a moment's thought. 'No there isn't,' he concluded. 'A few towns and then the land gets progressively wetter until it turns into water. Except no one's been able to find the exact point it does so. One minute you're thinking, "this ground is very soggy" and the next, "this water's a bit on the firm side." Either way, you get wet.'

'You'll see, you'll see,' Brody crowed slightly, waving an arm towards the east.

The direction of the journey was all very well, but getting across the road was not proving to be easy. There was so much use of the thoroughfare that there were no gaps. As soon as you could see space behind a cart heading south, you'd see there was a horseman on the other side going north. And there was no rhyme or reason for where anyone was on the road. It infuriated Hermitage that there was no sign of any organisation at all. People going in one direction were constantly having to adjust their path to avoid someone going the other way.

All the thing needed was a bit of coordination. He immediately saw that if all the people going north went on one side of the road, and those going south on the other, the whole thing would run much more smoothly. He also suspected that if he suggested such a thing the accusations of witchcraft would soon be flying.

Naturally, the most pressing question would be which side? Should people drive their goods and livestock on their left or their right? Did it matter? Of course it did, he concluded. And there was an absolutely definitive answer to the problem. Our Lord sat on the right hand of God, so people should drive on the right. Problem solved. And not a witch in sight.

He had heard it suggested that people travel on the left so that their right hands were free for their swords. But that was ridiculous. Who could afford a sword, for goodness sake?

Very satisfied with his reasoning, which he looked forward to explaining in some detail to the others, he jumped when he was grabbed by the scruff of the neck and hauled across the road.

Cwen had spotted a gap and gone for it. There had been someone approaching but a simple glare had slowed them enough for the route to open. There were some shouts of rage as people's travel was disturbed and a loud suggestion that people like them shouldn't be allowed on the road if they didn't know how to use it.

Once on the far side, Cwen hurled her own insults back into the flow of people. She even stooped to pick up a rock, which Wat gently took from her hand.

Hermitage feared for the future if people couldn't even travel on the roads of the country together without coming to blows.

. . .

Back at the ford, the blows were coming thick and fast. When Nicodemus and Athan arrived at the water there was no offer of a cart. Word of their parsimony had been spread very effectively by the boy from the tavern and the whole of the town seemed to have gathered to see them on their way.

It started with some simple stares of aggression and challenge but these soon developed into shouts and boos and it wasn't long before the first object was thrown. At least it was soft and so did little damage but it was the principle of the thing. More followed, and the small turnips did make an impact.

Even Athan, who would normally be more than a match for some stupid townsfolk could do nothing; there was no telling who in the crowd was throwing what. He picked something off his habit and held it between thumb and forefinger for Nicodemus to examine.

'Who on earth is throwing leeches, for goodness sake?' Nicodemus turned up his nose.

Athan turned his glare on the crowd and pointed at them in a very threatening manner. There were several, colourful suggestions as to exactly where he could put his threatening finger but no one actually stepped forward to assist.

'This treasure better be worth it,' Athan said through clamped teeth as he splashed across the ford, objects of a various, but consistently unpleasant nature landing around him.

'If it really is the Monasterium,' Nicodemus replied, 'you'll be able to come back here and either curse the place to the darkest corner of hell or buy it, three times over.'

The look on Athan's face made it quite clear which he'd prefer.

Caput VIII

The Valley in The Water

Their route following the group in front thereafter was relatively straightforward, being mainly across open country. Asking anyone if they'd seen someone leading a smart-looking man, a girl and a monk usually brought clear directions.

As they drew further east, Nicodemus grew confident that they must be going to Sleaford and so keeping close track of their prey was unnecessary. They could afford to increase the distance between them and so reduce the risk of being seen. In fact, before they approached that town, the group ahead had turned slightly south. So confident was Nicodemus that he and Athan found themselves in Sleaford asking about a monk, a girl and a weaver, and getting some very strange looks.

Retracing their steps, they needed to find the way once more. Passing along the bank of yet another nondescript body of water that could be a river, or a pond, or a drain or just lost itself, they found what seemed to be a person, although it wasn't immediately obvious.

Sitting gazing out at the water with no sign of action was a small, grey man who took no notice of their approach or their enquiry for directions.

'Have you seen a monk, a girl and well-dressed man pass by?' Nicodemus asked loudly, imaging that the man might not speak English, they were so far East.

'It's the eels,' the man eventually replied.

'Is it?' Nicodemus sighed his disappointment at finding yet another idiot in front of him. He sometimes felt they must be queueing up somewhere, just waiting for him. Except they couldn't even organise waiting properly.

'And have the eels seen a monk, a girl and a well-dressed man?' he tried.

The strange figure seemed to light up at this suggestion. 'Indeed,' he said, in a lively manner. 'Indeed they have. Although they were only the spirits of a monk, a girl and a well-dressed man.' He waved off towards more of the marshes and waters.

'That's what I meant,' Nicodemus explained.

'But the eels have gone now,' the man complained. 'Not been a decent catch for years.'

'Probably because they saw you coming,' Nicodemus muttered.

If this was an old eel fisherman he appeared to have taken on a lot of the qualities of his catch. He was long and thin with no shape to him at all. His eyes seemed to be heading round the sides of his head, which was decorated with wisps of grey hair, greasy and sticky and looking alarmingly like tentacles. His skin had taken on some sort of sheen which gave the distinct impression he might glow in the dark. This did not look like a man to trust.

'I can show you where the spirits went,' the fisherman offered. 'I can try to summon a shoal of eels to bear us through the waters.'

'It's all right.' Nicodemus smiled and took a step back. 'We can walk.'

'Just as well.' The man shook his head in disappointment. 'The eels don't answer the summons like they used to.'

Even taking directions seemed a doubtful chance but this creature was the only help they had.

'What's that way?' Nicodemus asked loudly, pointing in

the direction the man of the eels had indicated.

'That way?' the man asked, apparently aghast that anyone would enquire of such a place.

'Yes, that way,' Nicodemus repeated sounding as cross as he could.

The old eel-man beckoned them close.

As they drew near they could tell that even if there were no eels anymore, this man had spent so long in their company that they had left an indelible mark.

'Good Lord man,' Nicodemus took a step back, covering his nose and gagging slightly. 'You stink.'

'Aha,' the man laughed and nodded. 'So the eels know me,' he explained.

'I think even the eels will draw the line somewhere.' Nicodemus tried to wave the smell away. 'And that direction?' he repeated the question.

'That way,' the man announced in tones of awe and amazement, 'lies,' he paused for effect. 'Spalding.'

'Spalding,' Athan said with frank disappointment. 'And is there a monastery there?'

'You're the monk,' the old man pointed out. 'Don't you know?'

'Would I be asking?' Athan's fists were clenched in the way they normally were when anyone questioned him.

The eel man shrugged, 'Probably,' he acknowledged. 'There's monasteries in most places.'

'And the monk, the girl and the man?' Nicodemus enquired. 'They were heading for Spalding? They were on the Spalding road?'

'Aye, aye. That they were.'

Nicodemus and Athan convened a brief conference. 'I'd be surprised if the monastery was in Spalding,' Nicodemus speculated. 'Too busy. Too normal. If the Monasterium was there, everyone would know about it.'

Athan had to agree. 'I once had a novice who was born in Spalding,' he commented in a manner that did not invite further enquiry.

They returned to the old man of the eels.

'What's beyond Spalding?' Nicodemus asked.

'Beyond Spalding?' The man was truly shocked at such a question. 'No one knows what's beyond Spalding,' he explained in awed tones. 'Probably nothing.'

'Nothing?'

'The end of the world.' The old man even held his arms aloft to emphasise the point.

'The end of the world is the other side of Spalding?' Athan snorted with contempt.

'Don't ye mock,' the man retorted. 'Go beyond Spalding and you will fall into the mouth of the eel at world's end.'

'The what?' Nicodemus asked, despite his instincts telling him to leave this mad man to his eels.

'The eel that eats its own tail,' the old man's eyes were as glazed as his skin.

Athan huffed, 'How are we going to fall in if its mouth is already full of its own tail?'

The eel man pointed a withered finger at them. 'Beware,' he wailed. 'Beware the great eel, Eeloreelus. Mock ye not.'

'Yes, yes,' Nicodemus said, indicating to Athan that they should move away quite quickly now. 'We won't mock. And we'll look out for the eel and send your regards.'

'And say hello to the monks,' the eel man added in a surprisingly normal voice.

Nicodemus and Athan both stopped as if frozen.

'What monks?' Nicodemus asked, carefully.

'The monks who guard the eel of course.' The eel man obviously thought even visiting idiots should know that.

'There are monks guarding the eel,' Nicodemus said. 'Of course there are. And they're beyond Spalding as well?'

'Don't know where else they'd be.'

'But they're just before you get to the end of the world I expect,' Athan remarked.

'Where exactly?' Nicodemus pressed. 'How will we find these monks?'

The eel man had started shaking his head and laughing lightly at the ridiculous questions these people were asking. 'You head east out of Spalding until you get to the End.'

'The end?'

'That's right. The End.'

'End of what? The road?'

'Just the End. End of everything. You'll know it when you get there because there isn't any more.'

'And the monks are there. In a monastery?'

'That's right,' the eel man nodded enthusiastically. 'That's what they call a place monks live. We're quite proud of it round here. It's a special one is the Monasterium Tenebrarii.'

'The what?' Athan demanded, after a pause to realise that the man had actually said those words.

Neither of them moved in case the eel man got distracted and started talking about something else. Something to do with eels, no doubt.

'Monasterium Tenebrarii,' the eel man repeated. 'That's what it's called.'

Athan was grinding his teeth in a manner that said he'd soon be starting on the gums. 'That's the place we're looking for,' he growled.

'Oh,' the eel man said brightly. 'You should have said. I'll show you the way if you like.'

Nicodemus's teeth couldn't grind as they were clamped together. 'That would be lovely.'

. . .

'Are you sure this is right?' Wat asked as the afternoon saw them walking along a path that seemed to be turning slowly to water with every step.

'Oh yes,' Brody replied. 'This is the way all right. It's the only way.'

The land hereabouts was so flat and featureless, and the water so featureless and flat that it was hard to tell the two apart. The sky was as grey as both and the horizon could be miles away or right in front of your nose. Trees obviously had no place here and had been left long behind on their path.

Many of the inhabitants of Spalding had given them signs of blessing as they left on the eastern path; clearly a route seldom trod, and only then by the brave or foolhardy. Brody had been recognised though, and several of the locals greeted him; a wave by a couple of local girls, a cheery smile from a tavern landlord or a demand for payment from several tradesmen which he promised he would sort out as soon as he got back to the monastery.

They tramped on through this desert of emptiness, the reeds and grasses blowing in a wind that had nowhere to go. It was a good job Brody knew the path because it was completely invisible to anybody else.

Hermitage followed along confidently, after all, Brody had brought them word of the Monasterium and all the details that went with it. He was starting to have his doubts now though. There was no sign of any building whatsoever, and he doubted that one could be built in this place at all.

One of his early monasteries had been on the Lincolnshire coast but that was much farther north where there was at least a coast you could put your finger on.

This bleak place seemed to be a simple dissipation of land into sea with no clear demarcation between the two. Perhaps Brody had made it all up and was simply leading them to their deaths in the water. Why he would want to do such a thing was beyond Hermitage. Maybe King William had decided they should be disposed of, and this was his method. No, he thought. Far too long-winded and complicated for William. A simple knife in the ribs would be a lot less trouble. In fact the King would probably just send the knife with instructions for Hermitage to do the deed himself.

'Erm,' he spoke up, hesitating to question their guide. 'I see no buildings at all in this direction my son, only a great expanse of water and a very tenuous smattering of land.'

'Yes.' Cwen was much more direct. 'Are you completely lost, or just some sort of idiot?'

'It's here, it's here,' Brody protested that they were doubting him. 'It's in a bit of dip, that's all.'

'Ah.' Hermitage nodded at the explanation. 'Just a minute,' he added after actually thinking about the explanation. 'A bit of a dip? How could it be in a bit of a dip out here? You can't have a dip in the water, everyone would drown.'

'That's the clever bit,' Brody winked.

'The clever bit?' Cwen mocked. 'The monks are so clever they don't drown underwater?'

'It's the dyke,' Brody said with obvious pride.

'Is it?'

'Yes, it is. The great dyke keeps the water at bay. And it hides the monastery from prying eyes.'

Cwen snorted and looked around, 'I don't think anyone would bother coming out here to pry at anything.'

'An excellent spot to conceal the Monasterium,' Hermitage noted.

'If we believe a word of it,' Cwen huffed.

They walked on even further now, having to brush tall reeds out of their path, although the ground did seem to become more solid under their feet. There was no telling, in this bland landscape covered as it was with tall grasses, whether they were walking along a riverbank, along the side of some stream, or actually on the bed of a waterway itself.

Surprisingly, the ground started to rise beneath them. It was no more than a small step, but in this place it felt that they had climbed out of a pit. They must be all of two feet above the path they had taken and had doubtless climbed out of some subtle river valley, onto these magnificent uplands.

'Nearly there,' Brody assured them.

The group moved on in silence. It still seemed very doubtful that there could be anything but a rude hut out here. The bewildering flatness and stark absence of any mark on the landscape seemed to demand silence.

Having escaped the robbers of the woodland, Hermitage was starting to think there might be people hiding in the reeds waiting to jump out on him. He thought there were people hiding in most places waiting to jump out on him. Sometimes he was right.

They now took to positive climbing, which Hermitage hadn't thought possible. Such was the solid mass of reeds and rushes that comprised the entire landscape, it was impossible to discern any variation. In fact there was a pretty substantial hill which they now made their way up. It too was covered in green, waving fronds, which served to make it indiscernible in the overall impression of green and waving.

A small path led up the incline, which, in terms of inclines generally was still pretty pathetic, but it did lift them a good ten or twelve feet above the surrounding land.

As they crested the top of the rise and saw what lay before them, Hermitage drew a sharp breath. He looked at his companions and noted that even Cwen was failing to disguise her look of complete surprise.

It was just as Brody had said, there was a great dyke and they were on top of it. It was entirely covered with the universal greenery, which only served to disguise its presence until you were there. It stretched off to left and right in a straight line for hundreds of yards. Dead level and very solid. It then turned at both ends and headed off straight away from them before joining the twin of the one they stood on, quite some distance away. The whole created a giant square bulwark, holding back the land and the water beyond.

On the far side of the distant dyke, the level scenery resumed and the sea could be discerned quite clearly. It was a flat and glassy looking sea which clearly had little depth, but it indicated greater waters beyond.

Within the huge square of dyke, in a space that must comprise several acres, the land resumed its previous lower level. In fact, to Hermitage's eye it was clear that the ground inside the dyke had been dug out. The drop down the other side of the hill was much deeper and steeper than that which they had climbed. There were even steps cut into the hill in front of them to aid descent.

Most remarkable of all, in the middle of the area enclosed by the dyke was a monastery. The Monasterium Tenebrarii. It had to be. What other monastery would be put in a place like this?

It was incredible, and Hermitage actually found himself rubbing his eyes.

'Told you so.' Brody was smug.

'Goodness me,' Hermitage breathed.

Wat too was taking in the scene before them. 'Holy bones,' he said. 'How did that get there?'

It was a very good question, if unnecessarily expletive. The construction of the dykes themselves was a simply magnificent achievement. Hermitage couldn't for a moment imagine how much earth had to be moved to build these great ramparts. Nor where so much earth had even come from in this watery bog of a place.

And then there was the monastery. It was not a great, huge construction as some places were, but it was substantial enough. From their height, Hermitage could see that there was an outer wall with a main gate that faced them. Square walls then followed the line of the dyke, their tops probably just below the peak of the dyke itself; doubtless a clever piece of design to ensure the place would not be discovered. There were towers in each corner of the monastery but they were fairly modest affairs, perhaps deliberately squatting down to avoid being spotted from afar.

Within the walls the normal distribution of a monastery was in place. That building must be the refectory, there was probably the dortoir, that was the cloister and over there the chapel.

He wondered for a moment if he would be able to spot the sundial from here. He could see that one would be needed in this place. Not being able to see beyond the dyke would mean that the world beyond was a complete unknown. Without the activities of a town or village, it would be impossible to tell what day it was, never mind the time. Mind you, the bland grey sky indicated that the sun might not visit these parts very often.

He couldn't see the sundial and chided himself for imagining that the body of Father Ignatius might still be in place. Even monks in this strange environment would probably remove a dead body after a few days.

There was though a small cemetery visible by the chapel. The brothers who stepped over the dyke to populate this place might never step back again.

Even more remarkable than the construction of the dyke and the simple presence of the monastery, was the fact that it was built of stone. Stone! Very few places were built of stone at all. Wood was the common method of construction. To go to the trouble of building here in stone made it a truly incredible construction. If the source of the earth for the dyke was a puzzle, the location of any stone at all was a complete mystery. It must have been shipped in from miles away. And Hermitage even doubted ships could get close, the water of the sea looking far too fragile to bear great vessels.

Mind you, the absence of trees meant that even wood was a rarity.

Brody was holding out his arms and basked in the magnificence of the sight before their eyes. 'God's dyke,' he announced.

'God?' Wat queried.

'Yes,' Brody confirmed. 'God cast the dyke from the ground of heaven to protect the monastery.

'God,' Wat nodded, appraising the buildings below. 'Not perhaps the Romans at all?'

'The what?' Brody asked.

'Never mind.' Wat spoke to Hermitage while they waited for Brody to finish basking. 'Looks like a Roman fort to me,' the weaver nodded towards the monastery.

Hermitage looked again, and could perhaps see some similarities to the old Roman constructions that still littered the land; until they were dismantled to build something new.

'Why would they go to the trouble of building this though?' Wat asked, clearly in some awe of the place.

Hermitage, prompted by the idea of the Romans, could see that it might be right. 'Good fertile land,' he explained. 'From some of the old histories I have read, it seems the Romans may have drained a lot of this land, built ditches and dykes and the like. A good salt marsh as well. This could be a remnant of their presence. They would have guarded their prize, and perhaps even created access to the sea.' He speculated further about the site before their eyes. 'It could be that as the sea began to encroach, they started the dyke, adding to it with each year until it got to the current height.'

Wat looked thoughtful. 'Clever people,' he said.

'They were remarkable,' Hermitage confirmed. 'Mostly heathen of course,' he dismissed the whole civilization.

'Come on then.' Brody was beckoning them down the hillside and they followed on the steps, which were themselves cut of stone but little used.

Once on the floor of the massive, enclosed space,

Hermitage looked back the way they had come. He felt a shiver of discomfort at being here, down below the level of the waters around them. 'What if the dyke fails?' he asked, always ready to spot impending disaster well before it had started impending.

'The dyke won't fail,' Brody said with confidence. 'God's dyke is hardly likely to fail, is it?'

Whilst this was obviously a very sound argument, it did nothing for Hermitage's confidence.

'I imagine,' Wat said idly, 'that if the dyke fails, the waters will flow in, everyone will drown and the place will disappear from the face of the earth.'

'Ah,' Hermitage said. 'Just as I thought.' He swallowed hard and hoped that this business of priests on sundials would be dealt with quickly.

Once at the gates of the monastery, Hermitage could tell that they had not been opened for many a year. Moss and lichen patched the surface, and the ground in front had not been disturbed for so long it was starting to become part of the marsh again.

Wat ground a bit of the floor away under his boot, a frown on his face.

'Problem?' Hermitage asked, imagining it would be quite a big one.

'Just wondering why the water doesn't come up through the floor.'

'Ah.' Hermitage hadn't been wondering anything of the sort but was now.

'Good God, look,' Wat said.

Frowning at the blasphemy, Hermitage examined the ground under Wat's feet.

'Stone,' the weaver said. He looked out across the great

expanses of the land within the dyke. 'The whole place is cobbled.'

There was nothing any of them could say which would encapsulate the awe they felt at the sheer scale of achievement this place in the middle of a marsh represented. What giants of men had created this from nothing? What mind had even conceived of such an unearthly scheme, let alone turned it to reality?

Hermitage wondered that it was perhaps modern men who were the insignificant dot on the last page of the Historia Brittonnum, and not those of history.

Brody called out to bring them from their reverie of wonderment. 'We have to crawl through the hatch in the door,' their guide explained. 'The doors won't open 'cos the hinges are broken. And the abbot reckons the devil will get in if we knock 'em down.'

Wonderment dispatched, they gathered at the door and sighed as they dropped to their knees and crawled one by one into the Monasterium Tenebrarii.

. . .

On the top of the rise behind them, more eyes were taking in the sight that the dyke revealed.

The eyes of Nicodemus glittered as they examined the vision. This really was the Monasterium. It existed. It was not a myth. No wonder it hadn't been found in all these years, hidden out here behind its walls. What an incredible place. The treasure had suddenly become an awful lot more real. And a lot more valuable.

Athan scanned the place, seeing an isolated monastery hidden from the world and its temptations. An institution that would allow its inmates to concentrate solely on their worthlessness, insignificance and ultimate destruction. He wondered if it needed a prior.

'You can go now,' Nicodemus said to the eel man, who was looking down at the monastery with disappointment that it was horribly dry down there. Not good country for eels at all.

The man held out his hand in the hope of reward.

Nicodemus looked at him, and then scanned the land around them. He was clearly wondering if anyone would notice if the world suddenly had one less eel man to worry about. There seemed little to gain though. People in these parts knew of the monastery anyway, and they'd asked directions of enough people that keeping their journey secret was a forlorn hope. No. Now was the moment to simply explain to the eel man that Nicodemus had no money anyway, and had never been going to pay anything.

When he turned back the eel man had gone. Vanished back into the reeds somewhere no doubt. Nicodemus shrugged; one less problem.

Now. Why were the idiots down by the monastery on their hands and knees?

Caput IX

Into the Monastery

𝔈ntrance to the Monasterium Tenebrarii, the great secret repository of the knowledge and treasures of Christendom was an uncomfortable and undignified experience.

They found that not only was the door shut firm but it was starting to rot and the splinters around the hatchway caught in their clothes. Wat was particularly annoyed as a thread from his jerkin was pulled free.

'You would think..,' he started on a consideration of why the monks of this place should be engaged in some routine maintenance. He came to a halt as he observed several pairs of sandals on the floor in front of them. Each pair full of feet. Dirty, nasty looking feet that looked like they'd already been dragged through the marshes.

They all scrambled to their own feet and stood facing the reception party.

One monk stood to the front, doubtless the abbot. Hermitage took a half step forward and bowed. 'I am Brother Hermitage, Father. We have received instruction from the king to attend upon you.'

He rose from his bow and looked the abbot in the eye. Or rather he didn't as the abbot's eye was directed elsewhere. A spindly arm rose slowly and a finger, more bone than flesh, pointed like some spirit directing doom. 'What is that?' the abbot intoned.

Hermitage followed the arm and saw where it was pointing. He was absolutely positive that Cwen would not welcome being referred to as "that". He could see that Wat had a very tight grip on her arm. She had a look on her face that said she would like to snap something spindly off an abbot.

'That is Cwen,' Hermitage explained, nervously. 'She and Wat have come at the king's directions as well.'

The abbot looked like he'd asked for the reliquary of Saint Thomas's knuckles and been given Beelzebub's bottom instead. 'A woman?' Two words managed to express horror, dismay and disbelief with a subtle hint of question as the abbot tried to remember if this was what women looked like.

'Indeed,' Hermitage confirmed. 'The king has sent us,' he tried to move on.

'We can have no woman in the monastery.' The abbot, sounded as if he were about to shout an alarm. Next to "fire, fire" it would be the one word guaranteed to get everyone running for their lives. He turned and delivered a very hot glare at Brody. 'You did this,' he accused. Brody stepped back to get some monks between him and the abbot. 'Who else have you brought? Is there a crowd of followers outside?'

'No Father,' Brody gulped. 'No one followed. And these were the people at the place the king sent me.'

'I shall deal with you later,' the abbot promised in a rising scream.

Hermitage turned but Brody was already gone. Probably very wise.

Unfortunately, the abbot's declarations of shock had reached other ears and several brothers appeared from various doorways and corridors. As they gathered to look at the new arrivals, several of them seemed very pleased to be reminded that this was what women looked like.

'How long have you lot been here?' Wat asked, taking a protective step forward in front of Cwen, and looking like he was getting ready to run.

'Shall we go somewhere private, to talk?' Another brother stepped forward from just behind the abbot. He held out an arm to direct the new arrivals away from the now gawping and muttering crowd, joined every moment by another monk from somewhere or other. This fellow looked well able to see off a band of inquisitive monks. He had the stance and build of a soldier and the worn look of someone who had been out in the world instead of being nurtured in the cloister.

'That would seem best, Brother,' Hermitage said. He had first-hand experience of what monks were capable of when they got together and were in a funny mood.

'Brother Egbert,' the monk introduced himself. 'I'm the Claustral Prior. The abbot's study is this way,'

'No,' the abbot forbade such an intrusion with a booming instruction.

'Oh, very well,' Egbert said impatiently. 'We'll go to Father Ignatius's chambers. Probably the best place to start anyway.'

He led them away from the main gate and across the compound to a plain rectangular building which was obviously the chapel. Or at least was now being used as the chapel. The abbot followed but he clearly wasn't happy about it. His sulking silence making a sixth companion.

The monks who had gathered to witness the miracle of Cwen dispersed to their own devices; probably a detailed discussion of the event, followed by a number of imaginative speculations as to how it could have been made much more interesting. One figure, a cowl pulled low over its face, loitered to watch the departing party. If anyone had been bothered to observe, they might have seen a very slight but slow and deliberate shaking of the head within the cowl.

. . .

As they walked, Hermitage grew confident that Wat was right. This place had been a Roman fort long before it was a monastery. The main gate opened onto a large rectangular area, the walls punctuated with watchtowers. The view he had from the dyke had revealed as much as there was to be seen. There were only three substantial buildings really, this chapel to the left, the dortoir towards the back of the site and the cloister area which joined the dortoir to the wall on its right.

Markings on the floor though clearly indicated that this place had once been much more crowded. Probably with wooden buildings that had fallen into disrepair, rotted away or been taken for firewood.

Other gates could even be seen on each of the walls facing north, south and east. They had long been blocked up with masonry, presumably to make the place more secure. Hermitage wasn't sure how effective that would be as the blocking looked of very poor quality and rather precarious.

Egbert had brought them to the door of the chapel now and put his shoulder to the task of getting the thing open. Despite much grinding and groaning resistance the door shifted enough to let them slip through one at a time.

Windows, high in the walls of the place let the grey light of the marsh drop to the floor where it lay in stagnant puddles. Hermitage examined the chapel briefly and without surprise. It was a plain but large room, the same as any chapel in most monasteries up and down the land. Seats for the brothers faced the front, and the altar area was raised with a simple lectern from where the lessons would be read.

Nothing here to mark the place out at all. Apart, probably, from that large, gold-looking cross on the altar itself. Come to think of it, Hermitage noted, it did look very large for a place of this size. And very gold. And there seemed to be lumps of coloured glass decorating it. It must be a very prized possession.

Egbert led them on down the chapel towards a door on the right side of the altar. The abbot muttered his way along and Hermitage turned to make sure Wat and Cwen were with them.

This time it was Wat and Cwen who were gawping; and theirs was even more intrusive, somehow. They too appeared to have noticed the altar decoration and were studying it in great detail. Hermitage was cautiously pleased. They so seldom stood in awe of the might and majesty of the church. In fact most of the time they were very rude about it indeed. It was good to see that a place such as this could have an effect even on such as them.

They walked down the chapel as if in a daze.

'It is magnificent, is it not,' Hermitage commented, holding his arms out to encompass the full glory of the chapel. His own thought was that it wasn't actually that glorious. Rather plain really. But if it affected Wat and Cwen, who was he to complain.

'It's, it's,' Wat seemed lost for words.

Hermitage smiled.

'Gold,' Wat found the word.

'And jewels,' Cwen found some more.

'In the gold,' Wat explained.

'Which wraps around the jewels,' Cwen added.

'Ah, the cross.' Hermitage saw what was interesting them. 'It is a rather magnificent piece for a place in the middle of a marsh.'

As they arrived at the altar, Hermitage saw that the cross was at least two feet high and very solid. The shards of coloured glass looked particularly well made.

'Oh my,' he said, when the ideas of the treasure of the church being hidden in this place, Wat and Cwen's awe and the very shiny nature of the cross got together in his head. 'Is that?' He couldn't bring himself to ask the question.

'Yes, it is,' Wat said, having already worked out the answer.

'Ah.' Egbert saw that they had all stopped. 'You've seen our little altar piece.'

Hermitage nodded while Wat and Cwen simply opened their mouths some more.

'Part of our burden of care,' Egbert nodded solemnly.

'Burden,' Wat repeated in an odd tone.

'Come,' Egbert instructed. 'To Ignatius's chambers. I am sure there is much you wish to discuss.

'Much,' Wat repeated in the same, glazed manner.

Hermitage had to grab Wat and Cwen by the sleeves to drag them towards the small door that led to the room beyond.

Reluctantly following, the party found itself in what must be the chambers of the Sacerdos Arcanorum.

'Erm,' Hermitage raised a question before they walked in.

'Yes?' Egbert asked.

'Ignatius isn't erm, in here? Is he?' He was never good with dead bodies, which he knew was a drawback for an investigator of murder. But it wasn't his fault. He didn't want to be an investigator in the first place.

'No, no,' Egbert reassured him. 'Father Ignatius has been interred.'

Hermitage nodded, contentedly.

'We couldn't leave him on the sundial,' Egbert explained. 'And bodies tend not to last very well in this neck of the woods. It's the flies, you see.'

Hermitage urged Egbert to lead them on before the description became as bad as the body itself.

Egbert pushed ahead through a large, solid, arched door set into the stonework of the chapel and beckoned them to follow.

As they entered the chamber of Ignatius it was Hermitage's turn to gawp. His mouth dropped open and sucked a body full of air in with one, languorous gasp. He turned this way and that but all around him the treasures were stacked from floor to ceiling. There was even a ladder to reach the higher shelves and the floor was a maze of stacked piles that had to be negotiated carefully for fear of knocking the priceless artefacts.

The room was huge. A great, timbered roof towered above their heads and solid, stone walls stretched off into the distance in either direction. It was big enough to contain the population of an entire monastery, never mind one priest. But then with all of these marvels in here it was a bit crowded

The abbot and Brother Egbert did not seem in awe of this at all, but then they had probably lived with it all the time. Hermitage had never in his life imagined that such a place as this existed, or even could exist. Surely there was not enough material in the whole of Christendom to stock a room such as this.

The fact that this proved the place they were standing in

was indeed the Monasterium Tenebrarii had gone from his head. His sheer joy at seeing all of this laid out before him imposed itself and firmly made it known that this was the greatest day of his life. All the trials and tribulations of his days at the hands of his brother monks, at the boots of King William and Le Pedvin, and in the company of murderers, liars, drunks and idiots faded into a nagging annoyance that was easily ignored. Whatever he had gone through, it was now worth it.

All he had to do was make sure that this day, this moment, never ended. If he had any say in anything at all in his long and obedient career, it would be that he never left this room until he died. The waters beyond the great dyke could do what they liked. He would succumb to their inundations a happy monk.

His look was so excited he didn't know where to let his eye rest first. He turned to share his amazement at this astonishing discovery with Wat and Cwen. They seemed a lot more controlled in the face of this revelation; perhaps the cross on the altar was as much as they could manage.

Wat did look about the place and gave a half-hearted cough. 'Books,' he exclaimed, not seeing anything in this room that warranted their attention. 'Plenty to read then, eh, Hermitage?'

'Plenty to? 'Hermitage was aghast. So shocked at the casual dismissal of the greatest treasure trove in the realm that he found his voice. 'Wat, this is the greatest body of learning I have ever seen. I think it's probably the greatest anyone has ever seen. I never even knew this many books existed, let alone that they were gathered in one place.'

Wat didn't look impressed.

Hermitage went on. 'It is rumoured that The Bishop of

Hereford has a magnificent private library. One of the greatest personal gatherings of books outside of Rome.'

'Really?' Wat looked round to see if any of the books were made of gold.

'Yes,' Hermitage persisted. 'And do you know how many books the Bishop of Hereford is rumoured to have in his private collection?'

'Er,' Wat made a play of thinking carefully about it as if it was on the tip of his tongue, the number of books in the Bishop of Hereford's library being a regular topic of discussion in his workshop. 'No,' he concluded.

'Eight,' Hermitage said. 'The Bishop of Hereford has eight books.' He held his arms out to indicate the rows and stacks of books there were in this one room. 'And how many are here?' he asked.

'Four thousand nine hundred and twelve,' Egbert replied.

Hermitage looked at him. The words made sense on their own, but not in the context of counting books.

'It was one of the facts Ignatius tended to share. Quite frequently.'

'Four thousand,' Hermitage breathed.

'And he shared how difficult a task it was looking after all those books when they were being kept in the middle of a marsh,' Egbert went on.   'Rather than helping with the other jobs around the place.'

Wat picked up on the sharp tone, 'Not a popular Sacerdos then?' he asked.

'I wouldn't go that far,' Egbert said. 'Kept to himself and his books, mainly. But he certainly wasn't invited to the late night,' Egbert paused and looked at his abbot. 'Discussions,' he concluded.

'I think we have more important matters to discuss,' the

abbot demanded their attention. 'He pointed his special woman-pointing finger at Cwen once more.

'Yes.' Wat was patronising. 'Cwen is a woman.'

'I can speak for myself, you know.' Cwen spoke for herself.

The abbot drew in a breath as if he'd just been shot.

'The king has sent me here.' Cwen laid it on rather thick. 'So you'd better get used to it.'

Hermitage frowned at her. That was a rather broad interpretation of their instruction.

'The king?' The poor abbot seemed rather confused and didn't know which was worse, letting a woman into the monastery, or defying the king. He came to some sort of internal conclusion. 'The king would not send a woman. Not to this place.'

'What if I was the queen?' Cwen retorted.

The abbot looked her up and down. He was clearly finding this conversation difficult to cope with. Egbert knew that the abbot was a man of fragile temper; it took very little to send it flying all over the place. Being faced with anyone who answered him back tended to produce spluttering fury. A young woman who answered him back might be more than he could cope with. 'You are not the queen. If there even is one, now I hear that Harold is gone.'

'Look,' Wat said. 'It's too late now anyway, isn't it? Cwen's here. She's in the monastery, in the chapel and in the dead priest's book place.'

'Library,' Hermitage corrected.

'Quite. So why don't we just get on with business and see where that takes us?' If Cwen turns out to be a problem, we can ask her to leave.'

'If you ask her to leave, she will turn out to be a problem,'

Cwen growled at them all.

The abbot still had a face like a thundercloud.

'She's in here now,' Wat repeated. 'Your only option is to take her out again. Past all those monks of yours. And by now I don't think there will be a single one who isn't fully informed of the fact that there is a woman in the monastery.'

'The first,' the abbot croaked out anger and disappointment. 'In all the years of the Monasterium there has never been a woman inside the walls.' He seemed to be taking this as a personal failure. His temper had found no escape and so had gone back inside where it seemed to be doing something rather unhealthy to him.

'Cheer up,' Cwen said unhelpfully. 'There's probably never been a murdered Sacerdos before either.'

The abbot simply groaned at this.

Hermitage, who was never comfortable when Wat and Cwen started arguing, never mind when even more people were involved, wandered off among the aisles of books, stroking some of them and cooing at others. His hands hovered in front of him clearly burning to actually pick one up and open it, but not daring to in case it vanished in his hands.

'About the murdered Sacerdos,' he heard Wat asking quite loudly. Hermitage paused to wonder whether he, as King's Investigator, ought to be back there asking questions. But there were so many books. It was a real conflict. But not a difficult one. The books won.

'Not popular,' Wat went on. 'So not popular that someone might have done for him?'

Egbert considered the question carefully. The abbot was too busy glaring at the world around him, more specifically at the woman in the middle of it, that he was in no state to answer questions.

'I don't honestly think so,' Egbert answered. 'In fact most of the brothers considered him a bit odd and tended to laugh behind his back. And in front of his back as well. He stomped about and shouted a lot but there was no bite in him.' Egbert's eyes wandered towards his abbot, clearly indicating where all the bite in the Monasterium was kept.

'If it wasn't personal, it was probably to do with his role here.' Wat speculated.

'That's what I thought,' Egbert agreed. 'The Sacerdos Arcanorum is unique and leads a secretive but privileged life. It could well be that some secret he held was of such value that someone wanted it very badly indeed.'

Wat screwed up his face in thought. 'Why now though?' he asked. 'How long had he been here?'

'Longer than me,' Egbert replied. 'I came some four years ago and Ignatius was already part of the stonework.'

Wat rubbed his chin as he considered his next question. 'It is a rather odd place,' he suggested.

'Not really,' Egbert replied.

Wat raised his eyebrows at this.

Egbert explained, 'It is a completely, uniquely, extravagantly odd place. They don't come much odder. Most of the world has forgotten the place is here at all and now that Harold is gone I expect it will vanish under the waters before anyone bothers about it again.'

'But the treasure?' Wat said with rather more avarice in his voice than enquiry.

'Don't worry.' Egbert read Wat's thoughts precisely. 'There's plenty more actual treasure around the place. But it was put here a long time ago. Most of the people who knew are probably dead. It was all a great secret at the time and remained so. More myth than monastery.'

'How did you come here then?' Cwen enquired, causing the abbot to sit down on a stool by one pile of books.

'Harold told me to come. Said it was a reward for my services.' The tone in Egbert's voice shouted out that if this was a reward, bring on the punishment. 'Apparently I had a special talent which perfectly suited me to life in a monastery built in a hole in a swamp.'

'And what was that?'

'He never told me,' Egbert shrugged at the futility of life.

'So,' Wat was thoughtful. 'If Ignatius was killed for being the Sacerdos Arcanorum,' he paused. 'I take it he was killed? Not an accident?'

'Not unless he was on top of a ladder cleaning the cloister roof in the middle of the night.' Egbert was clear that this was not the sort of thing Ignatius got up to.

'Then it must be something he knew, or had, or was going to do, or hadn't done?' Wat scattered the ideas about.

'That narrows it nicely,' Egbert observed, wryly.

'This king's door thing?' Cwen asked. The abbot gave an audible gasp.

'Ah, yes,' Egbert, held up a finger. 'The very nub of the matter. Ignatius was pointing at the king's door. Now, if I'd just been impaled on a sundial I'd have more important things to worry about, but Ignatius took his work very seriously. He wouldn't point at the door for no reason.'

'So we open it,' Cwen concluded.

The abbot stood now, he could clearly take no more. '*We* do not do anything,' he instructed. 'The monk sent by the king may have authority in this matter but I am fairly sure that you do not.'

Cwen opened her mouth to speak.

'And even if you do,' the abbot went on, 'I am in charge here and you are going nowhere near the king's door.'

Cwen took half a step forward.

'And if you think otherwise,' the abbot smiled, nastily, 'I shall have you restrained by Brother Bedly.'

Egbert's grimace made it clear that being restrained by Brother Bedly was not recommended.

Cwen scowled extravagantly.

'Hermitage,' Wat called out to the room as Hermitage could not be seen. 'We might need to open the king's door and you're the only one who can do it, apparently.'

'Have you seen this?' Hermitage called from somewhere at the back of the room.

'Er, no,' Wat said.

'I believe it's the actual Historia Brittonum. Did you ever see such a thing?'

'Was that the one I found down the back of the apprentice's bedding the other week?' Wat asked.

'It could be original,' Hermitage went on, oblivious to Wat's response. 'Brother Nemnivus may have touched these sheets himself over two hundred years ago.'

'Pretty old then,' Wat commented. 'Not got any new books?'

'It even tells of the Saxon invasion. Can you believe that? We have just been invaded by William and here is a book reporting the invasion of the people he invaded.' Hermitage appeared among the piles of books, cradling a large volume in his arms, looking like he had just rescued a baby from a fire. 'Brother Egbert,' Hermitage moved the book half an inch towards Egbert. 'Did you know this was here?'

'Hardly,' Egbert snorted.

'Really? But you seem familiar with this room and the fact that the greatest library in Christendom is contained within your walls.' Hermitage couldn't believe that any monk in this monastery would not study the texts that were so close. Perhaps it was part of the rule of this place. A very cruel one, he thought, if only the Sacerdos was permitted access to the books.

'Of course we didn't know it was here,' Egbert said lightly. 'Only Ignatius was any use in that area. None of the monks here can read. Not me, not the abbot, not the lowest novice.'

Hermitage simply looked at him and tried to take in the ghastly idea. He knew that reading was not a common skill but among monks it was more widespread. And surely in a place like this? Putting monks who couldn't read in charge of a library? Well, it was like, it was like.., He tried hard to think of something more ridiculous that it was like. All he could come up with was that it was like putting monks who couldn't read in charge of a library.

Egbert was looking thoughtful. 'Bit of a coincidence, that, come to think of it.' He shrugged his shrug once more as he looked at all the books in the room. 'Quite a lot of trouble to go to, finding a whole monastery's worth of monks who can't read and sending them here.'

'And the Sacerdos was the only one who could,' Wat speculated. 'And now he's dead.' He paused to give someone else a chance to draw a conclusion.

Hermitage raised a finger. 'Perhaps it was something he'd read.'

Caput X

Open the Door, No, Take the Treasure

𝔑icodemus and Athan had reached the doors of the monastery. They were confident they had not been spotted as the place seemed to be completely dead. No signs of life emerged at all, never mind a monk toiling outside, or doing some of the basic repairs it looked like the place desperately needed.

Having successfully negotiated the ground from the dyke top to the entrance, they were now a bit lost as to what to do. There was no monk in attendance at the door, little sign that the thing had ever been opened and the hatch that the others had disappeared through was firmly shut.

'Just hammer on the thing and demand entrance,' Athan huffed as he stood staring at the door as if that was enough to frighten it out of his way.

'Excellent idea.' Nicodemus was his usual sneering self. 'Then Brother Hermitage can identify us straight away, tell the abbot of the place who we are and we can be drowned in the marsh by nightfall.'

'That mewling pool of cat sick wouldn't say boo to a deaf goose from half a mile away.'

'But the weaver is not so timid,' Nicodemus explained. 'And doubtless Hermitage is here in his official capacity. He will carry more authority than either of us; no matter how many people you thump.'

Athan's muttering under his breath was expected. 'You could say you're in the king's service as well.'

'You are full of marvellous suggestions today. I'm here on behalf of the king to have all the great secrets of the

Monasterium handed over please. Who am I? Oh, I'm his builder.' He gave Athan the look he used to wither things that were already dead. 'The question is,' he went on, 'how do we get in? And then once we are in how do we find out what's going on without Hermitage and his little friends spotting us?' He surveyed the walls. 'The place isn't big enough to hide us all.'

Athan coughed his own contempt. 'What do you think the cowl on a habit is for?'

Nicodemus looked at him askance.

'Just pull it over your head and cover your face. It's what I do when I want to give someone a surprise.'

Nicodemus could imagine what sort of surprises Athan liked to give. 'I think the brothers of this place will notice if two new habits appear. It doesn't look like the sort of establishment that gets many visitors.'

'What was your plan for when we got here then?' Athan demanded. 'Don't tell me there's something you hadn't got a plan for.'

Nicodemus said nothing. This was clearly a point of some sensitivity.

'A situation the great Nicodemus had not expected or prepared meticulously for?' Athan could do sarcasm quite well when he put his mind to it. 'Another one?' he added with a very large point. 'First De'Ath's Dingle and now the Monasterium Tenebrarii. What is the world coming to?'

'All right, all right,' Nicodemus retorted. 'We just need to think rather than go at it in your usual manner. This gate's too big even for your bull head.'

'I don't know why I put up with you,' Athan grumbled.

'The same reason I put up with you,' Nicodemus replied. 'Lack of choice.' He resumed his study of the monastery, gauging the height of the walls to see if climbing would be possible. Just as he was coming to the awful conclusion that Athan might be right, and they would have to knock, there was a movement of the hatch at their feet.

A section of the door swung back and an arm appeared, swathed in the rough cloth of a habit. The hand at the end of the arm mysteriously beckoned them close. Nicodemus reasoned that any monk's arm that beckoned through the hatch of the door to a monastery no one thought existed, qualified as mysterious.

He exchanged looks with Athan that said this was not the sort of thing they'd usually contemplate but an offer was an offer. They squatted down by the hatch and peered in, not willing to actually stick their heads through a hole that had some strange monk on the other side.

'Are you sent?' a voice on the other side asked. It was a hoarse whisper as if the speaker was trying to hide his identity.

'Sent?' Athan asked. Nicodemus waved him to silence.

'Yes,' the hoarse whispered. 'Sent?'

'Yes,' Nicodemus replied, confidently. 'We're definitely sent.'

'Then enter, Brother,' the voice croaked out. The hand withdrew as mysteriously as it had appeared and the hatch was held open.

Shrugging that they had nothing to lose, Nicodemus ducked through the hatch and was followed by Athan.

Once inside, they stood and saw their beckoner was indeed a monk, but with his cowl up and pulled over his face.

'That's how you do it,' Athan pointed out.

The monk before them crossed both arms across his

chest then put his right palm straight on his forehead – or where his forehead would be under his cowl – and bowed low.

Nicodemus raised his eyebrows at Athan with the clear indication that they'd got a right one here. Nonetheless he thought it wise to respond with the same gesture and waved a hand at Athan to instruct him to do likewise.

Shaking his head at the futility of all this mucking about, Athan crossed his arms, smacked his hand to his forehead in an entirely different gesture, and bowed.

'Aha,' the cowled monk said, 'you know the sign. This is good.'

Nicodemus could not stop a quiet, 'Ye God,' creeping out his mouth. 'You just made it to me brother,' Nicodemus reprimanded. 'I think you should be more careful in future.'

'Ah, of course.' The monk was very angry at himself for his stupid mistake and beat his fist hard against his leg. Very hard. And it looked like he had a knotted band of leather wrapped around his knuckles, specially designed for this very purpose. 'You'd better come with me.' The man turned away from them with a bit of a limp and a quiet groan of pain. 'The king's man has been sent and we must act if all is not to be lost.'

'Yes, yes,' Nicodemus agreed, 'we must. Indeed we must.' He felt it safe to make clear to Athan with a roll of his eyes that he had not a clue what he or the monk were talking about.

Hurrying as fast as his leg would allow, the monk took them away from the gate and towards the cloister, the man's head darted left and right to make sure they weren't seen. There was absolutely nobody about the place so the risk was pretty low. At the far end of the cloister he led them round a pillar and onto the top of a staircase leading down into some sort of crypt or cellar.

'A cellar?' Nicodemus exclaimed in wonder. 'Here? How on earth do have a cellar in this place?'

'It does get a bit damp at high tide,' the monk explained, pointing out the water mark well up the side of the wall as they descended.

Athan and Nicodemus hesitated.

'It's all right, it's low tide now,' the monk reassured them.

Nicodemus blinked. The uniform blankness of the watery landscape had given no hint that they were even on God's earth anymore, let alone about the state of the tides. 'How can you tell?' he asked.

'The cellar's not full of water,' the monk helpfully explained.

'Not a very good place for a cellar at any time I'd have thought,' Nicodemus observed.

'It was fine 'till we took all the cobbles off the floor to build a wall. After that the water started coming in twice a day.' The monk sounded like he had made no connection at all between these events. 'So between times it is a good place for us to meet.'

'Excellent,' Nicodemus said as they stood completely alone in a dark hole, waiting for the tide to turn.

The monk looked around the dark hole once more, checking that the empty room was not full of people listening in.

Nicodemus rested his face in his hand.

'There is talk that the king's door is to be opened,' the monk hissed his whisper.

'We have heard this as well,' Nicodemus said - which seemed to please the monk no end.

'And of course, this must not be permitted.'

'Of course,' Nicodemus agreed after a short pause.

'Just a minute,' Athan growled in his ear.

Nicodemus waved him quiet. He beckoned the monk to draw close. 'We have been sent, obviously,' he spoke conspiratorially. 'But our despatch was very hurried and we were not given full instructions. We were just told to report here and take guidance from you.' He paused to see if he had said entirely the wrong thing. The hooded figure appeared to be still listening. 'You think the king's man is here to open the door?'

'Of course,' the monk replied. 'Why else would he be sent?'

Nicodemus gave a good impression of deep thought, 'Perhaps to investigate the death of Ignatius?'

'To do what to him?' The monk sounded disgusted.

'Investigate,' Nicodemus explained with a sigh. 'It means to look into the murder. To track down the killer. From *vestigo, vestigare*, to track.'

'What will they think of next,' the monk lost his whisper and sounded very impressed.

'Perhaps the door will remain sealed and there's nothing to worry about.'

'Hm,' the monk gave this some thought. 'But what about Ignatius pointing at the door from his place on the sundial?'

'Ah, that, yes,' Nicodemus was grateful that listening in to the king's private conversations was so useful.

'Even if the king's man has come to inveigle himself with the dead body, he'll want to know why Ignatius was pointing at the door.'

'You are probably right, Brother.' Nicodemus sounded serious and sombre. 'You are far better informed than us in these matters.' He gave a thoughtful pause while he considered how far he could go. Athan's impatience was almost glowing in the dark. 'But if it is the king's man and it is the king's door, is it not the case that he is entitled to open it anyway?'

The habit containing the monk froze as if turned to stone, or a pillar of salt. Nicodemus glanced at his accomplice indicating that if this went badly, Athan might have to do what he did best. The ex-prior rolled up a sleeve of his habit in preparation.

Eventually the monk breathed again. 'And bring down judgement day upon us? Here and now?' His tone was one of complete horror at the suggestion.

'It must come at some time,' Nicodemus pointed out.

'Not until the next millennium,' the monk explained as if every fool knew this.

Nicodemus's surprise was genuine. 'The year,' he paused while he worked it out, 'two thousand?' he asked in disbelief that so advanced a time even existed.

'Just so.'

'And you're going to guard the king's door for another nine hundred years?'

'Not personally,' the monk replied as if it was quite a reasonable question. 'But we shall guard the brotherhood.'

Nicodemus was nodding gently to himself now as if all this was perfectly sensible. And he didn't need to worry at all about being in a cellar with this man. 'The Brotherhood,' he confirmed his understanding.

'The Trusted Brotherhood guard the secret of the king's door and we are the brotherhood that protects the Brotherhood.'

'Absolutely.' Nicodemus tried to sound as if this had been

his life's work as well. 'But if the king has sent his man and the door is key?'

'Then the king's man is misinformed and must be dealt with,' the monk said simply.

The sound of Athan rubbing his hands in what passed for glee, disturbed the silence. 'And we are just the people to deal with him,' he said very deliberately.

'Excellent,' the monk's grim smile could be heard, if not seen. 'The king's door must remain sealed, that was Ignatius's dying wish.' The monk was getting quite excited now. 'He also wanted all those who seek to tamper with destiny destroyed.'

'Did he?' Nicodemus asked, surprised that so much information could be contained in one pointing finger of a dead man.

'Of course. The death of the Sacerdos Arcanorum must inspire us to greater heights of devotion. Ignatius obviously sacrificed himself to protect the secret of the king's door and we are prepared to do the same.'

Nicodemus's nod was less than half-hearted and Athan's mumbled "not likely" was very quiet.

'Perhaps,' Athan suggested, 'we should go and deal with the king's man now, before he gets any ideas in his head about door opening. Maybe take his head off completely. That sort of thing.'

The cowl shook slowly from side to side. 'He is with the abbot and Egbert now in the chambers of the Sacerdos. There are others are with him as well, the ones who arrived with the king's man.'

'Hm,' Athan said thoughtfully, 'that probably is too many at once.'

The cowled monk sounded shocked. 'The abbot is our

leader, and Egbert his prior.'

'But if they want the door opened,' Athan gave a shrug, 'they'll have to go as well.'

'The abbot would not want the door opened. It has been part of his sacred duty to protect it. No. the king's man is the one we must worry about. Him and his companions.'

'Fine.' Athan clapped his hands together in eager anticipation.

'But,' Nicodemus's tone was a very direct tone and was aimed straight at Athan, 'we must make sure no hidden treasures are damaged or lost by precipitate action.'

'Good job there's two of us then,' Athan replied. 'You can guard the king's door and the treasures while I take care of the damage.'

'We know what is to be done then,' the cowled monk confirmed. 'We must return to our watches, make sure that no actions are being taken.'

'And what about us?' Nicodemus asked. 'The king's man may see that we are here if new faces appear around the place.'

'Aha,' the cowled monk raised an arm, indicating that he had a very well worked out plan for this. 'Just pull your cowl over your face like this. No one will notice.'

'What a good idea,' Athan said. 'Why didn't we think of that?'

'I will go and alert the other brothers to your presence,' the cowled one explained. 'You go and attend to the king's door. It's in the far corner of the cloister. Whatever you do make sure it is protected. Even if it comes to,' he hesitated to say it, 'violence.'

'You say that like violence is a problem,' Athan commented.

The cowl gave what looked like a reluctant nod. 'If we all succumb this day it will have been a life well spent when the king's door remains closed. Whatever befalls us, one thing must remain at the setting of the sun. The king's door must still be closed.'

They were about to leave the cellar, which Nicodemus had noticed was starting to make his feet feel wet, unable to believe their luck that they had just been put in charge of the door with the treasure behind it. Before they could climb the steps a voice called down.

'Brother, Brother? Are you there?'

'Yes, Brother,' the one brother replied to the other.

'Come quickly.'

'What is it?'

'The king's door.'

'What about it?' the one called up.

There was a gasping sob from above. 'They've just opened it.'

Caput XI

That's One Way of Opening It

The dark of evening was descending on the scene of the king's door laying open before them as Egbert, Wat and Hermitage held the abbot back and prevent him reaching Cwen's throat.

Hermitage had been reluctantly dragged from the library, where he would have been happy to spend the rest of his days. They reminded him that they were here to look into the death of Ignatius and that this king's door seemed to be at the middle of things. They promised him that the books wouldn't leave while his back was turned.

They had gathered at the door and looked at it for a long while. It really was not prepossessing at all. From the surrounding stonework, it was clear that there was some sort of chamber behind it but apart from that, there were no clues at all. It was an old, wooden panelled door, set low in the wall and was only big enough to let one person at a time pass through. And then they would have to duck.

It was arched in shape to match the gap it filled and could easily have been a simple tool store or the way to the privy.

The debate had ranged far and wide, at times pleading and demanding, at others speculative and enquiring. Was Hermitage really the king's man as he had not been instructed directly by the king? Should they perhaps find Brody? In any case, did the king's man have the authority to open the door at all? Should it not be the king in person? And the Sacerdos? With Ignatius dead, there was no official to attend any opening.

Wat had suggested they could dig him up and prop him

117

in the corner while they opened the door but he was roundly castigated for this improper and disrespectful suggestion.

It was when they observed that the door looked very weak and might fall down at any moment that Cwen stepped forward. With a muttered, "for God's sake make your minds up," she kicked the thing in.

Egbert, Wat and Hermitage had had to move very quickly to get to the abbot before he got to Cwen. For an aged bag of bones, the man moved with remarkable agility and the look on his face said he was going to do something very nasty straight away. His mouth was open but he had obviously not prepared any words for this occasion. All that came out were strangulated croaks and gurgles.

'Look,' Cwen said as if it was going to help, 'you were going to open it anyway, I just helped you make your minds up.'

Hermitage scowled at her and Wat indicated that the trouble he was having restraining this abbot was all her fault.

Sensing that the abbot was losing some of his strength Hermitage risked releasing his grip a little. He had been the last on the scene and so was kneeling on the ground holding the old man round the top of his legs. This must surely be the least pleasant part by which to grab any old abbot, particularly one whose last new habit had been donned the day he entered this place. A fateful day indeed, as it had been the last time he had a wash as well.

Egbert and Wat also realised that the abbot had exhausted his anger and cautiously let go. The old man dropped to the floor and sat staring at Cwen. He raised a gnarled finger and pointed at her. 'Blasphemer,' he cried, rather weakly and pathetically. 'What have you done?'

Cwen at least had the grace to look a little shamefaced under the sad gaze of the abbot.

'Since the millennium that door has remained closed,' the abbot moaned. 'I am only the third abbot of this place and I am the one to fail in his sacred duty.' He held his head in his hands.

Cwen looked positively put out and turned to the others for some support. There was none as Egbert, Wat and Hermitage all shook their heads in silent condemnation of anyone who would be so mean to an old man.

The abbot drew his face up again and looked once more at Cwen with an interesting mix of hatred, sadness and a deep wish that he was young again and could jump up and throttle her. He took a deep breath of resignation at his failure. 'I knew I should never have let a woman in here,' he concluded.

Cwen was back to her old self. 'You don't have to go in you know,' she snapped at the abbot. 'It's only a bit of wood. If you like it so much, build a new one. You obviously never bothered repairing the one that was there.'

'Bit of wood.' The abbot was talking to himself now, something inside the man appeared to have broken.

'And not a very good bit at that,' Cwen concluded, folding her arms.

There was a long pause as they all looked at the space previously occupied by the king's door.

'Well?' Cwen asked. 'Is a woman going to have to be the first to go through the thing or do you all need another month to make your minds up about that too?'

'We're waiting,' Egbert replied.

'I can see that. What for?'

'To see if anything happens.'

'What's going to happen?'

'We don't know,' Egbert said, rather pointedly and with some impatience. 'The king's door has never been opened before.'

Cwen tutted.

'And,' Egbert went on, 'I imagine the Sacerdos Arcanorum had a whole ritual ready for the moment. The king would be here, perhaps the great nobles of the land and the leaders of the church. There might be days of prayer and preparation before the solemn moment fell upon us. He probably didn't have anything in his book about a girl coming along and kicking the thing down.'

Wat clapped his hands together in a sign of impending action. 'We are where we are,' he said.

Hermitage frowned and found his attention diverted from the door in hand, or rather on the floor, in bits. 'What does that mean?' he asked.

'Eh?' Wat looked bemused.

'We are where we are,' Hermitage repeated. 'What on earth does that mean?'

Now Wat frowned. 'It means we are where we are,' he explained carefully.

'But that doesn't tell us anything. We are where we are,' Hermitage tried it again. 'We're always where we are. If we weren't where we are we'd be somewhere else and then we'd be there, not here. When we got there we could say we are where we are again.' This sentence had made sense when he set off, but somehow he had lost his way. 'Who's going to say we aren't where we are? Or we are where we aren't?'

'It's just an expression, Hermitage.' Wat shook his head in gentle despair. 'In this situation it means that the door

120

has been opened and so we have to advance from here. We can't go to some other place where the door is still closed.'

'But we shouldn't be here in the first place,' Hermitage argued. 'It's no good saying, "we are where we are" when you're halfway down a cliff heading towards the rocks. You shouldn't have jumped off the cliff in the first place. Far better to think about where you want to be and go there instead of just finding yourself in places. Some careful planning, that's all you need.'

Wat and Hermitage simply looked at one another. It was clear that neither had the first clue what the other was talking about.

Cwen grabbed their attention with a snort. 'I shall kick something where you are in a minute,' she explained, with a very clear look on her face.

Hermitage and Wat forgot about being where they were.

Wat beckoned towards the door with an arm. 'I think you'd better go first, Hermitage. After all, you are the nearest thing we've got to a king.'

Hermitage decided he didn't like being where he was. But then that had been true for as long as he could remember anyway. He looked to them all to see if anyone was urging him not to do anything. Unfortunately the abbot looked like he really was somewhere else altogether and the others weren't expressing any concern one way or another.

'Brother Egbert,' he tried, 'you are prior here. With the abbot, erm, indisposed, and the Sacerdos even more indisposed, I think you are probably the community leader.'

'Thanks, Harold,' Egbert muttered. He paused for a moment's thought. 'You are here from the king, brother.' He addressed Hermitage. 'Or, as master Wat says, as close as we are going to get. The king's door lies open for whatever reason,' he gave Cwen a glare of disappointment. 'It could be that this is the path the Lord intends us to follow. No great catastrophe has befallen since the door was opened. No demons have issued forth and the day of judgement appears not to have dawned.' He paused again to let them all take in the silence that confirmed that no, the seven horned lamb with seven eyes had not popped its head out.

Hermitage took a long, slow breath and saw that he had no choice. That was very normal as well. He took one step towards the door and paused to confirm to himself that he really was going to do this. He took another step and started to bend so that he could get through the door. As he got closer he saw that he was going to have to get on his hands and knees to pass through. That would make it more difficult to get out again quickly if he found there was something dangerous in there. With a last look back at his companions, a rather pleading one which was crying out for a final call to come back - a call which did not come – he ducked forward.

. . .

'I'd better kill him now,' Athan hissed in the ear of the cowled monk.

The other held up a hand, much to Athan's frustration.

'He's going through the king's door!' Athan suddenly sounded very enthusiastic about the whole concept of the sanctity of the door.

'The prior may be right,' the cowled monk commented. 'Nothing has happened.'

'It smells a bit,' Nicodemus observed, sniffing the musty air that had issued from the door after its rude departure at the hands of Cwen's feet.

'Mayhap the Lord will take care of his own,' the monk speculated.

'Meaning?' Athan asked.

'That the monk who enters the room will be struck down with a mighty blow.'

'I could do that,' Athan complained.

'From here?' the monk asked. They were hiding behind the fateful sundial, looking over the space of the courtyard towards the small gathering by the door.

'I can get over there very quickly,' Athan promised.

'It is too late.' The monk wailed slightly as the figure of Hermitage disappeared through the door.

Athan observed this event with poorly contained disappointment. He gave the situation a moment's thought. 'I'll kill him when he comes out then,' he offered.

The cowled monk at last threw back his cowl and looked at Athan. The face was thoughtful. It was also a bit bizarre with some sort of scar on its forehead and a look in the eyes that could make dogs walk away backwards. The man was of middling years but they had all been spent in the depths of his sacred duties which had done nothing for his health. Take the cowl off, lay the man down in some pale dust and he would probably disappear completely. The head was properly shaved and the jaw was bare of beard but the slight twitch in the cheek and the smile which wasn't even a distant relation of nice gave even Athan a moment's concern.

'Have you got a name?' Athan asked, perhaps thinking that giving this creature a title would ease the encounter somewhat.

'While in the brotherhood we have no names,' the monk explained. 'We are simply called brother.'

'Brother Brother?' Athan asked, frustrated and annoyed.

'No, of course not,' the monk retorted. 'How would that work? We'd spend all our time saying Brother Brother this and Brother Brother that. The whole thing would be ridiculous.'

'Then how do you know one another?'

The Brother slowly pointed a significant finger at the scar on his forehead. It could be construed as being roughly star-shaped; if it had been deliberately made by someone who had once had a star described to them by someone who had never seen one. 'We all bare the secret mark,' he said, significantly.

'All of you?' Nicodemus asked with some surprise.

'All of us,' the Brother replied seriously.

'In the middle of your heads?'

The Brother frowned disappointment at Nicodemus's questioning of the mark.

'Just saying,' Nicodemus said, quietly. 'Wouldn't have thought it's the best place for a secret sign, that's all. Middle of the forehead?'

'That's why we wear our cowls,' the Brother explained with a sigh.

Nicodemus nodded. 'So no one can see the sign. I see.'

The Brother seemed satisfied.

'Even your other brothers,' Nicodemus concluded.

The monk turned to Athan and looked back to the door. 'Perhaps dealing with him when he comes out would be good,' he suggested. The voice, when buried in the cowl had been neutral if insistent. Now it was paired with the face the combination was positively alarming. 'But the Abbot, and Egbert and the others,' the monk pointed out.

Nicodemus appraised the group. 'The abbot appears to

be beyond recovery. The girl won't be any trouble, although the weaver can handle himself. That prior looks strong though.'

'He came to us recently from the king's service,' the Brother explained.

'Ah,' Athan smiled grimly. 'Some sycophantic monk from the soft belly of the court.'

'No,' the Brother replied. 'I gather he was in the king's army.'

Athan's smile became slightly less grim.

'Quite well thought of, according to the abbot.' The Brother mused, 'Although rather more deaths surrounding him personally than one would normally like in a monk.'

Athan re-appraised the situation. 'Perhaps we'll wait and see what happens.'

'And what do we do then?' Nicodemus asked, with some impatience. 'You can see that the king's door has already been opened. We cannot allow them to start removing the treasures.' The tone of high greed tinged with envy and anger was not quite the one he'd been aiming for. 'I mean, it would be a tragedy,' he tried to recover. 'Surely it's the duty of the erm,' he tried to recall which brotherhood was which, 'the Trusted Brotherhood to protect them?'

'Naturally,' the Brother retorted, with some irritation. 'And we protect the Brotherhood. It is not our place to go barging through the king's door and even see the treasure, let alone deal with it. That is for the Trusted Brothers. Our protection of the door has failed. Castigation awaits.' He said this as if he was quite used to castigation.

'I, erm,' Athan peered around from their hiding place. 'I don't actually see anyone else?" He gave the Brother a hard stare.

'Of course you don't.' The Brother seemed astonished at their ignorance. 'You would not see the Trusted Brotherhood. No one knows exactly who the Trusted Brothers are.' He looked at them both through narrowed eyes. 'Are you sure you were sent?'

'Oh, definitely sent,' Nicodemus reassured him brightly. 'Sent as sent could be.'

'Hm.' The Brother did not seem so sure.

'Attack when the King's man emerges from the door then,' Nicodemus tried to distract him.

The Brother thought about this carefully. Eventually he nodded. 'I think so.' Athan cracked his knuckles. 'When he leaves the chamber we will be ready. I will summon the other Brothers to assist.'

Nicodemus checked, 'That's the first lot of Brothers, not the Trusted ones?'

'Was any of this explained to you at all?' the Brother asked with disappointment.

'Just making sure,' Nicodemus tried a smile, not something he was very good at.

'Quick,' Athan called, 'he's coming.'

They looked over and Hermitage's head was indeed appearing through the door again.

The Brother looked around urgently, probably to see if any of his companions were nearby and ready. As he realised he was on his own, he saw that the king's man had stopped.

. . .

Hermitage beckoned to the others who were still standing and waiting. Apart from the abbot who was sitting and wailing. 'You've simply got to see this,' he beckoned them with the hand of enthusiasm. 'It's absolutely wonderful.'

Wat, Cwen and Egbert exchanged looks. Being relative strangers to this place, those looks were mostly of surprise that the old door really did hide something of significance.

'I've never seen anything like it,' Hermitage said as he turned back to the chamber, naturally assuming that the others would follow. 'In all my days,' his voice continued, 'I never dreamed that I would see the like of this.'

Despite their best efforts, Hermitage's enthusiasm was proving infectious. They started to lower themselves for the crawl through the door.

'Don't get your hopes up,' Wat cautioned. 'Bear in mind that he did get quite excited by a library.'

Caput XII

Them Bones

'Look.' Hermitage held his arms wide to take in the majesty of the sight before them.

Once through the door, they found that they could easily stand in quite a tall chamber that in sophistication was as rude and simple as the door concealing it. There was a small window high in one wall, but it looked like it opened on to some stone recess and so was hidden from external view. This also meant it was pretty effectively hidden from light and so the inside of the chamber was gloomy. Gloomy as well as damp, musty and carrying the distinct impression that some animal had died in here not long ago; quite a big one. The smell indicated that the cause of death was probably some revolting disease. The three new arrivals gagged slightly at the thick and pungent air.

The room was just large enough for four people and Wat noticed that they had not tripped over piles of treasure when they entered. The floor was bare as were three of the walls. It was the final wall to which Hermitage was directing their attention.

Wat peered through the darkness. 'What is it?' he asked, in a mixture of disappointment and disgust.

'Why it's an altar of course,' Hermitage explained. 'And a remarkable one at that.'

'That's it?' Cwen asked. 'An altar? Where's the treasure?'

'This is the treasure.' Hermitage sounded very sure that this jumble of something or other propped against the wall was very valuable. Or more likely very interesting - which was much more of a disappointment.

'An altar?' Egbert stepped up to the end of the room and studied it.

It was a fairly simple table, still hung with a cloth that looked like it had been put there nearly seventy years ago. It might have been blue once but was now faded and ragged. Perhaps the dead animal had tried to eat it as a last resort. Two large candlesticks stood at each end of the table and a jug sat dusty and unused.   It looked pretty clear that they weren't made of gold.

At the centre of the altar, at the back of the table stood a carved cross. This was obviously the focus of devotion but it was a confusing mess of bits and pieces that had either been put together by a sculptor with some devious plan of what it was he was representing, or one who didn't have the first clue what he was doing. It could almost have been taken straight from the tree, polished up a bit and stuck on a plinth.

The thing was a good three feet high and two wide and it dominated the room. But the harder it was looked at, the harder it became to figure out what it was supposed to be. It resembled nothing so much as a tangle of thick rope shaped into an upright and cross-piece. Carved lines weaved around here and there with a unique texture that invited you to leave them alone.

Egbert bent in to examine it more closely and took a start backwards as he thought he saw a pair of eyes peeping out at him from the midst of the confusion of carved shapes. 'What is it?' he asked. He sounded genuinely intrigued, and a little disturbed by the shape of this thing.

Hermitage breathed his announcement. 'This is the lost altar of the Tangled Bones.' He turned his attention back to them to share their marvel at the discovery. They didn't look very marvelled at all. Wat and Cwen he could perhaps understand, but even Egbert looked non-the-wiser. 'The altar of the Tangled Bones,' he repeated, hoping that might help. It didn't. 'Saint Botwulf,' he explained in language so clear even a child would get this.

Wat and Cwen exchanged the look they usually shared when Hermitage started going on about saints; complete ignorance of both the subject matter and the fact that it might be of any interest to anyone.

'Saint Botwulf,' Egbert repeated. It sounded like he knew what he was talking about.

'And Saint Athwulf, of course,' Hermitage added, his enthusiasm nodding his head up and down as if it had been waiting for a moment just like this.

Wat and Cwen opened their eyes wide at one another confirming that Hermitage had said the names of two saints they'd never heard of.

Hermitage himself gave a simple "tut" at the lack of even then most basic knowledge. 'Saint Botwulf of Thorney, as we all know,' he began, despite it being obvious that most of his audience did not, 'was an abbot and is patron saint of travellers.'

'I thought that was Christopher,' Cwen interrupted.

'And Botwulf,' Hermitage carefully explained.

'Can you have two then?'

'Oh, really,' Hermitage exclaimed. 'Did no one teach you anything when you were young?'

'Well, they did,' Cwen replied, looking down. 'But I don't think they're the sorts of things you want to hear about.'

Hermitage controlled himself again. 'Yes, you can have two. In fact, Saint Christopher looks after plague as well as travellers.'

'Handy,' Wat observed, to a scowl from Hermitage.

'If I could go on?' Hermitage asked. 'Thank you. Where was I? Oh, yes. Botwulf was an abbot and founded the monastery of Ikanhoe, probably not far from here. He was a very devout man who died hundreds of years ago but he was greatly revered.'

'Devout, revered and dead,' Wat said as if he was checking a list.

'Just so. And he had a brother, Athwulf.'

'A saint as well?" Cwen sounded surprised.

'And also an abbot,' Hermitage went on, enthusing all over the place. 'Both of them abbots of the monastery at Ikenhoe, where they were buried.'

'Quite a family,' Wat observed.

Hermitage let a small grumble wander round his throat. 'Unfortunately the monastery was sacked by the Vikings.'

'Happened a lot round here,' Egbert added helpfully.

'And,' Hermitage raised his voice to stop these annoying interruptions, 'about a hundred years ago the new monastery at Thorney was erected and it was decided to move Botwulf's body,' he held his hand to stop Cwen before she could speak again. 'Because he was the much more well-known of the brothers. By this time he was being called Botolph.'

'Ah,' Wat and Cwen said as if this made everything clear. Hermitage suspected they knew no more now than when they came in the room.

'But what they found in the tomb was that Athwulf and Botwulf's bones were so mixed up it was impossible to separate them and so they had to be moved together.'

'Hence the altar of the Tangled Bones,' Wat concluded.

'Exactly. It was reputed to have been made at the time of

the internment but was lost to history.'

'And now it isn't,' Cwen noted with little interest.

'Now it isn't,' Hermitage said with great pride.

They all looked at it and examined it more closely now they knew the story. It was indeed a carving of tangled bones and yes, Egbert had seen eyes, or at least eye sockets, as two small skulls had been skilfully built into the middle of the altarpiece.

Wat and Cwen then looked around the room again to confirm there was nothing but the altar of the Tangled Bones.

'So.' Wat clapped his hands together.

Hermitage looked at him with interest. Perhaps he had something to contribute to their reflections on the lives of Athwulf and Botwulf. He thought this unlikely but he lived in hope.

'What does it do then?' Wat asked.

Hermitage gazed at him not quite understanding the words, even though they made sense on their own. 'What does it do?' he repeated.

'Yes. What does it do?'

'It doesn't do anything. It's an altarpiece. A famous, missing altarpiece that dates back a hundred years.'

'Very nice.' Wat rubbed his chin. 'I'm just wondering why dead Ignatius was pointing at a door with this behind it? And why there's such a fuss about the king's door if this is it.' He gestured to the altar in a rather dismissive manner.

'This is a great discovery,' Hermitage protested. That he was the one to discover the altar of the Tangled Bones was proving to be the highlight of an already happy day. This was not what he'd expected at all, being sent on a mission from the king. He knew what he had expected and yes, the abbot had proved a difficult fellow and there was a dead priest to consider but still; a whole library full of books and now this. He didn't know if he'd be able to take much more excitement.

Wat and Cwen did not look excited at all. Even Egbert seemed to be taking all this in his stride. The prior looked thoughtful and eventually spoke. 'It does seem odd that Ignatius should go to the trouble of pointing here, and that there should be such legends and rumours about the king's door if this is what it contains.'

Hermitage's disappointment that the others weren't as excited by this as he was, was palpable.

'It is, of course, a fascinating discovery in its own right,' Egbert encouraged. 'I am sure that there will be many who want to hear the tale of its finding and see the great object itself.'

Hermitage could only agree with this, although when he put his mind to it he couldn't immediately think of an actual individual by name.

'But as master Wat says,' Egbert went on, reluctantly, 'it doesn't quite have the significance we might have expected? What with the door being opened by the king and the millennium and all?'

Hermitage had to accept that this was probably true. After all, it was a plain altarpiece, albeit it one of interest to the church. But then maybe the whole idea of the king's door had been simply blown out of all proportion in the years it had been closed.

'And if Ignatius's dying gesture was to point us to this place, what did he want us to do?' Egbert asked. 'You'd hardly go to the trouble of pointing out an interesting liturgical object when you've got a sundial in your back if it wasn't important.'

They all pondered this question in their own way. And in their own ways came up with nothing at all.

'I have to confess it hardly seems to be central to the role of the Sacerdos,' Hermitage observed, gazing at the altar again. 'Or indeed a key to anything particular. It is absolutely fascinating, of course, but I'm not aware of any great significance surrounding Botwulf and Athwulf.'

Egbert held up a finger in thought. 'Do you think he even knew it was here?'

Hermitage looked at him, questioningly.

'The king's door has been closed for nearly seventy years,' Egbert went on. 'Ignatius was its guard. If he carried out his duties with devotion he would not have opened the door to find out what was in there.'

'Perhaps he knew anyway?' Hermitage suggested. 'As part of his general collection of secret knowledge. It could even be in one of his books.'

This wasn't getting them much further. They looked around the room some more, including at the ceiling to see if there were any secret messages painted up there. There weren't.

'The books!' Hermitage exclaimed suddenly, which made everyone jump as they were in a dim and dingy room with a rather worrying altarpiece of carved bones.

'For goodness sake, Hermitage,' Wat snapped. 'What about them?'

'Ignatius wasn't pointing at the door,' Hermitage explained.

'I can assure you he was,' Egbert said. 'I may not be the most attentive person in the world but bodies on sundials pointing at things are hard to ignore.'

'I mean he was pointing at the door.'

'Good.' Egbert's tone was the one used with people who talked to rocks.

'But that's only because it was all he could point to. Being stuck on a sundial and everything. He could hardly stagger to his library, pull out the key volumes for his successor, prepare a note of explanation and then die at his own convenience.'

'Not while lugging a sundial around behind him, that's for sure,' Wat added.

Hermitage ignored him. 'Instead, Ignatius pointed to the door, which he may well have known contained the altar. He didn't point at the cloister, or the chapel or the dortoir which he could easily have done. Well, not easily but you know what I mean. By means of his pointing, he is telling us to look to his role. His job as Sacerdos Arcanorum. The king's door was his to protect, as are the books. Specifically ones about Botwulf or Athwulf.' He was very satisfied with his deduction.

'Or books about bones,' Cwen suggested.

'Or Vikings,' Wat added. 'Or door construction.'

'Perhaps we should stick to saints to begin with,' Hermitage tried to be insistent.

'And what's that going to tell us anyway?' Wat asked. 'Ignatius was killed. He pointed at the door. We find a book. Then what?'

'We shall see,' Hermitage said with interest. 'It could be that Ignatius hid his most important secrets in the library. Everyone knew of the king's door, perhaps some sinful individual would have been tempted to break it down and steal the secrets therein.'

'There aren't any secrets therein,' Cwen said, taking it as a personal slight that breaking the door down had been thought of as so troublesome when this was all that it contained.

'There aren't now,' Hermitage agreed. 'Ignatius or one of his predecessors may have moved things out of the chamber for safer keeping. What better place to hide knowledge than in over four thousand books? We could go through the Bishop of Hereford's library in a morning. This place could take a lifetime. Ignatius needed to tell us where to look. Botwulf and Athwulf are the clue.'

'Clue to what?' Cwen asked.

'Well, we don't know, do we?' Hermitage replied. 'It wouldn't be a secret otherwise.'

'So how do we know it's worth bothering with? It might be the secret location of another altar with fewer bones.'

Hermitage sighed. He supposed it was understandable, but Wat and Cwen really had no idea where they were. 'This is the Monasterium Tenebrarii and we are dealing with the secrets of the Sacerdos Arcanorum,' he said. 'The greatest secrets in Christendom were entrusted to his hands. It could be anything. The Holy Grail, the Crown of Thorns, the Spear anything.   One thing we can be sure of is that it will be something of the greatest significance. After all, would you go to all this trouble to protect something that didn't matter?' He held his arms out to encompass the whole of the monastery and all that went with it.

Wat and Cwen had to acknowledge that it was pretty impressive and a lot of trouble to go to for a carving of some bones.

Hermitage rubbed his hands at the task ahead of him. 'We go to the library and see what we can find.'

'Among thousands of books?' Egbert queried. 'When

you're the only ones who can read?'

'It will be a challenge,' Hermitage noted. 'But we must recall one thing that gives the secret even more significance.'

'What's that?' Cwen asked.

Hermitage took a breath, 'Someone probably killed Ignatius for it.'

All their thoughts were sombre as they exited the room once more to pick up the abbot and head for the library. That old man was sitting on the cloister floor muttering about women and the king's door and what disasters were going to be rained on them from heaven. He seemed to have little awareness of what was going on around them so Egbert suggested they should take him to his cell for a bit of a lie-down.

When Cwen offered to put him to bed, Hermitage suspected quite mischievously, the poor man nearly had a fit and ran off of his own accord.

. . .

'Did you hear that?' the cowled brother hissed at Nicodemus and Athan with barely contained excitement as they squatted behind a pillar outside the King's door. 'The Holy Grail, the Crown of Thorns and the Spear.'

'No,' Nicodemus corrected in his condescending way. 'They said it might be one of those things. And of course it might not.'

'But it's just come to me,' the brother insisted. 'It all makes sense.'

'It'll be the first thing that does.'

'Think about it. We all know that Saint George killed the dragon.'

'What?' Athan snapped. 'What the devil has that got to do with anything?' He looked over to see if Nicodemus was making any sense of this. He wasn't.

The brother tutted at Athan's ignorance. 'When Saint George cut the dragon open he found the Holy Grail in its stomach.'

'Did he?' Athan, not renowned for his own theological prowess, clearly thought this was a monk with some very strange ideas.

'Of course. The dragon had been at the last supper and the crucifixion. It swallowed the Grail and George got it back.'

'If you say so.' Nicodemus was clearly dismissing this nonsense.

'And Saint George is patron saint of England. Of course the door will lead to the Grail. That's where George must have put it. In England. Here.'

'Or, maybe the trail leads to the dragon?' Athan said, with some menace. 'Who probably isn't very happy about having grails cut out of him.'

The Brother looked worried at this. Then his face relaxed. 'Don't be ridiculous. George killed the dragon, didn't he?'

'Could be its ghost.' Nicodemus said, sounding very serious.

The Brother looked like he wasn't so keen on knowing where the secrets from the door were anymore. 'Perhaps we'd better follow,' he said, quickly forgetting about grail swallowing dragons but giving the door very worried looks. 'And it may be a good job we didn't deal with them immediately.'

'But what about the secrets?' Nicodemus asked, sarcastically. 'I thought you were protecting them. If this lot go and find everything out, where will that leave you?'

The Brother sighed that he was having to explain this yet

again. 'We protect the Trusted Brotherhood. They protect the secrets.'

Nicodemus pursed his lips. 'I haven't seen much sign of any trusted brothers.'

'Well of course you haven't,' the Brother explained with his own fair measure of condescension. 'They're hardly likely to go round wearing some sort of insignia, are they?'

'Like a scar in the middle of their heads, for example?' Athan asked.

This point missed the Brother completely. 'When the moment comes that the secrets themselves need action, the Trusted Brotherhood will come forth.'

'I look forward to it,' Nicodemus said.

'But even then you probably won't see them, so mysteriously do they move,' the Brother said, with awful significance. 'In the meantime, we will do what we can to control the actions of those who seek the secrets.'

Nicodemus shook his head slowly. 'This all seems terribly complicated for quite a simple task.'

The Brother held him with a gaze which the monk probably thought carried great significance, but which Nicodemus thought bore signs of slight insanity. 'No one can be trusted,' the Brother explained slowly.

'I'm with you there,' Nicodemus agreed.

'So there must be layers within layers. Perhaps even the Trusted Brotherhood does not know the secrets, only that they must be protected.'

'Let's get along to the library then,' Nicodemus waved them on. 'After all, can't have the unknown secrets being revealed to those who don't know what they are by people who wouldn't know them if they saw them, can we?'

The Brother led them across the courtyard to follow the

party to the library. He paused at the sundial and laid a weighty hand on it. 'This is where Ignatius met his end,' he said, solemnly.

'I see.' Nicodemus glanced at a fairly nondescript sundial.

'You can see when he died,' the Brother pointed a finger.

Nicodemus paused and closed his eyes for a moment. 'I beg your pardon?'

'You can see when he died,' the Brother explained with quiet dignity. 'Here,' he pointed to a spot on the face of the dial. 'half-past vespers.'

Nicodemus peered over and saw that there was indeed what appeared to be a bloodstain halfway between the marks for Vespers and Compline.

Nicodemus spoke slowly and carefully. 'You're saying that the mark on the sundial at half-past Vespers shows that that's when Ignatius died?'

'That's right. The mark is as clear as day.'

Nicodemus looked to Athan, who, while not being exactly the brightest lamp in Christendom, was frowning deeply at the monk's reasoning.

'Indeed, the mark is clear.' Nicodemus wondered if this was worth the effort. 'But it doesn't really work like that, does it? Would you like to have another think about this?' He folded his arms and waited while the convolutions of complex thought wormed their way across the monk's face.

'Ah,' he said, after a very long pause. 'I see the problem.'

'Good.' Nicodemus was relieved.

'Yes,' the Brother explained. 'We don't know whether he died at half-past Vespers in the day or half-past Vespers at night.'

'No.' Nicodemus, remained remarkably calm but was running a hand over his face. 'That's not it. Have another go.'

The monk looked puzzled.

'The sun is a clue,' Nicodemus prompted. 'Sundial. Sun?'

The monk looked to the sky to see if it would help.

Nicodemus moved his head until he had the monk's undivided attention. 'Do you know how a sundial works?' he asked, slowly and carefully. 'Be careful now, it is quite complicated.'

The monk stood proud, 'Yes,' he proclaimed. 'The will of God.'

Nicodemus took a deep breath. 'How remarkable,' he said, 'Ignatius dying at half-past Vespers like that. Well spotted.'

Caput XIII

The Revelation of Books

Nicodemus and Athan were led round the side of the chapel, where the Brother assured them there was a secret way they could gain access without being seen. Nicodemus was no longer sure that he could trust this man to know the way to his own feet, but he was all they had. Walking in on Hermitage and the others would almost certainly cause all talk of secrets to be quickly dropped. He knew that the sight of Athan alone might be enough to make the young investigator drop dead from shock. Or, if that didn't happen, drop dead from being hit by Athan.

They passed the chapel on their left and headed towards the rear of the building where the bulk that formed Ignatius's chambers spread itself outwards and upwards. Beckoning them on, the Brother moved around the back of the main wall to a point where it looked like the stonework had either fallen down or was waiting to be put up. If this was a building site it was long deserted, the blocks being covered in moss and lichen.

Worming his way between several larger stones, they were led to what was basically a hole in the building. This was not some carefully planned and executed passage that had been laboriously constructed. This looked like a mistake, plain and simple.

'There is an outer wall and an inner,' the Brother explained. 'Between the two there is space to climb up to the eaves of the roof, from where the chamber may be observed.'

Nicodemus gave the building a rough appraisal. He

caught Athan's eye and saw that they shared the opinion that climbing up the inside of this place would be like entering the bed-chamber of the old Earl of Northumbria; something heavy could well fall on top of you.

'You do this often, do you?' Athan asked, peering into the hole they were expected to enter.

'Oh yes,' the Brother nodded. 'The stones don't fall very often.'

'Very often, eh?' Athan scowled at the stones as if warning them to be on their best behaviour.

'And there is no other way?' Nicodemus asked.

'Not without knocking on the door.'

With one last look at the masonry, which reminded him of nothing so much as the monastery at De'Ath's Dingle - a place was always on the brink of falling down - he beckoned the Brother to lead the way.

Inside, the gap between the walls was actually quite large. Nicodemus suspected, this was not because the place had been carefully constructed of a double-skinned wall to protect its contents, but because one building and been put up inside another; probably some builders' ruse to avoid having to put on a decent roof.

The space was dark, but as their eyes grew used to it some faint light could be seen filtering down from above. Probably where the builders hadn't put the interior building together properly.

The Brother led them on along an uneven floor, strewn with stones, until they came to a step. It wasn't a proper step in any sense of the word, rather it was a large piece of stone sticking out of the inner wall and not quite reaching the outer. It was easily big enough for two people to stand on side by side but its purpose was unclear.

Nicodemus appraised it. Doubtless, this was supposed to be a tie-piece to hold the two buildings together. While he had never actually lifted a tool himself, he had been involved in enough building works to know when the noble, or the church who commissioned the work was being robbed blind. Tie-pieces that didn't actually tie were a common method of the builder having to be brought back for years afterwards to try and work out why the walls kept moving, and to be paid exorbitant fees for repairs.

The Brother climbed up on the first tie-piece, from where further stones could be seen leading up the wall. Some of them actually did join the two walls together. It was never good practice to have the building fall down completely until a reasonable time had passed and the builder could legitimately blame ground movement, storms or the other builder who had done the work in the first place and who everyone knew was a rogue, if only they'd asked.

As the party disappeared into the walls of the chapel, a single, darkly cowled figure moved among the stones outside. It cautiously approached the opening to the wall and slowly moved its head around the corner of the wall to peer at the interior. Apparently satisfied that it was not spotted, it entered the space and stood carefully considering the tie-stones that led up the wall. Coming to some sort of conclusion, a smile of sorts played across the face - in the way that magpies play on the bodies of dead things.

. . .

The climb became ever more precarious the higher they went. Not because the stones were loose or too small to stand upon, but because the fall would be a pretty final one as you bounced off each of the tie-stones on the way down.

Eventually the Brother, who had been leading the way,

turned and beckoned them to silence as he crept up the last two steps. He hoisted himself up onto some sort of parapet and Nicodemus and Athan followed.

The view behind them was not so bad as they could really not see how high up they were. The tie-stones fell away into the darkness and the ground might be just below their feet. On the other side of the wall, the floor of Ignatius's chamber was clearly visible about thirty feet below. A small groan escaped from Athan.

Nicodemus turned to the fearsome friar who, even in this dim light, was looking a bit pale.

'Problem?'

'If the Lord had intended us to be this high he would have given us longer legs,' Athan grumbled, closing his eyes and looking as if he was about to be very ill, all the way to the floor beneath.

This would have done nothing for their concealment as even Hermitage would have noticed someone being sick on him from a great height.

The Investigator and his companions were gathered directly below them and were encircling Ignatius's desk which had a few books and sheets on it.

Nicodemus strained his ears to hear the conversation but it was not difficult as the size and shape of the room let words wander freely into whatever ear wanted them. The group below was not making any attempt to keep their discussion secret, probably not expecting people to be in the roof, listening.

'There must be an index of some sort,' Hermitage was saying.

'A what?' Egbert asked, looking at all the books around him as if they were capable of doing him some damage.

'A list, if you like. With this many books it would be impossible to simply know what they all were and what was in them. There would be a master list of all the titles, their locations and with any luck a brief description of them.'

'Sounds very organised,' Egbert said in some surprise.

'It is a library,' Hermitage reminded him. 'Of course it's organised. That's what a library is. An organisation of books.'

Egbert looked at the books with great suspicion. Any large number of books that were capable of organising themselves were not to be trusted.

'But we don't even know what we're looking for,' Cwen pointed out, waving her arms at the very large number of books there were. 'She opened a book that was on Ignatius's desk, probably the one he'd been working on last. She glanced at the page. Then she looked at it quite hard. Then she got her nose close and peered at it. 'What on earth is this?' she asked, standing up and waving towards the book.

Hermitage stepped over and studied the text. 'Ah, good heavens above,' he said with great pleasure, clapping his hands together and clasping them tightly. 'I do believe this is Abbot Aelfric's Hexateuch.'

'I imagine he misses it,' Wat said with a look of complete ignorance.

'Hexateuch,' Hermitage repeated, impatiently. 'It's the first six books of the Bible. And beautifully illustrated.' He gazed in rapture at the page. 'See here,' he pointed to the page and read. "*Fæder ure þu þe eart on heofonum*".'

'Ah,' Cwen recognised the words. "Our Father that art in heaven" eh?' She peered at the words again. 'So that's what it looks like written down.'

'That's what it looks like?' Hermitage was lost. 'I thought

you said you could read?'

'I can. Few bits of Latin here and there, and the odd French. Never read English though. What's the point?'

'What's the point?' Hermitage was horrified. 'This is your own language. And Abbot Aelfric's Hexateuch is the Bible in English. A bit of a Wessex dialect, I admit, but still.'

'Not going to be much use when we all speak Norman,' Cwen snorted.

Hermitage didn't know which way to turn.

'So,' Egbert observed, 'that's two of you who can read for four thousand books.' He folded his arms, waiting for the next steps.

Hermitage looked questioningly at Wat.

'I can read English,' Wat answered the unspoken question. And some French and Latin.'

'Good.' Hermitage felt some relief.

'Yes,' Wat confirmed. He stepped over and felt the weight of Aelfric's Hexateuch. 'Book this size?' he put his "estimating" face on. 'This many pages. This many words?' He studied the page. 'Should be able to get through it in about a month.'

Hermitage looked at them all one at a time. And then he looked at the room and all its books. He came to a conclusion pretty quickly. 'This is hopeless,' he said.

'And as I believe I mentioned earlier, we don't know what we're looking for.' Cwen added helpfully.

Hermitage couldn't think of the answer at all. Perhaps repeating the problem would help. 'This was Ignatius's chamber.'

'So far, so good,' Wat agreed.

'Ignatius was killed and died pointing at the king's door, which we now know contained the altar of the Tangled

Bones. The bones mean saints Botwulf and Athwulf.'

'Which he may not have even known,' Egbert pointed out.

'Even so, someone killed Ignatius for some reason and it was to do with the king's door, otherwise why would he point there? Something in this room must tell us what he was working on, or what connection there is from his death to the role of the Sacerdos Arcanorum.'

'Maybe,' Wat was thoughtful, which got Hermitage's attention. 'Maybe people just didn't like him and the sundial was there, and one thing led to another?' he shrugged.

'Not helpful,' Hermitage replied. 'And even if that was the case, he was still pointing at the door.'

Hermitage gazed around the room, hoping that some feature would leap out at him. He looked again at Aelfric's Hexateuch. He couldn't think that anything in that would be motivation for murder. Hardly a secret document, the Bible. His eyes ranged over the stacked shelves and the floor piled with volumes and he thought that if he could just be left alone in here for a few years he'd sort it all out.

His eyes lifted from the floor and took in the sheer height of the room, all of it crammed with books. It filled him with a sense of hopelessness at the task. He could probably skim through some titles quite quickly, but Wat and Cwen sounded like they were going to be roughly useless.

Perhaps he should focus on the index. It must be here somewhere. If he could at least find that, it would make the search easier. He couldn't believe the Sacerdos would work without one. Unless of course it was memorised to maintain secrecy? His heart sank again. Then again, if the index was the key, it might be hidden itself. He looked around the room once more and wondered how to imagine where the index would be hidden.

His eyes fell upon the ladder that was propped against one section of shelving. It looked very well used, the treads being smooth and worn. He reasoned that if there was a regular spot Ignatius had to visit, he would leave the ladder there, to save moving it about all the time. The most regular thing he would need would surely be the index. His eyes followed the ladder upwards to see if there was anything remarkable about the high shelves at that point.

He saw something right up in the eaves of the roof that made his heart skip a beat. Then it skipped another one and had to be coughed into life to get it going again. He raised a quivering finger and pointed up towards the roof where the revelation had presented itself.

'Hermitage,' Cwen called, 'what is it?' She stepped quickly over to the young monk who was looking in a complete state of shock.

He moved his mouth around a few times to prepare it for the words that had to come out. He swallowed and gulped and tried to speak.

'Spit it out,' Wat instructed.

Hermitage's finger had not moved from its target in the roof. 'Up there,' he managed to croak.

They followed his gaze and peered into the gloom of the roof timbers to see what the fuss was about.

Hermitage got his senses back and managed to breathe the name that has stunned him so. 'Saint Botwulf.' His pointing finger was steady in its aim at a small wooden statue that sat atop one of the supporting trusses of the roof.

. . .

Athan looked along the parapet from where they were propped and saw the statue some thirty feet away. He nodded his head towards it for Nicodemus's benefit.

Nicodemus returned the nod and indicated that they should keep quiet and listen to what came next.

. . .

It can be no coincidence,' Hermitage said. 'There are no other statues in the room.'

Wat squinted to try and make out the statue in any detail. 'How do you know it's him?'

'Well, of course it's him,' Hermitage waved a hand. 'Just look.'

'I am looking and all I can see is a small shape. How can you tell it's Botwulf?'

Hermitage didn't really understand the question. 'It looks like him.'

'It looks like him,' Wat repeated. 'How long ago did you say this saint died?'

'Oh, hundreds of years.'

Wat peered at the statue again. 'And that looks like him.'

'Absolutely.' Hermitage was anxious to get on. He made his way quickly over to the section of the library under Botwulf's gaze. 'Ah, yes,' he said, as he examined the titles. 'This makes perfect sense.'

The others gathered around him.

'Demons,' he held out his hand towards the books.

Wat, Cwen and Egbert took a sharp step backwards.

'What do you mean, demons?' Egbert asked from a safe distance.

'Botwulf drove the demons out of the marshes of the east,' Hermitage explained, happily. 'It is only natural that his section of the library should be concerned with demons.'

'Demons, Hermitage,' Cwen squeaked a bit.

'Yes?' Hermitage wondered why they were making such a fuss.

'It might not be safe.' She took another step back, just to be on the safe side.

Hermitage laughed, lightly, 'I think books about demons under the watchful gaze of Saint Botwulf will be perfectly safe.'

'You can read them then,' Wat said, not going any closer.

'For heaven's sake,' Hermitage shook his head. 'You and Cwen are the first to mock the works of the church and to cast aspersions on its leaders, yet the first hint of a demon and you hide behind a monk's habit.'

'Yes,' Wat explained, 'demons.'

'It isn't a very healthy topic,' Egbert spoke up. 'I saw a demon take over the spirit of a cat once.'

'A cat?' Hermitage asked.

'That's right. The demon rose out of a fire and turned the cat mad.'

Hermitage frowned. 'By any chance had the demon taken the shape of a shower of red hot embers?'

'That's right,' Egbert said, with some awe at Hermitage's learning.

'Which landed on the cat's fur.'

'Yes, they did,' Egbert's tone was hushed. 'Do demons do that?'

'I don't think you have anything to worry about.' Hermitage found it a strange turn of events to have Cwen and Wat lurking in the background while he faced up to the terrors of the world. Except of course they weren't terrors of the world. These were just books on demons, it was ridiculous to be frightened of them. If a real demon turned

151

up he would be the first to leave.

He turned his attention to the shelves and started pulling books out one at a time to see if anything helped in their search for clues about Ignatius or the king's door. These were all rare and precious texts but pretty much stuck to their subject.

Here was a volume on Saint Guthlac and how he was given lessons on how to fight off demons by Saint Bartholomew - along with a big whip. Here was a charming book of Revelation with most of the demons in beautiful colour. And this one was.., well, that was odd. Hermitage looked at the volume in his hand. It was a small book, easily held in one hand, but he couldn't immediately understand what it was doing here.

Wat noticed his puzzled look. 'Something wrong?' he asked nervously, in case this book was the one with the demon in it.

'Must be in the wrong place,' Hermitage held the book up. 'I imagine with thousands of books to manage it is not uncommon to have one on the wrong shelf.'

Now it was Wat's turn to frown. 'I imagine,' he countered, 'that if this library was put here for a special purpose and that its books are the greatest treasures,' he didn't sound convinced of this, 'and that there is one man whose job it is to look after said books..,'

'Yes?'

'They don't end up in the wrong place by mistake.'

Hermitage considered the title in his hand. 'You mean it might be here on purpose.'

'If that's the opposite of being there by mistake, then yes.' Wat folded his arms. 'What is it?' he nodded at the volume.

Hermitage held the book open, its title page on display.

'It's called De architectura,' he read out. 'Written by someone called Marcus Vitruvius Pollo.'

Blank looks in the room said no one had heard of him.

'And it looks like he signed this one personally.' Hermitage translated the Latin on the front page. 'To Caesar Augustus with respect.' They all shrugged again at the meaningless names. 'This seems to be all about how to build things. Apparently there are many volumes in the work but this one has a lot about forts and military buildings.' He looked up again at the statue of Saint Botwulf. 'I'm absolutely positive this has nothing to do with Botwulf. If it was a book on how to build a monastery, I could understand.'

'Aha,' Wat said.

'Aha?' Hermitage enquired. Did Wat know something of Saint Botwulf's hitherto unknown interest in construction? He thought it unlikely.

'It's as I said,' Wat explained. 'This isn't a monastery.'

Hermitage was about to interrupt.

'Well, it is now but it wasn't when it was built. It's a Roman fort. Or was.'

Egbert looked around with a deep frown on his face. 'Come master Wat,' he chided, 'I have been here four years and I can assure you that it is, without doubt, a monastery. Just look at it. There's the main gate to the East, the dortoir, the chapel, the cloister. Yes, there is sign of some old gates in the walls at the other quadrants,' he acknowledged. 'And there may have been some other buildings within the walls at some point in the past.' He went on. 'And the towers in the corners of the walls could be used for defensive purposes and of course the dyke itself and cobbles inside are major feats of engineering.' He stopped and looked confident that

153

his argument was sound and accurate. He took another breath. 'It's an old Roman fort, isn't it?'

'Yes it is,' Wat said. 'And that book is about Roman forts. And it's in the section of the library under the statue of saint what's-his-name, whose altar is hidden behind the king's door that the dead priest was pointing at. There you are.' He said this as if the whole mystery was solved. The book did it. 'Hermitage,' he asked, 'is there anything marked in the book? Any particular sections?'

Hermitage worked his way through the pages which were well-thumbed but crammed with detailed descriptions and remarkably accurate drawings and diagrams of a whole range of buildings. He was nearly at the end of the book. 'Oh,' he said, 'yes, look.' He held the book with its tiny writing for them all to see from ten feet away in a gloomy library.

'Very nice,' Cwen said. 'What does it say?'

'It's a section on dedication to the Gods. The Roman Gods,' he added hastily. 'Complete nonsense, obviously, but it was a long time ago. It looks like someone has marked one section with chalk or something.'

'Which section?' Wat asked.

'Erm,' Hermitage read the text, his lips moving as the Latin was taken into his head where it was converted into English. He read the words, translating as he went. 'Sacrifice to the God Cloacina.' He coughed his derision at the idea of sacrifices. 'This will ensure that the construction proceeds to plan and that the final design will operate effectively and to the benefit of the populace.'

'Design of what?' Wat asked.

'Erm,' Hermitage read on to try and find the right section. 'Oh,' he said as he read the title. 'The drains.'

After a short silence both questioning and embarrassed, Cwen spoke up. 'The Romans had a God of the drains?'

'It seems so.' Hermitage was not really taken with the idea himself. 'Although the Romans called them the cloaca and I believe the Normans call them sewers.'

'Doesn't make it any better,' Cwen observed.

'And what's it got to do with this place?' Wat asked.

'We have them,' Egbert spoke up.

'Have what?'

'Drains, clocums, sewurs. Under the ground somewhere.'

Hermitage found this hard to believe. 'How can you have drains in this place? It's already in a drain.'

'Don't ask me,' Egbert replied. 'All I know is that there are holes in the ground the stuff goes down, and it doesn't come back. Well, not unless there's a really strong tide.'

'Is there a way in?' Hermitage asked, which generated a cacophony of disgusted groans from the others.

'A way in?' Egbert asked. 'To the drains? Well, there's the normal way.' He didn't seem quite sure what Hermitage was asking.

'No,' Hermitage explained, 'I mean a way to get into the drains. According to the book, these cloaca are quite big. More like tunnels than holes. If there was a way in, it might be that this is where the secret to Ignatius's death is hidden. He has left us a clue. Why else would drains be sitting under Saint Botwulf?'

Wat snorted. Hermitage frowned disapproval.

Egbert was thinking hard. 'There's the stink-hole, I suppose.'

'The stink-hole.' Hermitage thought that sounded exactly like the entrance to a drain.

'That's right. In the far back corner of the walls there's a covered area where all the smells seem to come from when the tide's in the right direction.'

'Excellent,' Hermitage said. 'That must be it then.'

'I'm not going there though.' Egbert was very clear.

'A few smells will not deter us, Brother,' Hermitage encouraged.

'It's not the smells,' Egbert protested, 'it's the ghosts.'

. . .

High above them, Nicodemus had hold of the Brother by the scruff of the habit. 'You know where this place is?' he hissed harshly.

The Brother nodded, but the terror in his eyes said he held the same opinion as Egbert.

'Good,' Nicodemus was less bothered about smelly ghosts. 'Take us there,' he gestured back down the wall. 'If we get arrive first we can find what there is and leave the idiot Hermitage to his own devices.'

'Or get on with removing him completely,' Athan suggested.

The three of them turned quietly away from their parapet and began the descent back to the ground. Athan was taking it very cautiously, seemingly convinced that getting down was just as dangerous and being up there in the first place.

He was starting to gain confidence that the ground would be getting nearer as he put his foot out for the next step; which wasn't there anymore.

As he pitched forward, his thought was not that he might be about to fall to his death, but that the person who had removed the step was going to have a very bad time when Athan got hold of him.

As he bounced, chest-first into the next step down, he

could only feel resignation in the face of the inevitable as he heard Nicodemus and the monk falling quite rapidly in his direction.

. . .

Thirty feet below, Hermitage was putting the book back where he had found it. As he did so a slip of vellum fell from the back cover. He stooped to pick it up and replace it. Hardly surprising that the book was falling apart after all these years. He found that it was a folded page which he opened out of interest. Because that's what you did with folded pages.

'Oh my,' he breathed.

'What now?' Wat turned back from the door.

Hermitage held up the sheet for them all to see.

'Ah,' Wat said after he'd taken a moment to digest the Latin.

Even Cwen and Egbert raised their eyebrows at the diagram.

Hermitage turned the page back to himself and read to the title. 'By Marcus Vitruvius Pollo; how to construct a sundial.'

Caput XIV

Investigation Can Be So Draining

Leaving the library, the volume of Vitruvius was still clasped in Hermitage's hand. Given the significance of sundials to the demise of Ignatius he thought it sensible to keep it to hand, in case someone tried to remove it. When asked who was likely to remove it, as no one else could read to see what it was, Hermitage explained that it was just a precaution. He hated to admit that having a book from this great library in his possession was a huge pleasure. Just feeling the weight of the thing reassured him somehow that the world still had value and could create great works. It was not full of killers.

Having decided that the tunnels under the monastery were where they needed to go next, Hermitage had assumed that was what would happen. Egbert though had other ideas; or rather he changed his ideas quite frequently.

To begin with, he had just been nervous about the ghosts but had reluctantly agreed to take them to the right spot. Then, as the right spot came into sight he changed his mind and concluded that he was going nowhere near the place as the ghosts and spirits of the dead would rise up from the ground and eat his soul.

Despite reassurances that this was extremely unlikely, Egbert promised that they would be able to see the ghosts for themselves when they got close enough, and he would keep his distance.

Dismissing this nonsense, Hermitage led in the direction indicated until they drew near to the far corner of the monastery compound where the walls to the east and the south drew together. Into this space a shelter had been built using the main walls of the place to support a simple roof of wooden tiles. The whole space was about thirty feet square and under the shelter of its roof it did look pretty dark and uninviting.

Doubtless, it was the log store or something similar and so Hermitage put his concerns behind him and strode confidently ahead.

His concerns jumped out in front of him again as he thought he saw a white shape in the back of the enclosure. A rather human one, standing tall and still.

'The ghosts,' Egbert wailed.

'There are no ghosts,' Hermitage was firm, although just at the moment he was having his doubts. 'It's simply a trick of the light.'

'What light?' Egbert asked, disarmingly. It was true there was no light in the store, or whatever this building was. And it was getting quite dark now. A good moon was rising in the sky, which did nothing for mysterious figures hidden in dark corners.

Hermitage found that his feet wouldn't move. Egbert's were taking him slowly backwards and Wat was squatting down to try and see what was there before going further.

'Oh, for goodness sake.' Cwen snorted at the lot of them as she strode forward and passed under the roof.

'Eek,' Egbert said, perhaps expecting her to disappear completely.

After a moment she reappeared and beckoned them to join her. 'It's all right,' she said, in a mocking tone. 'I've told the nasty ghosts they've got to behave.'

No one moved.

'There are no ghosts,' Cwen shouted. 'You idiots,' she

added, for good measure.

Egbert seemed happy to remain an idiot and stayed where he was. Hermitage and Wat stepped cautiously forward, Hermitage bending as he approached to try and see what was there before he went too far.

'Ah,' he said when the contents of the covered area were revealed but turning his nose up at the smell that went with them. 'More statues.'

'Lots of them.' Cwen walked among the figures, most of them slightly smaller than life-size but very well made of some bright stone. There were figures of men and women, many draped with clothing carved so well that it looked ready to flow in the breeze.

Unfortunately, many of them weren't draped with anything at all and the sight of so many naked people gathered together, albeit stone people standing on plinths, was enough to bring a flush to Hermitage's cheeks. Whoever had made these figures had clearly prized accuracy in their art; an accuracy which was revealing things Hermitage had last seen in one of Wat's tapestries.

'Well, well.' Wat strolled amongst the works. 'This gives me a few ideas.' He pointed out one statue which Hermitage hadn't noticed, or perhaps of their own accord his eyes had told him not to look at.

This one was of a man and woman. Neither of them were clothed and they had their hands upon one another. 'What manner of people would allow something like this to be even thought of, let alone realised in stone?' Hermitage gasped.

'Romans.' Wat grinned. 'Magnificent people.'

'Ahem,' Hermitage coughed, anxious to move on. 'These must have been cast aside when the place became a monastery.'

'But not destroyed, eh?' Wat winked for some reason. 'I expect the monks popped back now and again to make sure they were all right.'

Egbert had cautiously joined them and was peering at the statues. 'I was told they were ghosts,' he complained.

'I bet you were,' Wat said.

'If we could concentrate on the matter in hand,' Hermitage tried to get them back on the subject of drains.

'This one's got quite a lot in hand.' Wat pointed at another statue that was even worse than the first one.

Despite himself, Hermitage looked over and gasped. He knew men and women were built like that but surely they should be minding their own business a lot more than these two were doing. Although the statues were predominantly of raw stone, one or two still bore traces of the paint that must have coloured them originally; and the paint in this case was predominantly pink. 'Let us look for an entrance to the tunnels,' he insisted.

'This one's got an inscription,' Cwen called out from the back of the statues.

Hermitage made his way towards her, hoping that this would take their attention away from the representations staring them in the face. As he approached he worried that the inscription might be just as bad.

Thankfully, he found quite a modest statue. It was still a female figure but at least the drapes and coverings had been put in the right places. There was still a bit too much bare flesh for Hermitage but at least none of it was actually improper. He peered at the Latin inscription adorning the base of the statue.

'Adeorna,' he translated. 'Goddess of the journey, guard

our steps.' He turned to the others. 'How ridiculous,' he said. 'A goddess for a journey. What sort of people were these that thought there was a God just for journeys? They probably even prayed to her. No wonder they have vanished in the dust of history with pagan, sinful behaviour like that.'

Wat nodded at Hermitage's statement. 'Not all like Saint Botwulf then.'

Hermitage couldn't see what that had to do with anything.

'A patron Saint of travellers who probably gets prayed to before a journey.'

No, Hermitage couldn't get what Wat was on about.

'And Christopher,' Wat added. 'That's two saints for travellers.'

'Yes,' Hermitage agreed. 'What's your point?'

'Oh nothing, really,' Wat shrugged with a smile for some reason or other.

'This one's Cloacina,' Cwen called again, beckoning them over. 'Isn't she the one in charge of the drains?'

They all gathered at the statue that looked pretty similar to the Goddess of journeys. The name of the God was clearly spelled out on the plinth.

'How did they tell them apart?' Hermitage asked, shaking his head. 'They all look alike.'

Wat was still smiling. 'Good job we've got you to tell us which saint is which. After all, they don't all look alike at all.'

Again, Wat was going on about saints. Perhaps Hermitage's constant nagging was having an effect at last.

Cwen was strolling around the statue, which was placed almost against the wall. She disappeared around the back of the statue. 'And here's her drain,' she called.

Hermitage dearly hoped that wasn't a rude term for something.

In fact, at the back of the statue there was a hole in the ground. It was a very neat hole, about four feet across with stone edging and it clearly served some purpose. The purpose at the moment seemed to be to let the most appalling smell come up from below.

'Definitely the drain then,' Wat observed with a wrinkle of his nose.

'And it is more like a tunnel.' Hermitage noted that the size of the hole would make it very easy for someone to climb down.

'A big, dark tunnel.' Cwen stuck her head down into the opening, which seemed a remarkably brave thing to do.

'And Ignatius sent us here?' Egbert asked, with a look of disgusted disappointment on his face.

'He did,' Hermitage confirmed. 'So we must go down and see what he has sent us to find. Perhaps the secrets of his life and death are hidden below. It would be a good place. No one is likely to stroll down there by mistake.'

Wat appraised the entrance to the drain. 'Some secrets are perhaps best left secret.'

'Having come this far, we must go on.' Hermitage was disappointed that Wat had seemed terribly keen when it was all about treasure. 'We can't back out now.'

'We could,' Wat suggested.

'Yes, we could,' Cwen said, her hands on her hips and that look on her face that usually got Wat to do what she wanted. 'And we could leave the treasure for the next person to find.'

'Pretty smelly treasure.'

'It'll wash,' Cwen replied. 'Like your clothes,' perhaps

neatly hitting the reason for Wat's reluctance to think about climbing into Cloacina's drain.

Hermitage appraised the opening and the darkness coming out of it. 'We'll need a light of some sort,' he said.

'There were oil lamps in Ignatius's chamber,' Egbert said.

'Good,' Hermitage nodded. 'Although we'll have to be careful. I know that putting a lighted flame into an enclosed space such as this can give rise to a great conflagration.'

Egbert looked impressed, 'Knowledgeable, isn't he?' he said to Wat.

Wat smiled, knowingly, 'He had a bad experience with a lighted flame and a privy once.'[3]

Egbert frowned and looked a lot less impressed as he went to fetch the lamps.

Hermitage used the time to prowl around the covered space, ignoring the most explicit statues and trying to focus on the opportunity for learning about the ways of the Romans. After three new statues, he had learned far more about their ways than ever wanted to. He returned to the drain opening. 'Where do you think it goes?'

Wat joined him, a piece of cloth delicately held against his nose. 'I think we can tell which way one end goes,' he observed.

'Presumably the other must go out to sea,' Hermitage looked in that direction, beyond the wall of the monastery.

'Best place for it,' Cwen said.

Hermitage looked at the ground around him and at the wall of the monastery and frowned. 'But how? As far as I can tell the sea is already higher than the ground here anyway. Why isn't the drain full of seawater?'

---

[3] *The Garderobe of Death*; full of bad experiences.

Wat shrugged, 'Maybe Cloacina's down there holding it back. Either her or the God of keeping the sea out of your pipes.'

Hermitage coughed, 'Be serious. Look.' He waved his arm in the general direction of where they knew the sea was. 'We all saw the water. Why isn't it in here?'

'Clever people,' Wat nodded to the statues.

There was no time for further debate as Egbert returned carrying four simple oil lamps. They were plain clay, about the size of your hand and were a simple flat container with a spout at one end holding the wick.

'Roman as well,' Hermitage observed.

Egbert took one of the lamps into the shelter of the building and produced a bundle containing flint from his habit. A couple of simple strikes and the oil lit to a gentle flickering flame. Applying this to the other lamps they were soon prepared for their journey into the drain. Well, as far as light was concerned anyway.

Hermitage took his lamp to the edge of the hole and, leaning back as far as he could, he lowered his arm in, turning his face away as he did so. When nothing happened he took a cautious look into the drain. 'It seems fine,' he reported.

The others came and looked over his shoulder down into the space. The light from the lamp was virtually no help whatsoever, so Hermitage lowered it as far as he could reach.

They saw that in the bottom of the space was a trickle of water that didn't bear close examination. What it was running in was a remarkable sight. An almost perfectly circular tunnel ran to left and right, every inch of it lined with equally spaced and identical bricks. Hermitage couldn't immediately imagine how anything like this could be built at all, let alone why anyone would go to all this trouble for a drain. A drain was a simple trench dug where you needed it. When it collapsed or got blocked, you just dug it out again. This thing looked like it was built to last a hundred years. What a waste of effort. These Romans clearly had too much time on their hands.

The drop to the bottom of the tunnel was at least five feet and to walk along inside would be easy. Never mind the thing being built of brick, why was it so big? Hermitage imagined that a fort full of Roman soldiers might well be able to fill a thing this size. A handful of monks would barely trouble it.

It still worried him why the tunnel wasn't sloshing with seawater, being five feet below ground which was itself lower than the water.

'In we get then,' Wat said with strained enthusiasm. 'Though goodness knows what we're going to find in here.'

'We'll know it when we see it,' Hermitage assured him. 'Just as the altar led us to the library, so the book leads us here.'

'Persuaded into a drain by a book,' Wat huffed as he sat on the edge of the entrance. 'Are you sure this is..,' He never got to finish the sentence as Cwen pushed him in the back.

The language which emerged from the drain put the smell firmly in its place as Wat went into some detail about what he would do to Cwen when he got hold of her.

Cwen simply grinned at the onslaught and went over to lower herself as well.

'Have you seen the state of my shoes?' Wat could be heard remonstrating with Cwen as she joined him.

Egbert followed and dropped into the hole with agility.

Hermitage sat on the edge and looked down into the blackness below. Rather like a dog trying to find the right place to sleep he twisted and turned looking for the best grip to lower himself without injury. Eventually he found himself laying on the floor with his legs over the edge, unable to go backwards or forwards. 'Erm,' he said. This was followed by 'Eek,' as someone pulled him from below.

. . .

In the shadows of the statue of Salacia, goddess of seawater, adorned with the inscription "Oh, Goddess, please don't drown us", something stirred as the last head dropped down into the drain. A figure, most certainly not stone, detached itself from the darkness and moved over to Cloacina's drain. Satisfied with something or other, it moved over to the back of the shelter, where it started to shift a large stone tablet that was propped against the wall. The tablet was a fascinating record of the life of Marcus Vertigius Rex, last commander of the fort and it explained an awful lot - if anyone had been able to read it.

Behind the tablet, emerging from a slot in the wall specifically made for the purpose, was a large lever. Another inscription, carved with great skill and artistry, explained the purpose of this device. To any learned eye, the very large and capitalised letters would be taken as a warning. This figure was not learned and had not a clue what any of the markings meant. He knew what happened when you pushed down on the sticky-out bit; which he now did with a rather worrying smile on his face.

. . .

Wat had led the group away from the sea and in towards the monastery buildings. Hermitage argued that surely this was the most unpleasant direction of travel, but Wat suggested that if anything was hidden, it was most likely to be closer to the monastery than out near the sea where anyone might find it. Hermitage wondered who would be wandering in from the sea to find anything at which point Wat offered to split the group in two. The monks could head for the sea, on their own, while he and Cwen explored inland. Hermitage decided that he'd rather be in their company.

As they walked along, the tunnel became no less impressive. The standard of construction was maintained and the lamps revealed markers in the wall, indicating the distance travelled.

Hermitage's amazement was undiminished as well. 'What people would go to all this trouble for a drain?'

Wat was hobbling along with one foot either side of the stream to try and keep his feet out of the worst of it. 'Probably people who had five hundred Roman soldiers up above doing their best to fill the thing on a regular basis. Don't know about you, but I'd rather spend a bit of time and effort up front than have to go into the drains every night to try and clear them.'

Hermitage could see the sense of that but he was still puzzled. 'What I don't understand is how they work at all. The water you're standing in doesn't seem to be going anywhere.'

Wat looked down and tutted that he was, indeed, standing in the water again. 'How did that happen?' he lifted his foot and shook a soggy shoe.

Hermitage examined the floor of the tunnel. 'The water does seem to be deeper here,' he observed.

'How can it be deeper?' Cwen asked. 'The tunnel isn't going downhill.'

Hermitage was impressed with her reasoning. In his library browsing, he had come across a book by one Boethius which concerned something called geometry. That seemed to be all about lines and slopes and things. Perhaps there was something in the volume of Pollo that might help. By the time he had thought about this, the water appeared to have got deeper still. 'Do you think people are, you know, using the drains?' he asked with some distaste.

They all looked at the floor. Wat sniffed the air. 'Do you detect a certain salty tang to it now?'

They all sniffed and looked none the wiser.

Cwen nodded back the way they had come. 'It seems to be moving in from that way.'

Hermitage looked back down the tunnel, and then ahead of them. There was definitely something odd going on. He pondered the problem for a moment. 'I say,' he said, 'I've just had the most marvellous idea.'

'Do tell,' Wat said with a hint of impatience that the water was now approaching his ankles.

'Well,' Hermitage explained his idea. 'If you had a drain like this, down below the sea, as it were, what you could do is put a gate on the end where it comes out in the water.'

'A gate?'

'That's right. Then, when the tide is high, you open the gate and seawater rushes in and fills the tunnel with nice clean seawater. When the tide goes out again, it takes all the water and the filth with it and you close the gate.'

Egbert was rubbing his chin at the explanation. 'But if the water is always higher than the end of the tunnel, it will never run away.'

'Hm,' Hermitage pondered. 'That is true.' He gave the problem some more thought. 'Perhaps there was a wheel of buckets..,'

Wat held a hand up to stop him. He spoke slowly and there was worry in his voice. 'Did you say a gate could be opened that let the sea in?'

'Well, that's the theory,' Hermitage nodded. 'But, as Brother Egbert points out, there are several practical problems relating to the height of the water.'

Wat's voice was now getting positively excited, 'And what would you say the practical problems would be for anyone who was in the tunnel when the gate was opened.'

'Oh my,' Hermitage said. 'That wouldn't be very wise at all. Who would get themselves in such a position?'

'We would,' Wat shouted as he pointed down the tunnel towards the wall of water that was coming their way. 'Run,' he added, unnecessarily.

They did run, and there was only one direction to go, but Hermitage wasn't sure where it was going to get them. If the tunnel filled up with water, where could they go?

'Look for a privy,' Wat shouted, guarding the flame on his lamp very carefully, 'and climb up it.'

The noise of the rushing water was intense now, blocking out any chance of discussion, or even thought. It wouldn't be long before it fell upon them and carried them down the tunnel whether they liked it or not.

'Perhaps there's another drain hole,' Hermitage shouted. 'Like the one we came down. At that moment the water did catch up with him, taking his feet, swarming over him and bowling him along like a skittle. The lamps were all extinguished and in the darkness he found himself thinking it was quite good that the water was deep as he wasn't hitting himself on the walls of the tunnel. Then he concluded that deep was a bad thing as it might stop him breathing.

The drag of his habit increased as it absorbed more than his own weight in water and his swimming ability, which did not exist, did nothing to aid his buoyancy. He managed to get his head above the pounding water to take a breath before he was dragged under again and thrown around like something small and brown in a sewer full of water.

At the moment that he started thinking he would quite like to take a breath, he found he was still under the water. It felt that he was being dragged along the bottom of the tunnel and if he could get his feet under him he could push upwards to the air. The water had other plans for his feet though and seemed to be trying to remove them completely by shaking them from side to side.

He knew that he had to take a breath really very soon now and felt compelled to do so, underwater or not. His reasoning was still sufficient to tell him that if he did this, he would drown, but his body wasn't listening to his reason.

He thought that this was ridiculous. He was in a relatively small tunnel with seawater running through it. Drowning happened in big rivers, or over the side of a boat. It didn't happen underground. This situation was simply unacceptable.

It was just crossing his mind to try and take his habit off, to prevent the thing dragging him to his death. Naturally this would be enormously embarrassing should Cwen be there when he emerged, but probably not as embarrassing as being dead.

He started to heave at the rope around the waist of his garment, which had unhelpfully swollen with water and he could not untie the knot. Suddenly he felt a pull on his shoulders. Perhaps someone was trying to help. He hoped it wasn't Cwen.

The pull grew stronger, dragging him upwards until he at last emerged from the surface of the water and could take a gasping, gurgling breath. He coughed and spluttered and managed to get his feet underneath him as the arms from above held him firm. He looked up and saw those strong arms clothed in the simple garb of a habit. Egbert did look like a very capable man, thank the Lord that he had been on hand. This must be another drain outlet which they had luckily come across.

'Brother Hermitage,' the voice above called as it hauled him from the deadly stream.

Hermitage looked up and gave a weak smile to his rescuer.

Then he screamed. As he faded into unconsciousness his reason still told him that it must be Brother Egbert. His near-drowning had confused him and done the most appalling thing; it had replaced Egbert's face with that terror from his past, Prior Athan. Still at least when he woke up everything would be back to normal.

Caput XV

Swimming Lessons

𝔚aking up to find that normal included Prior Athan gave Hermitage a strong inclination to jump back in the sewer. That Nicodemus was standing next to him holding an oil lamp, made him think that he was back in De'Ath's Dingle. How could that have happened? Perhaps he had started drowning in that awful monastery and all the intervening time had been a dream. Or a nightmare. There was no King William, he wasn't King's Investigator. Back to normal then. What a truly horrible thought.

He looked around, dragging his terrified eyes away from Athan. Wat and Cwen were there, along with Brother Egbert and some other monk he'd never seen before who had his cowl pulled low over his face. So it was true, all his memories were accurate. King William was real, he was King's Investigator and Athan was in this small room with them.

There was another opening from the drain here but it seemed to be into a simple square stone room with no immediately obvious way out. Perhaps it was some feature of the drain's construction. Nicodemus and Athan had obviously arrived some time earlier as they were bone dry and had two oil lamps burning to illuminate the drear scene. Definitely a nightmare then.

'What?' he managed to say.

'We just dragged you from the tunnel full of water,' Athan growled at him. 'Although personally I'd have let you float away.'

Same old Athan then.

173

'How? Who? When?' The questions tripped over themselves as he found his voice.

Nicodemus brushed Athan aside and looked down at Hermitage who was still soaking all over the floor. 'We too have been sent by the king, young Hermitage,' Nicodemus said, in that manner that made Hermitage clasp his habit close before it was stolen from his back. 'And fortunate that we were, it seems. Rescuing you and these,' he waved a dismissive hand, 'people from almost certain death.'

'But, but, but,' Hermitage butted. 'At the monastery in De'Ath's Dingle? The king? I thought..,' He thought that the king had put Nicodemus and Athan firmly in their place and that they might at least be in a dungeon somewhere by now. If not actually dead. It hadn't even entered his head to think he would ever see either of them again. If it had, of course, he would have worried himself sick over the prospect. Now he had to get sick very quickly.

He tried telling himself that Athan wasn't his prior anymore and so wouldn't simply start hitting him again. He confirmed to his mind that he wasn't in De'Ath's Dingle anymore; that Wat and Cwen were here to protect him. It didn't help much when Athan was glaring at him in that way he had. The way he looked at everyone.

'Ah,' Nicodemus said in his knowing way. 'Poor King Harold.' He shook his head in the manner of a sad person but without any sadness. 'Taken from us so soon after his encounter at De'Ath's Dingle. And now King William.' Nicodemus rubbed his hands. 'He appears to have given us both work to do.' Nicodemus smiled the smile of a toad in a bucket of worms.

Hermitage just swallowed. He looked at his companions and saw that they were not in a much better state than he was. They all looked bedraggled and had obviously shared his experience of Roman drainage. Cwen seemed a bit more alert and was glaring at Athan with the glare she only used on special occasions.

It occurred to Hermitage that there must have been some discussion between people while he was out of his senses. From the look of that glare it had been a lively conversation and Cwen was still harbouring some ill intent towards Athan in particular. Cwen's harbour for ill intent was a capacious facility.

Wat was looking generally disgusted. 'I think I swallowed some,' he said, with a grimace.

'But at least you are alive, master weaver,' Nicodemus sneered with disappointment. 'You and your little friend.' He waved a hand in Cwen's direction.

Cwen held up a hand, bidding Nicodemus to wait a moment as she had something to say. She coughed and wiped her hair free of the water. 'As soon as we're fully recovered,' she croaked and spluttered, 'I'll come over there and dip you in the drain until your head stops working.'

Athan took half a step forward and got the full brunt of that glare. 'And you,' she said as if Athan had been scraped off the bottom of the sewer. 'I've heard all about you from Hermitage.' Athan had clearly been accused, tried and convicted in his absence. And now Cwen was ready to do the execution bit.

The ex-prior paused, perhaps seeing something in Cwen that reminded of himself. He contented himself with an inaudible grumble.

Wat interrupted the hostile atmosphere. 'Charming as this reunion may be, any chance of discussing just what in God's bristling beard is going on?'

Hermitage's state was such that he couldn't even raise objection to Wat's usual profane language. Athan was in a small room with him. All of his terrors were running around the inside of his head, trying to decide which one of them should take charge.

'Of course,' Nicodemus was suddenly all lightness and charm as if considering what colour they should paint the walls. 'Someone is trying to kill you,' he said simply.

'Not you?' Hermitage blurted out before he could stop himself.

'No, funnily enough.' Nicodemus was not in the least disturbed by the accusation. 'Someone else altogether. Now normally this would not worry me at all, but they appear to be trying to kill me as well.'

'That I can understand,' Wat said.

'The questions are why and who?' Nicodemus went on.

'I think my question is what the devil you are doing here?' Wat appeared to have recovered most quickly of all of them. 'Last time we saw you two the king had just expressed a very low opinion of the pair of you. I find it hard to believe King William has taken you into his trust. At least not if he has the faintest idea what sort of people he's dealing with.'

Nicodemus waved the criticism away.

'And this is the Monasterium Tene-what-not,' Wat went on. 'Supposedly a repository of great treasure. I can only assume that you are here to get your hands on it.'

Nicodemus and Athan looked like they weren't listening.

'The king sent Brody off to get Hermitage here,' Wat was thinking as he went. 'We came to look into the death of Ignatius.' He narrowed his eyes and drilled them at Nicodemus as if he could drag the truth out of the man. 'I reckon you happened to hear about it and came of your own accord. Probably by eavesdropping on the king. Trying to better yourself at the expense of others. As usual.' He smiled, content with his own deductions. 'And who's your little friend?' he gestured at the cowled monk who looked like he was trying to vanish into the stonework.

'No idea,' Nicodemus replied. 'Just some monk.'

Egbert dragged himself to his feet, water running from his habit which was just as soaked as Hermitage's. He stepped over to the monk and whipped the cowl back without any ceremony. 'Brother Lefric? What on earth are you doing here?'

'Aha,' Brother Lefric looked surprised to find himself in this dim and dingy hole as if he had wandered in when he wasn't looking where he was going. 'Just, sort of, erm, got caught up, you know.'

'Got caught up?' Egbert examined Lefric's habit. 'You're bone dry. You must have come in with these two.'

'Erm,' Lefric looked around, perhaps hoping that the answer to the question was written on the wall somewhere - which would be no help anyway as he couldn't read. 'Just showing them around.'

'Showing them around?' Egbert was aghast. 'Just showing some total strangers around the most secret monastery in the kingdom?'

'Well,' Lefric began, but went no further.

'And ending up in some underground chamber with the sea running by underneath?'

'Ah,' Lefric seemed to appreciate the true depth and breadth of the hole he was in.

'We shall have words, Brother,' Egbert said, making it quite clear the words weren't going to be nice ones. He turned to Nicodemus and Athan. 'And what do you mean, someone's trying to kill us?'

Nicodemus held his hands out, an innocent look on his face saying that he was only reporting facts. Unfortunately, innocent looks didn't fit on Nicodemus's face and he looked like he'd just robbed his grandmother's grave and was selling the contents to his grandfather. 'I think someone opened the sea gate while you were in the tunnel,' he said. 'And believe me, if I'd done it I wouldn't hesitate to take the credit.'

Egbert frowned at the suggestion but had no immediate reply.

'And,' Nicodemus continued, 'I suspect this may be the same person who removed a tie stone in the chapel wall which nearly made us fall to our deaths.'

Egbert glared for an explanation.

'We just happened to be passing by the inside of the chapel wall,' Nicodemus observed as if they'd been strolling in the woods. 'We were sort of up near the roof and when we came down again, someone had taken away one of the steps.'

'Up in the roof of the chapel listening to us,' Wat concluded. 'Before hurrying down to the drain before us in order to steal whatever there was and be off.'

'Nothing of the kind,' Nicodemus reassured them. 'In fact, you're lucky we were here or you'd all be the drowned bodies frightening the monks in their privies by now.'

'Yes.' Hermitage tried to move the conversation on as he was always uncomfortable when the people around him weren't getting on. He also hoped it would take his mind off Athan. 'What is this place?'

They all looked around the room and could see no obvious function. Through the hole in the floor the seawater still bubbled and frothed, although the first strength of its arrival had faded. At least it wasn't coming up to join them.

'Must be part of the drain construction,' Wat speculated. 'Perhaps an overflow, or somewhere the builders used when they were putting the thing together in the first place.'

'There doesn't seem to be a way out,' Hermitage observed. Well, there was, but it was full of seawater now and he was pretty sure that he would not be able to swim back underwater to the point they came in. He'd be able to drown quite easily but that defeated the object rather.

The stones of this chamber were very closely packed and any gaps that there were had mortar pressed neatly into place. The ceiling, the floor and the walls were all the same. There appeared to be no door and there was certainly no window.

'How do we get out?' Hermitage asked.

'Wait 'till the sea goes down again?' Egbert suggested.

'Why would it do that?' Wat asked. 'Now that it's been let in.'

'Low tide?'

'I think we'd need Moses to make this sea go that low.'

Hermitage tutted at the suggestion. He was starting to feel his old self again. 'Is it getting warm in here?' he asked.

The others looked at him and the expressions on their faces said that yes, they were starting to feel a bit warmer.

'Probably all the people,' Cwen said. 'Why don't these three jump in the water?' she waved a hand to cover Nicodemus, Athan and Lefric.

'Why don't we throw you in,' Athan suggested. 'You're already wet.'

'This is not helpful,' Egbert tried to exert some authority.

179

'There are quite a few of us in a confined space with the water blocking the only way out. We just need to think.'

Hermitage did so. 'I say,' he burbled with enthusiasm, 'I think I've just had a thought.'

'Oh God,' Athan mumbled, not really to himself. 'I'd forgotten just how annoying he could be.'

Egbert waved him to silence. 'What is it, Brother?'

'I think we're suffocating,' Hermitage said, brightly. Very pleased at having worked this out so quickly.

'We're what?'

'Suffocating?' Hermitage sounded fascinated. 'From *suffocare*, to choke? Itself from *sub*, below and *fauces*, the throat. You see the room is tightly sealed all around us and the water is filling the hole below. This means that no life-giving humours can get it in.'

They all looked completely lost.

'It's been well known for many years,' Hermitage explained. 'The ancient Greeks understood. The four humours?' He was disappointed that his audience appeared completely ignorant of these very basic facts. 'Blood, yellow bile, black bile and phlegm.'

'Which have what do with air?' Wat asked, wiping a bead of sweat from his brow.

Hermitage shook his head. He really was going to have to go back to basics. 'The humour, blood, is associated with the element air. Earth, air, fire and water, yes?' There were at least some half-hearted nods at this. 'We all know blood is produced by the liver.' No nods this time. 'So, therefore, if there is no air our livers will stop working, we'll run out of blood and we'll die. Suffocation. See?'

'Oh great,' Cwen complained. 'Nice to have it explained.'

'So we just need to get some air. Our livers are

over-excited and are making us hot.'

'And how do we get air in a sealed box?' Athan demanded.

Hermitage didn't have an answer to that. He thought he'd explained the problem very well, surely he didn't have to think of everything.

'Knock a hole in the wall?' Egbert offered.

'Be my guest,' Nicodemus gestured to the solid walls that surrounded them and the complete absence of hole-knocking tools.

'Search the walls,' Wat instructed them all. 'See if you can find a loose stone or some weak spot we can have a go at.'

They all moved, slowly and with much panting, to the walls and started to examine them closely. They were now blinking sweat out of their eyes and found simply standing up to be quite exhausting. Even Nicodemus's oil lamp was guttering as if its liver was giving up as well.

'They're very well made,' Hermitage said, admiring the quality of the workmanship that had gone into what might turn out to be their tomb.

Nobody was saying anything as they gave their attention to the task right in front of their eyes.

'Anything?' Wat asked the room.

Mumbled negatives filled the air.

'Well,' Cwen called from her corner, 'it's not a gap but I don't know what it is.'

The whole group made their way to the section of wall Cwen was pointing at. Having seven people crowding round one small section of wall was not conducive to seeing anything at all.

'Get back, get back.' Wat pushed them all away. When there was space he looked at the wall. 'What?' he demanded of Cwen, not seeing anything at all.

'That.' Cwen pointed at one of the large stones of the wall which had a definite symbol carved in its surface.

'So?' Wat asked, not seeing anything that was going to help his liver.

'Well, I don't know do I?' Cwen snapped back. 'It's different from the rest though.'

Hermitage pressed his way through the crowd to see what the fuss was. 'Ah,' he said, seeing the image carved on the stone. 'That's the Fasces.' The shape on the stone was a series of parallel lines, each closed off at both ends with the clear outline of an axe head at one end of the lines.

'Faskays,' Wat repeated. 'And that helps how?'

'No idea. But as Cwen says, it is different.'

'I expect,' Athan said with enough weight in his voice to sink through the floor, 'Brother Hermitage is going to explain what it is.'

Of course he was. 'It's a bundle of rods bound together with an axe in the middle.'

'Excellent,' Athan concluded. 'That's explained that then.'

'Generally a symbol of authority,' Hermitage went on, invited or not. 'The magistratum or court would use it as a mark of their status.'

'What's it doing there?' Cwen asked. 'Who'd have a court down here? Fishes?'

'Well, no one,' Hermitage acknowledged. He thought that it was indeed a very strange place to bother with a mark of this sort. Perhaps the stone had been somewhere else originally and was re-used for the drain. Or perhaps.., 'This could be what Ignatius sent us to find,' he said, with excitement.

'A stone with a mark on it in a drain?' Wat asked, clearly

thinking that Ignatius must have been very stupid indeed.

'Yes, but what a mark. And here. And us directed down here by the book.' Hermitage thought it was obvious. It didn't look like anyone else did. He stepped forward to examine the stone more closely. The mortar around it still looked firm and even but the texture of the stone itself seemed more worn than its neighbours. 'So,' he said, very slowly, as his thoughts ordered themselves. 'Someone stuck down here might demand an exit with some authority.'

'Oh, come on,' Wat said, seeing where he was going but thinking it was completely ridiculous.

Hermitage gave a weak smile and stepped right up to the stone. He placed both hands on the symbol of the Fasces and pushed. The stone slid smoothly back into the wall and a rush of fresh air blew across their faces, stimulating their livers no end. They all took grateful breaths, pleased that their blood started to cool down quite quickly.

'Do we get out this way?' Cwen asked, looking at the size of the stone which might be enough to squeeze her though but there wasn't anyone else in the room who'd make it.

Hermitage examined the stones surrounding the symbol. 'I think the rest of these will move as well.'

Egbert, Wat and Athan stepped up now and pushed the stones below the Fasces which all slid neatly backwards and off to the left. Once they were clear, a staircase could be seen behind, leading up out of the room.

'Perhaps we should go up this?' Hermitage suggested.

'I think we should,' Cwen said with some urgency.

'Very well,' Hermitage nodded.

'Because for some reason,' Cwen went on, 'the sea seems quite keen on coming in now.'

They all turned and saw that the sea from the tunnel was

bubbling up and over the edge of the hole and seemed determined to fill the chamber up quite quickly.

'Now that is interesting,' Hermitage observed as his feet started to get wet once more. 'I wonder if..,' he didn't get a chance to complete his speculation, which was going to be quite a good one.

'Up, up,' Wat commanded, ushering everyone out of the room and up the stairs.

There were only half a dozen steep stone steps until the passage ended at a slab of wooden panelling.

'It's shut,' Cwen called back to those behind her.

'Shut,' Athan scoffed. 'Let me through.'

They all shuffled about a bit until Athan could get at the wood. He examined it briefly, took a slight swing back and threw his shoulder at it. Like most things facing an angry Athan it collapsed completely and splintered out of the way.

The whole group swarmed through the opening and away from the still-rising sea. They burst into a simple room but at least a normal one this time. It looked like nothing more than a straightforward monk's cell, albeit a large one. A barred window ahead of them let in the grey light of the moon and a further door out into the corridor stood open.

The only remarkable thing about the room was the cot in the corner. The cot which had the abbot on it, blubbering and pointing at the huge crowd that has just climbed out of his wall.

Caput XVI

Let's Frighten the Abbot

'Master Abbot,' Egbert said, half in acknowledgement, half in surprise.

The abbot's eyes were wide, his head was ranging from side to side as he tried to take in the sight that had materialised in his cell, but most of all his pointing finger had found its life again and was singling out Cwen. 'Doom, doom,' he moaned.

'There will be in a minute,' Cwen agreed, 'if we don't find some way to make the sea go backwards.' She was glancing back down the staircase they had climbed, where the sound of the gurgling sea was getting slightly louder with each passing moment.

They were all crowded into the abbot's cell, which really wasn't built for such numbers. As the leader of the community, he had greater space than any other but this was really so that he could retire here and work, as well as sleep, not have gatherings with seven extra people, four of them still soaking wet. Cwen and Wat were pressed against the back wall with Athan, having been the first to enter the room. Egbert was jostling with Nicodemus for space in front of the abbot's bed and Lefric was half in and half out of the staircase entrance.

Hermitage had found himself bundled over towards the door. While he'd rather have been with Wat and Cwen, he found being close to the route of escape from the place quite comforting. Small spaces with many people in them had never been easy for him. A small space with several unwashed monks in sopping wet clothes that were starting

185

to smell was positively unpleasant.

'What are we doing here?' he asked, looking around the bland and featureless room. He considered the group, which, confined in the space of the abbot's chamber, seemed to be unnecessarily large now, considering it was supposed to be carrying out a delicate mission in a secret monastery. 'I mean why are we in the abbot's chamber?' he explained, spotting a number of unhelpful comments being made ready. 'Why would the trail from the altar to the library to the tunnel, lead here?'

No one appeared to have anything useful to say on this question.

They turned to face the abbot as if he ought to know why this mysterious path had brought them to his bedside.

The old man appraised them all, managing to drag his gaze away from Cwen for a few moments. 'I don't know you,' he said, now pointing at Nicodemus and Athan.

'We are sent by the king,' Nicodemus answered quickly.

Wat coughed, 'I doubt that.'

'More?' The Abbot queried. 'Why does the king send so many people to trouble me?' He was returning to his wailing, worrying self.

'Fear not, father,' Lefric spoke up. 'All is in hand.'

The others all stared at him as if they hadn't noticed he was there until then. He had the grace to look put out by all the attention. 'The secrets will be protected,' he sounded very sure about this.

Athan took the opportunity to step up and grab the monk by the scruff of the neck. He looked like he really needed to grab something and Lefric was in the right place at the right time. 'What secrets?' he demanded. 'We've only got your word that you don't know them.'

Lefric looked offended. 'Well I don't know, do I? They wouldn't be very secret if everyone knew them.'

'But you protect those who do know,' Nicodemus pointed out.

'Er.' Cwen was first to ask the question. 'What?'

'This monk,' Nicodemus explained, 'claims to be in some sort of secret brotherhood.'

Lefric was tugging frantically at Athan's arm, which still had hold of him, while making blatant "shut up" signals, which were being ignored.

'Oh, don't be ridiculous,' Nicodemus waved him away. 'We all know why we're here now. No point in trying to keep any more secrets than the ones we don't know already.' He turned back to the rest of the room. 'Apparently this monk is guarding some other monks who are guarding the secrets.'

Egbert frowned deeply, 'Is this true, Brother Lefric?'

Lefric looked at the floor.

Egbert sighed, raised his arms slightly and slapped them down on his thighs with a grunt. 'What have we told you about secret societies?' he folded his arms now, just like some parent or teacher, waiting for the humble confession of wrongdoing to be spilt.

Lefric looked at the floor a bit more deeply.

'Well?'

'Mumble, mumble,' Lefric said quietly.

'We didn't hear you,' Egbert said, much louder.

'We're not supposed to have them,' Lefric snapped, with simultaneous defiance and submission.

'You're not supposed to have them,' Egbert repeated the lesson. 'The abbot's told you. I've told you. We've told everyone. No secret societies. They're sinful, they're unhealthy, they're a breeding ground for all sorts of questionable goings-on.'

Lefric didn't have a reply.

'And who are these other monks you're supposed to be guarding? Secrets within secrets. Do you know who they are?'

Lefric looked at his prior. 'No,' he muttered. 'It's a secret.'

'A secret!' Egbert coughed the word. 'We're all used to keeping secrets brother. They are quite well cared for by the whole monastery. That's why it's here. It's already the biggest secret society there is, we don't want any more. Everything is quite well managed by the abbot and the Sacerdos.'

'The Sacerdos who is dead,' Wat pointed out. 'And who appears to have sent us on a goose chase all over this place looking for something he hid from the rest of you.'

'Be that as it may.' Egbert tried not to be distracted by Wat's quite reasonable point. 'The monks have been told in the strongest possible terms that they are not to start secret societies. Where are we going to end up if everyone is in a secret society?'

'One big not-secret society?' Cwen suggested.

'But they don't do that, do they?' Egbert went on. 'They all go off and start their own little groups getting up to goodness knows what. All of them sneaking around trying not to let anyone know what they're up to.' He peered hard at Lefric, some realisation creeping up. 'Is that what those blisters on your head are all about?'

Lefric drew his cowl close.

'I knew it,' Egbert announced, throwing his arms around again. 'I should have stamped on it as soon as I saw the first one. I knew there was something going on.'

'Are there many with this mark then?' Hermitage asked, trying hard to keep up with developments.

'Lefric here,' Egbert said, 'Brother Gardon, and that's it. As far as I know.'

Lefric did not contradict the information.

'Two of them?' Nicodemus burst out, sounding very disappointed. 'There are two brothers in this great secret guarding group?' He glared his annoyance at Lefric.

'And Brother Gardon would be challenged to find his way out of a cell with one door,' Egbert commented. 'I wouldn't trust him to protect his own head if the roof fell down.'

Nicodemus gave all his attention to Lefric, who was clearly wishing he'd never opened his mouth. 'And who exactly appointed you to the role of protecting this Trusted Brotherhood?'

Lefric looked completely horrified. 'What are you doing?' he wailed. 'You were sent. Why are you revealing that which must not be revealed?'

'Because you're an idiot,' Nicodemus concluded. 'Sent. Pah! We just turned up at the gate and you let us in. Without any invitation you told two complete strangers all about your secret and led us into the heart of the monastery.'

Lefric had his head in his hands now.

'Why am I not surprised?' Egbert shook his head slowly, in disappointment. He directed his comments at Lefric. 'You've let the monastery down, you've let the abbot and me down, but most of all you've let yourself down.'

Lefric's face emerged from his hands and it seemed to have taken on a new defiance. A slightly mad one, from Hermitage's point of view.

'Well, you're all doomed now,' Lefric said with a clear hint of the loon about him. 'You can't go talking about the secrets without consequences. The Trusted Brotherhood will deal with you all directly.'

'Trusted Brotherhood,' Nicodemus snapped his fingers in dismissal. 'The leader and only member of the Trusted Brotherhood is probably the monastery cat.'

'Someone took the tie-stone away,' Lefric pointed out, with rather wild enthusiasm. 'And someone opened the gate to let the sea in.'

'And,' Hermitage pointed out, from the back of the room where he was being largely ignored. 'Someone killed Ignatius.'

That did give them all pause for thought.

Egbert was the first to speak. 'I'm pretty sure Lefric and Gardon couldn't work out which was the sharp end of a sharp thing. I can't see either of them dealing with Ignatius in such a manner. They're probably scared of the sundial because it's magic.'

'Then there is another,' Hermitage concluded. 'At least one. And one who wants to deal with all of us, it seems.'

'Ha, ha,' Lefric skipped a little skip. 'Isn't it wonderful,' he sang. 'The Trusted Brotherhood is going to kill us all.'

'Including you,' Wat explained.

'I know, I know.' Lefric seemed to think this denoted some sort of favourable treatment.

'How do we know that the Trusted Brotherhood is any more capable in the head than this one?' Nicodemus gestured dismissively at Lefric.

'Does it matter?' Hermitage asked. 'If they've got the wherewithal to throw a priest on a sundial, remove bits of buildings and let the sea flood the place? Personally, I'd rather not be killed by anyone.'

'Oh.' Lefric was clearly leaving more of his sense behind with every passing moment, 'I'd love to be killed by the Brotherhood. What an honour.'

'After you,' Cwen said.

'I kept hoping they'd invite me to join,' Lefric was off on a fantasy of his own. 'But the call never came.' He shook his head, sadly. Then he looked up at the room once more and his eyes narrowed in thought. 'Perhaps if I killed you all they'd let me join?'

'You can have a go.' Athan invited Lefric to take part in a "Strongest monk" competition, knowing that he wouldn't win.

'Begone!' The abbot brought them all to silence with a loud shout, part command, part desperate plea. 'Foul demons of my dreams, cease to disturb my waking hours with your caterwauling.'

'Erm.' Egbert gave the abbot a rather worried look.

'I have discerned your plan,' the abbot said knowingly; mostly mad, but a bit knowingly. 'You are not real. You are not sent by the king at all. You are sent by the fallen Angel. The Devil himself tempts me with the shape of a woman in this place.'

'I didn't tempt him with anything,' Cwen said, sounding mightily offended. 'Silly old fool.'

'And now you appear from the walls of my cell. You are not real I say. Begone.' The abbot didn't know whether to cover his ears or his eyes and so tried to do both at the same time, his hands running over his face as if they had a life of their own.

Egbert drew his breath through his teeth. 'Perhaps we'd better move on? I think the abbot is a bit tired.'

'He's certainly a bit something,' Cwen commented.

'But, but,' Hermitage said as the crowd started to press towards the door. 'We still don't know why Ignatius led us here. What is there in this chamber that we should be discovering?'

'We've discovered a mad abbot, if that helps,' Wat observed.

'Brother Egbert,' Hermitage called over the press. 'Ask the abbot if Ignatius left him anything.'

Egbert shrugged as looked at them leave. 'I can have a go but I'm not sure it will make much sense even if he does tell me.'

As the last one left, Egbert pushed the door to the cell shut and turned to his abbot. To his surprise, his leader was beckoning him to sit by his side. He did so cautiously, not knowing if this was some sort of trap.

His caution turned to alarm as the abbot grabbed the hem of his own habit and started to haul it upwards. The man may have lost a lot of his senses but this really was going too far. 'Father, please.'

'It's in here somewhere.' The abbot bent his head to the task in hand and was delving around inside his clothing in a manner even a flea would think twice about.

Egbert was leaning towards the door, ready to jump up the moment the abbot revealed anything that no one should be expected to see.

'Aha,' the abbot called out in triumph. 'Got it.' He sat back on the cot and held out his hand to show Egbert what he'd retrieved.

'Oh,' Egbert said with the most enormous relief. 'A key.'

'Of course.' The abbot looked around the now empty room as if something might be going to leap out of the walls again. 'Now that the demons have gone,' he spoke in a very conspiratorial manner, 'I can let you have this.' The key was a simple slim rod of iron about four inches long with a small 'T' at one end for inserting into the barrel of a padlock. The T would release the padlock's internal spring and open the lock. It seemed the abbot had regained some of his senses, although what this key was for, Egbert had not a clue.

He patted Egbert on the knee. 'The demons clearly know where I am now and will only try to take the key again. Best I entrust it to you. You will know what to do.'

No. Not regained any of his senses at all.

'And what do I do?' Egbert asked.

The abbot looked at him as if he'd just located the biggest idiot in the room. 'You don't open the padlock.' He stated the blindingly obvious.

'I won't.' Egbert allowed a long pause. 'Which padlock?' he added.

The abbot shook his head with disappointment that this wasn't perfectly clear. 'The one to the Sacerdos's secret passage.'

'Aha.' Egbert nodded knowingly. He paused again. 'Which secret passage?'

The abbot sighed. 'For goodness sake, Egbert. If I knew that it would be the abbot's secret passage, wouldn't it? I know perfectly well where the abbot's secret passage is, thank you very much. This is the Sacerdos's secret passage.'

'But he's dead.'

'Exactly.'

'So we don't know where this passage is.'

'What is wrong with you?' the abbot asked, clearly puzzled why Egbert seemed unable to follow this simple matter.

"What's wrong with *me*?" Egbert thought.

'Ignatius entrusted me with the key to his secret passage while I gave him the key to mine.'

'Very equitable.'

'We were to use them if anything happened.'

'Without knowing where the passages are.' Egbert noted.

'Exactly.' The abbot appeared to consider that the most cunning part of the plan.

'But you haven't looked for the passage?'

'Of course not.' The old man was mightily offended at the very idea.

'Even with Ignatius impaled on a sundial? Surely that counts as something happening.'

'It could have been an accident,' the abbot nodded to himself. 'No need to get carried away just because one priest ends up on a sundial.'

'I see.' Egbert had no desire to argue the point.

'But now the demons have appeared.' The abbot looked warily about his cell. 'Did you see them?'

'Er, yes father, I saw them.'

'A whole host there was.'

'Indeed.'

And a female demon. They're the worst.'

'Are they?'

'Oh yes. They are temptation.'

Egbert couldn't immediately imagine even a female demon from the heart of hell being inclined to offer the abbot any temptation whatsoever. They must have some standards, after all.

'They've obviously found me and want the key. Doubtless, they will return to drag me to the pits of hell but they shall not have the key.'

Egbert looked at the key which was a straightforward device. It could probably open any padlock, so how he was expected to find the one to a secret passage was beyond him. 'Right then, father,' he said, as he made a move to get up from the cot. 'I'll get off to not open the padlock to the passage then.'

'Excellent.' The abbot rubbed his hands. 'We shall defeat the demons and then what a welcome we shall have in paradise.'

'Aha. Yes.' Egbert was slightly surprised that he managed to stand and get to the door without the abbot grabbing him to impart some more madness. Still, at least a key was a significant find. 'I'll, erm, see you later then,' he said as he slowly opened the door and started to sidle out.

'Ah,' the abbot cried.

Egbert sighed. He had been so close.

'The fires of hell come for me too soon,' the old man wailed.

Egbert frowned at this nonsense, but his leader did seem to be in an even worse state than the one he had started in. 'I'm sure not father,' he tried to reassure.

'But they are cold,' the abbot sounded very confused. 'Why are the fires of hell cold, Egbert?'

'Erm.' Egbert dragged his mind for some explanation which might calm the man.

'And wet,' the abbot added. 'Do they drown you first when you get to hell? I hadn't been told about that.' He now sounded quite offended that there was some detail of eternal damnation that had been withheld from him.

'Oh Jesus!' Egbert cried out.

'He comes to save us?' The abbot looked around.

'Not exactly.' Egbert stepped forward again to pull the

abbot from his cot. 'I erm, I think the demons have another plan.' He directed his leader's attention to the cell floor. The room sloped slightly with the cot in the lowest corner. This explained the man's distress as the ever-deepening inch of seawater that had climbed the stairs from below lapped at his feet.

Caput XVII

Up Ignatius's Passage

'What's that?' Hermitage asked as Egbert emerged from the abbot's cell bearing the key in his hand.

Egbert looked at the key and then at Hermitage. 'It's a key,' he said, clearly wondering what sort of life Hermitage had led if he couldn't recognise keys.

'I know it's a key,' Hermitage explained. 'Perhaps I should have said what's it for?'

Egbert looked puzzled at Hermitage's ignorance again. 'You use them to open things.'

'I mean what lock is it for?' Hermitage spelt it out.

'Ah,' Egbert got it. 'The Sacerdos's secret passage, apparently. So effectively secret that the abbot doesn't know where it is.'

Egbert was now joined by the abbot, hopping on one foot as he shook the water from his sandal. He glanced at the crowd in the corridor, gave his attention back to his footwear for a moment before realising what he had seen. 'The demons!' he cried, hopped smartly back into his cell and slammed the door.

'Father,' Egbert called after him with a very weary tone. 'They're not really demons. They're just people.'

'You are deceived,' the voice replied from the cell with a mixture of complete confidence and utter madness.

Egbert shook his head at the others, indicating that he really couldn't be bothered to retrieve his abbot. 'He'll float out when the water gets high enough.'

'What water?' Hermitage asked.

'The water from the tunnel.' Egbert explained, before

197

slowing somewhat as he seemed to understand the full implications of what he was saying. 'It doesn't seem to be stopping.'

Everyone gave this a good long think. As Hermitage pondered the inevitable outcome, his face became very pale indeed.

'I expect it will go down, eventually,' Lefric offered.

Hermitage explained his thinking in a cold and fearful tone. 'If someone has opened a gate to the sea I think it will only stop when it reaches the same level as the surrounding water.'

They all looked at him, impressed.

'I read it in a book somewhere,' he explained, imagining that they all saw the terrible outcome that was heading their way.

'If that's the case,' Wat said, thoughtful in his own way, 'It'll stop just after this whole place vanishes under the waves.'

'With us inside,' Lefric burbled with wide-eyed enthusiasm.

'Not if we get out first,' Cwen said.

'Oh, we can't do that,' Lefric protested. 'If the Trusted Brotherhood want us drowned we have to stay here and get on with it.'

Cwen just coughed at this suggestion.

'And there's still the matter of Ignatius's death,' Egbert pointed out.

'And the treasure,' Nicodemus added.

'Which won't matter a jot if our livers have run out of blood,' Wat reminded them.

'The water's coming it pretty slowly,' Egbert said. 'I think it would take quite a while to fill the dyke. If we can't find some way to stop it.'

'Can we close the gate again?' Cwen asked.

'Not if we don't know where it is,' Athan scoffed.

'We know where it is,' Cwen retorted, firmly. 'It's at the end of the tunnel somewhere. Here's an idea. Why don't you pop back down there and see if you can find it. I'll hold your head under for you.'

Athan just snarled at Cwen and Cwen growled back.

'Lefric,' Hermitage asked anxiously, trying to ignore all this irrelevant chatter, 'do you know where the sea gate is?'

Lefric screwed his face up as the effort of thinking distorted his features. Eventually he came to a conclusion. 'Out near the sea, I think.'

'Very helpful,' Wat commented. 'We'll just have to get a move on here then. I could go to the chapel and rescue that cross.'

'I'm sure.' Hermitage was not really surprised at Wat's priorities. 'But there are greater treasures we must bend our efforts to rescuing. And I'm not even sure we will have the time for all of them.'

'Oh, yes?' Wat rubbed his hands. 'Have you worked out where they are then?'

'Of course. They're in the library.'

'The library?' Wat sounded very disappointed. 'But we just came from there. Why did we go to all the trouble of nearly drowning?'

'Oh, Wat,' Hermitage sighed. 'The treasures are the books.'

'The books?' Wat clearly couldn't understand what Hermitage was talking about. 'What books?'

'The books in the library. If the monastery is to disappear under the waves we must save the books.'

'Which ones?'

'All of them, of course.'

'All of them?' Wat sounded like he'd been asked to stop the tide with a small piece of damp cloth.

'Of course. It is our absolutely sacred duty. We cannot leave such boundless knowledge to be lost.'

'There's thousands of them.'

'Which is why we need to start straight away. If we get all the brothers of the monastery to the task, I'm sure we can ferry the volumes up to the top of the dyke.' He turned to Egbert. 'How many brothers are there?'

'About thirty,' Egbert replied.

'*About* thirty?' Hermitage asked, puzzled by the inaccuracy.

Egbert shrugged. 'It's a remote place and no one keeps count. Occasionally we lose the odd one.' He gave a half-hearted smile. 'We find them eventually and have a burial.'

Hermitage shook his head to get his thoughts back to the problem in hand. 'Thirty monks carrying, say, ten books each, would be erm,' he considered the numbers. 'Quite a lot,' he concluded.

'Three hundred,' Wat provided the answer. 'Which would mean just over sixteen trips to clear the place out.'

'We'd better get started then,' Hermitage was happy that this had been sorted out.

'And the real treasure?' Wat asked. 'The one Ignatius has hidden with all his messages and symbols and the like? That could be much more important than your books.'

Hermitage wasn't convinced. What could be more important than all the knowledge contained in the library?

'The Monasterium Tenebrarii?' Wat prompted. 'The

Sacerdos Arcanorum? Can't all be just for a few shelves of books.'

Hermitage thought that actually, yes, it could well be. He did also acknowledge that there should be more though. A magnificent collection of books could be anywhere. This place had been established for something far greater, he had no doubt. Fascinating though it was, a Latin book on how to build drains could not be counted as a treasure of the church.

'Very well,' he concluded. 'If Brother Egbert can organise the brothers and the books, we can use what time we have to follow the rest of Ignatius's trail.'

From the look on Egbert's face, he shared Wat's view about rescuing a lot of books when the sea was sloshing at your ankles.

'The brothers will want to leave anyway,' Hermitage reasoned, 'when they see that the waters are rising. They just have to take some books with them.'

'And then come back for more,' Egbert pointed out the difficulty. 'Fifteen more times. While the waters are rising.'

'The sooner they start, the better chance they'll have of not drowning.' Hermitage was quite frustrated with the lack of appreciation for the books.

Egbert gave a resigned shrug, 'Please yourself.' He handed the key over to Hermitage and wandered away from the group, off up the corridor. 'But if you find the treasure,' he called back, 'I shall want to know about it. It does belong to this monastery, don't forget.' He seemed to be making this point at Wat, Nicodemus and Athan specifically.

'Of course.' Hermitage was quite taken aback that someone had done as he asked. He wasn't used to that at all. 'Now then,' he turned back to the matter in hand. The matter in hand was the key, which he held up as if it would have the location of its lock written on it somewhere. 'The Sacerdos's secret passage. How on earth are we going to find that?'

'And if we do find it,' Cwen piped up, 'it could be as full of the sea as the last one we had a go at.'

'I know.' Lefric was suddenly full of self-importance.

'What do you know?'

'I know where the Sacerdos's passage is,' he boasted.

Hermitage frowned that this seemed unlikely. 'Really?'

'Of course. Everyone knows where the Sacerdos's passage is.'

'Except for your abbot and prior, it seems.'

'Well, naturally. We're not going to tell them, are we?'

'Why not?'

'Because it leads outside.'

'Beyond the walls?'

'That's it. If any of the brothers feel a need to perhaps visit the nearest village, or receive goods that the abbot might not approve of, we use the Sacerdos's passage.'

'I imagine the Sacerdos didn't know about this use of his passage either.'

'Oh, heavens no.'

'So why are you telling us?' Cwen asked. 'I thought you wanted us to stay here and be drowned by the Brotherhood.'

Lefric looked at her hard. 'Oh, bugger,' he said, and smacked himself on the leg a few more times.

'You're really not cut out for this secrecy business, are you?' Nicodemus observed.

'I think you better take us to it.' Hermitage tried to make it clear that Lefric had given the game away now and so there was no point trying to hide anything else.

The monk pulled his cowl back over his head and grumbled and mumbled as he scuffed away along the corridor. 'Hasn't got a lock on it anyway,' he was saying, half to himself. 'So there's no point having a key, is there Brother clever-monk?'

Through winding ways and corridors that dipped and rose, Lefric led them. Hermitage was feeling quite alarmed that some of the dipping corridors were starting to get quite wet. He couldn't really imagine that anyone would deliberately flood the entire monastery just to get at them. The great secret that had been maintained all these years sacrificed because someone turned up asking some questions? It was a bit extreme, surely? The loss could not possibly be justified.

But then there was the death of Ignatius to consider as well. If this was all connected somehow, perhaps outlandish measures were called for. But much easier, surely, to simply stab them in the back, or drop some rocks on them or get a bucket of water if drowning was so important.

Once again, he found himself wondering how on earth he had wound up in this situation. He found himself wondering how he ended up in situations far too often. In fact, whenever there was a situation with him in it, he had not a clue how he had got there. When this one was out of the way he would have to sit down and give himself a good talking to. And next time he would stay under his bed.

While Hermitage mused upon his lot, Lefric had brought them out of the dortoir, across the cloister to the chapel once more. Passing through the main door, Hermitage saw the golden glaze come over Wat's eyes once more as the great cross on the altar called out to the weaver. This time

Nicodemus and Athan were there to consider it as well and an almost palpable tension arose between the three of them, like three rats who just had spotted a wounded sparrow.

Hermitage was grateful to see that a small chain of monks was weaving its way from the entrance to the library, up the chapel and towards the door. Each brother had a number of books in his arms, some more, some less, depending on the size of the volumes. Egbert's voice could be heard directing the activity to remove the books from the shelves and organise their transport. In the light of the moon it was a very strange sight.

Even Brody was there, looking like he had been given an armful of treasure to do what he liked with. This did cause Hermitage some concern as he imagined Brody would think nothing of taking the books over the dyke and selling them to the first person he found who could read. As the first of the monks approached the new arrivals, heading for the exit, Hermitage could hear the conversations they were having.

'Apparently we're to pile them up outside to stop the sea getting in,' one was saying.

'No, no,' his brother replied. 'We put them in a big heap, set light to them and the heat will drive the water away.'

'You're both wrong,' a third called out. 'We build a great big tower and climb up it so the water won't get us.'

Hermitage couldn't believe his ears. How on earth had his instruction to Egbert become distorted into this load of nonsense? 'Brothers, brothers,' he called to the room.

The parade of book-laden monks came to a stop.

'You are simply to take the books to the top of the dyke and place them out of harm's way. Then you come back and get some more until they are all safe.'

The looks on the faces said that the monks plainly

thought this was a completely futile exercise. However, their looks also said they were well used to futile exercises and so they shrugged and carried on.

'Can I trust them to carry out the instruction?' he asked his companions, but none of them seemed particularly concerned either.

'The passage is this way,' Lefric gestured to the back corner of the chapel.

Hermitage was torn between protecting the books and following the Sacerdos's trail. At least the monks in the chapel now seemed to understand what they were to do with the books, even if they had no idea why. He reluctantly followed Lefric and the others as they moved across the chapel floor. His confidence in his decision was dented when he heard one of the monks in the chapel call out to his fellows. 'Hey, look. This one's got pictures in it.'

Casting many a worried glance back to the parade of monks, Hermitage eventually came to the far corner the chapel, to the left of the altar, opposite the entrance to the library. All he could see was a wall of plain stone but after the experience in the drain, he could easily picture a section of the wall moving aside to reveal a well-trodden passage.

'Here we are then,' Lefric said with some pride. 'The Sacerdos's secret passage.'

Hermitage examined their surroundings as best he could, given that it was as dark as night in this far corner where no windows or doors gave any illumination at all. 'Where?' he asked.

'Here.' Lefric gestured towards the floor of the chapel. Perhaps there was a secret door in the flagstones, which would lift up if the right stone was pressed.

Lefric now got down on his hands and knees and

demonstrated that there was a gap between the wall and the floor. It was more like a failure in the building than anything as deliberate as a passage. It simply looked as if part of the wall had collapsed as it hadn't been put in properly in the first place.

'That?' Wat asked. 'Are you sure?'

'Of course.' Lefric sounded disappointed that they weren't very impressed with his passage.

'It's just a hole,' Cwen said.

'Please yourself,' Lefric huffed. 'Don't go through it then. See if I care.'

'You're sure this is Ignatius's passage?' Hermitage asked, trying to assuage Lefric's sulk.

'Saw him go into it often enough. That's how we knew it was here. One minute he'd be at the altar for the offices of the day, next thing, gone. Where did he go? We'd say. Back to his chamber, someone said. Never saw him go that way. Where else did he go then? Why don't we have a look? So we did.' Lefric held out his arm towards the crack in the wall, content that he had now given a thorough and comprehensive explanation.

'So you went through it as well,' Hermitage nodded.

'Not right then. We didn't want to bump into Ignatius in the dark. And we had no idea what he was getting up to in there. Could have been something horrible. No, we waited 'till night when he was in his chamber. Then we went in. And then we came out.'

'Came out?'

'The other side. We came out beyond the walls. That's handy, we thought. We could use this. So we did.'

'Very interesting,' Hermitage tried to follow this bizarre description. 'Where does the key come in?' He held the key up, it being perfectly obvious that the hole in the wall had no use for it.'

'No idea. Never needed a key.'

Hermitage could make no sense of this at all. The faces of the others said they were doing no better. The only thing for it was to go into the passage and see what they could find. The abbot had specifically directed them here so there must be something important about it. 'Lead on,' he directed Lefric.

'It's a bit dark in there,' the monk noted. 'We're used to it and can find our way. You might need a torch.'

Hermitage looked around the chapel, which was torch-less. They'd have to go and find one.

'There are two candles on the altar,' Nicodemus pointed out.

Well, that was a ridiculous suggestion. 'You cannot use an altar candle for lighting your way,' Hermitage said, knowing that there were some absolutely sacred truths in the world.

A few moments later he followed Nicodemus into the tunnel as the man lit the way with the sacred candle from the altar. Wat was holding the other one. He had thought about refusing to go as a protest at this sacrilege but they said it was them who would be punished, so he needn't worry. He was sure it wasn't as simple as that but didn't want to let them go on alone.

He was pleased to see that even Athan was scowling at this development. But then Athan scowled most of the time so it was hard to see if this scowl was for anything special.

The inside of the tunnel was no more organised than its entrance. It really did look more like a cave than a specially built passage. The stones and rubble of the walls around them looked perilous and Hermitage thought that one touch could bring the whole lot down on their heads. At least the floor was relatively level and still dry. If it dipped anywhere, it might get down to the level of the sea. And after they'd had to crawl in, the roof did at least rise to head height.

After several paces they came across what was clearly the outer wall of the monastery. This was much more regular and solid. The great stones, presumably put there by the Romans, looked quite capable of withstanding the centuries.

'There we are then.' Lefric indicated that a few steps more would see them outside the monastery.

Hermitage clasped the key in his hand, unable to see any reason for it in this place. The secret passage had turned out to be no more than a gap in the masonry. Granted it gave access to the outside but that seemed more by mistake than design.

'Perhaps there's a door on the outside of the monastery that it opens?' Cwen suggested, nodding at Hermitage's fretful clasping of the key.

'Aha.' He hadn't thought of that. It could well be the case that once outside the monastery there was indeed a door which led into another chamber. The chamber that would contain the answer to all of this. He was rather hoping it would be the answer as he was beginning to tire of being led places that turned out to be no help at all. Couldn't Ignatius have simply written a note? After all, no one here could read. Why go to all this trouble?

'Is there another door?' he asked Lefric.

'No idea. We tended not to hang around once we'd got out of the place.'

'Then we must look.' Hermitage led them out of the tunnel and into the fresh air outside the monastery wall.

If the tunnel had been oppressive, this space between the wall and the dyke was quite alarming. The monastery towered up at their back, a featureless wall of stone higher than seemed strictly necessary. In front of them the great dyke loomed menacingly. Its dread made even worse by the knowledge of what it held back. Although they were now in the open air, it still felt very much that they were trapped. The feeling was made less comfortable by the fact that the ground beneath their feet seemed a lot more soggy than it had been when they arrived.

Hermitage weighed up their situation. 'You go that way,' he directed Nicodemus, Athan and Lefric. 'We'll go this. First one to find a door calls out.'

'Tell you what,' Nicodemus said. 'Let's both go the same way.'

Hermitage frowned. 'But that will take twice as long.'

'But with half the chance of you finding the door and disappearing.'

What a distrustful and deceitful fellow this Nicodemus was. Imagine thinking something like that of your fellow man. Hermitage almost thought about saying something.

'Or,' Nicodemus offered, 'you could give us the key and we'll call out if we find a door.'

There was no way Hermitage was going to do that. He wouldn't trust Nicodemus with a blade of grass, let alone a key to the secrets of the church. 'We'll both go,' he agreed.

They walked along the outside of the monastery, examining the wall for any sign of a lock that might be missing Hermitage's key. Cwen went wandering ahead, not finding a large stone wall particularly fascinating. 'What about this?' she called from round one corner of the monastery.

They joined her and there it was, a simple wooden door set low in the wall with a plain barrel padlock on it. It could be a wood store for all they could tell, not that the wood would need locking up. Well, that was easy.

'Go on then,' Wat urged Hermitage on, 'try the key.'

Hermitage looked at the door and the lock and at the place on the outside of the monastery they had come to. He peered upwards to a small window set high in the stonework and almost completely obscured by the adjoining wall. He frowned.

'Well, get on with it.' Nicodemus complained.

'Erm.' Hermitage wondered how to broach the problem he had just spotted.

'What are you waiting for?' Athan joined in. Hermitage had never been very good resisting Athan.

He stepped forward with key in hand. 'I don't think you're going to like what we find,' he said. Perhaps warning them all in advance would stop everyone getting cross. Probably with him for opening the door.

Amidst a small chorus of complaint, he pushed the key into the simple lock and heard the springs click out of place. He slid the lock open and out of the clasp that was holding the door shut. He pulled it open and beckoned that whoever wanted to could enter.

Looking surprised that Hermitage didn't want this honour for himself, Wat ducked his head through the door. 'God's blood,' he swore and ducked his head out again.

'What is it?' Cwen asked with some excitement which quickly dissipated when she saw Wat's face.

Nicodemus and Athan looked cautious. And suspicious.

And demanding, and ready to do something about it if Wat didn't explain.

He took a breath and shook his head, 'It's only the blasted bone chapel again. We're right back where we started.'

Caput XVIII

The Secret Revealed

'What the devil is this supposed to mean?' Athan demanded. 'Where's the secret? Where's the treasure?' He had pushed Wat aside and stuck his head through the door. It came out looking a lot more cross than when it went in. He turned to Hermitage. 'There's just some altar in there.'

Hermitage shouldn't really be surprised that Athan's awareness of Botwulf and his brother would be marginal.

'This is your fault.' Athan pointed an aggressive finger. Well, that was expected.

'I only followed the pattern,' Hermitage explained. He knew that explanations were seldom what Athan was looking for when he demanded an explanation. He usually wanted someone to hold to account. Holding to account meant blame and blame meant punishment. Athan often skipped straight to the final stage.

'The king's Door gave us the chapel which sent us to Ignatius's chamber. That took us to the drain which led to the abbot's cell and the key. That brought us here.' He was very happy with this as an explanation as it accounted for everything and came to a nice neat conclusion. That it was of absolutely no value whatsoever, was just a detail.

'And what does all that mean?' Athan went on. Hermitage noticed that his old prior was quietly but firmly thumping his fist into the stonework of the monastery. One of them was going to have to give way, and from the specks of blood it looked likely to be the fist.

'What does it mean?' Hermitage asked. He hadn't given any thought to what it meant. He was perfectly satisfied

212

that it had come to a neat if completely circular conclusion. He looked at the group gathered around him and thought they all looked like they were waiting for him to explain. That was hardly fair.

'Erm,' he began. 'I suppose,' he carried on, still not having a single thought about what it meant. 'Ignatius gave the Abbot the key to this door.' He said. He often found that stating the obvious helped. 'And the door opened fairly easily.' Now, there was a thought.

Wat coughed and Hermitage realised that he had stood in silence for several moments while the ideas ran around inside his head. As usual, with the ideas inside his head, they had stopped the rest of him working.

'Sorry,' he came back to his senses. 'The door is obviously well used which means the abbot, or more likely Ignatius has been in here.'

No one got excited about that.

'They have been in the king's chamber. The one that is not supposed to be opened until Judgement Day.' Hermitage took some satisfaction from the "oohs" and "aahs" that ran round the group. 'So, if there was a great secret contained within, Ignatius knew about it all along.'

'And took it,' Athan growled.

'We don't know that,' Hermitage said, although he hadn't seen anything in the chapel that could be classed a treasure, great or otherwise.

'Well, there's nothing there now,' Athan pointed out, unhelpfully.

'Unless it's something we haven't spotted.' Hermitage didn't really believe this himself. 'Or perhaps,' he said, as an awful thought jumped out to scare him. 'Perhaps that was why Ignatius was killed.'

Again, none of the others seemed to pick up on this. Sometimes he really wondered what they spent their time thinking about. In Wat's case he had a pretty good idea what it was, but surely some of them were paying attention. 'Ignatius entered the chamber and took whatever was hidden there and that is why he was killed.'

Once more, there was a gaggle of the noises people make when the blindingly obvious is revealed.

'In which case,' Cwen spoke slowly and carefully, 'why wasn't it put back by whoever did for him?'

'Because Ignatius had destroyed the secret. Once the room was opened it wouldn't be safe anymore. Whoever took whatever it was has put it somewhere else.'

'Very helpful,' Wat said. 'This really has taken us a long way forward, hasn't it? A room which might have had something in it is now empty. We don't know what the thing was, who took it or what they did with it.'

Hermitage had to admit that this was a pretty neat summary of the situation.

'I do,' Lefric said with a broad grin. 'It was the Trusted Brotherhood.' He even did a little dance to celebrate the fact.

'Really?' Nicodemus was clearly having some trouble believing anything Lefric had to say. 'They got past the dragon then?'

'What dragon?' Wat asked, in some surprise.

Nicodemus waved the question away. 'It really isn't worth the effort.'

'Of course.' Lefric was ploughing on, regardless. 'The Brotherhood protect the secret. Ignatius entered the chamber, took the secret and so the Brotherhood had to deal with him.'

'By putting him, point first, on a sundial?' Nicodemus raised an eyebrow 'It's a bit public, isn't it? For a Brotherhood that protect secrets? Far better to take him out into the marshes and watch him sink. No one would be any the wiser.'

'It was a message,' Lefric explained, in tones of doom. 'A warning to all those who seek to follow Ignatius.'

'But hard to follow him when we don't know what he was doing anyway.' Wat complained. He held his hand up to get their attention, 'Aha,' he said, 'I've had an idea.' He sounded very enthusiastic.

'What's that?' Hermitage asked, thinking that the weaver must have spotted some missing element in the problem.

'Let's go home,' Wat said, still sounding very keen. 'The secret, whatever it was, has gone with the Brotherhood and no one knows who they are. We think they killed Ignatius but again, we don't know who they are. I say we just rescue that great big gold cross from the chapel and go home. We're not getting anywhere, we've gone round in one long and complicated circle and I am pretty confident that King William won't even be interested in any of this if we try to tell him. Also, my feet are getting wet. '

They all looked to the ground now and saw that there was at least half an inch of water over the whole area. And a strong smell of salt.

'The water must have sped quite up a bit,' Hermitage observed. 'It was rising quite slowly earlier on.' He gave this latest problem some consideration. 'Of course, it could be that the drain has collapsed under the force of the water coming in and increased the flow.'

'How absolutely fascinating.' Wat lifted one foot out of the water and shook it before putting it back in again.

'In which case,' Hermitage said urgently, 'we must move quickly.'

Wat seemed happy with the suggestion.

'We have to speed up the rescue of the books.'

. . .

Back in the chapel, in the face of Wat's continuing complaints, the brothers of the monastery were urged to increase their efforts, which Hermitage noted, seemed to have tailed off in the absence of his encouragement. Several of them were sitting around examining some of the books in detail. While this was gratifying, he felt it was not really the priority. His view was confirmed when he saw what books the monks were looking at. They seemed to consist mainly of medical texts, with illustrations showing what went on inside the human body.   The pages they were lingering appeared to focus on those bits of the body mainly visible from the outside.

He tutted and fretted and prodded them back into life. Examining the library, he was at least pleased to note that the number of volumes in the room had gone down appreciably. There were a lot left though, and the water on the floor was now increasing at a visible rate.

Waving the monks to speed up a bit and shooing them back through the chapel with their loads, Hermitage tutted at the struggle that had now developed between Wat and Athan over the safety of the gold cross. It was becoming quite physical. Each was arguing that they were the best person to hold on to it until its fate was decided.

Wat had suddenly developed a very pious streak which, together with his experience as a merchant, meant that he was the only appropriate refuge. He would be able to keep it safe, as he did with other treasures, the details of which he was not prepared to go into, and he would protect it for the church.

Athan's argument was that if Wat laid one finger on it he would get punched so hard in the head that his ears would swap sides.

Wat suggested that the prior would need a significant body of men to support him in this endeavour, but he was welcome to try.

The descent to a most unseemly fight in front of the altar was disturbed by Egbert, who appeared with a book under his arm. He reached out to the cross and took it from the altar. 'Thank you,' he said as he headed for the door.

Wat and Athan followed and Hermitage suspected it was not because they wanted to know what the book was.

'Take some books with you,' Hermitage called. 'We mustn't leave anything behind.'

Wat stopped in his tracks, but Athan carried on. It would have been the first time Athan did anything Hermitage wanted, so he shouldn't be surprised.

'What did you say?' Wat asked, in a rather strange tone, his head tilted over to one side. Hermitage's head did that when he was thinking. He always thought it was because his mind couldn't do too many things at once. Or that thoughts had weight and his neck wasn't up to the job.

'I said take some books with you.'

'No, after that.'

'Erm,' Hermitage didn't think it was that important. 'We mustn't leave anything behind?' He thought it had been something like that.

'Exactly,' Wat shouted and clapped his hands together.

Nicodemus frowned at the weaver. 'Exactly, what?'

'Exactly we mustn't leave anything behind. Nothing at all.

Everything must go.'

Hermitage thought that saying the same thing in different ways was hardly illuminating.

'The monastery is going to disappear under the water, yes?'

'Yes,' Hermitage agreed.

'So everything of value must be taken out before that happens. Gold crosses, books.'

'Of course,' Hermitage, got it. Quite quickly. 'And any other great secrets or treasures that are hidden about the place.'

'They can't be left to the tide,' Wat said. 'Even the secret we've been chasing will have to be taken to higher ground. Probably by the Trusted Brotherhood.'

Lefric paid attention at this point.

'If everyone and everything is up on top of the dyke, we'll be able to find out what all the fuss is about.'

'You'll never spot the Trusted Brotherhood,' Lefric said, with confidence. 'They are masters of, erm, not being spotted.'

'Perhaps they've got a big red mark on their heads and can't keep a secret,' Nicodemus suggested.

'We don't have to spot them,' Wat explained. 'We simply have to spot who's not them.'

'Eh?' Lefric couldn't keep up with this.

'We just have to look for the monks who are behaving differently. The ones who are keeping themselves apart, or who have something that they're trying to hide. Bit hard to hide anything when you're on top of a dyke.'

Hermitage saw that this was a good plan. He wasn't sure what they were going to do with it though. What if this Brotherhood turned out to be great in number? And what if they could rally the rest of the monastery to their cause? After all, every monk in the place was here to protect the secret. That was the point of the place. He doubted that even with Athan on their side they'd be able to fight off thirty monks. Particularly when those monks were probably quite disappointed that their home had just drowned.

'The sea will wash the secret out of the monastery like rats out of a drain,' Wat said with some glee.

'But if the monks are sworn to protect it?' Hermitage suggested.

Wat gave this a moment's thought. He grinned as he came up with the answer. Hermitage didn't like the look of that grin. 'You're the king's man,' said Wat. 'You're here with the king's authority.'

'So are we,' Nicodemus added.

'Hm.' Wat didn't give that any credibility. He addressed Hermitage. 'If you command the monks to hand it over, or reveal it, or explain it, or whatever it is you do with this whatever it is, they'll have to obey. The king's own investigator. Sent by the king. For just this purpose.' He held his arms out to illustrate that this was all perfectly obvious and wouldn't be a problem at all.

Hermitage could spot problems miles away. He was quite capable of worrying about the ones that weren't even heading in his direction, let alone those that had been given his name. And commanding people was not something that had ever gone well for him. Most of the time the people being commanded didn't seem to realise it was happening. They just carried on doing whatever it was they were up to without paying him any attention whatsoever. When he tried to impress himself upon the situation they frequently started laughing.

Standing in front of the strange population of this strange monastery, commanding them to do anything at all was a problem that not only had his name, it knew where he lived and probably had a private door to his nightmares.

'Erm,' he said, decisively. He thought about situations when he had seen people address large groups and tried to determine what it was that made it work. When he was in a group of listeners simple terror of the one doing the commanding usually did the trick. He didn't think he'd be able to drum up some terror, it simply wasn't in him. Some of the really terrifying speakers hadn't even said a word themselves. They just whispered in the ear of some attendant who did the speaking for them. They were so terrifying they daren't even speak directly. 'Wat?' he said slowly, 'I've just had an idea.'

. . .

By the time the last of the books was taken to the top of the dyke the night was full. A bright moon shone down, illuminating a scene that was going to need a lot of explanation. What all these soggy monks were doing climbing hills in the middle of the night carrying books was a question even the moon was probably going to try and avoid answering.

Hermitage was quite satisfied with progress, although he had to let several volumes fall to the flood as the waters rose with increasing speed. At least he had checked that these were well-known works and so the loss of these copies would not be a catastrophe.

Most of the monks seemed to think that getting their feet wet for a bunch of books was the catastrophe.

The last thing to be taken from the inundation of the

monastery was its abbot. Egbert had been quietly satisfied that the library had been cleared and stood looking down at the slowly vanishing Monasterium Tenebrarii. This great establishment, the one that had been hidden from the world for so long was about to be hidden in a much more permanent manner. Perhaps, in the days ahead, he would have the time to consider how all this had come to pass. The place had been so settled and secure it seemed inconceivable that within the space of one day it would disappear completely. An immediate connection between this catastrophe and the arrival of Brother Hermitage sparkled brightly in his head.

He had surveyed the brothers of the monastery gathered on the top of the dyke and thought grimly of the task that now lay ahead. How to get this lot to a place of safety. These monks who hadn't been outside for years.

As he examined the faces, some shocked, some confused, some with impenetrable thoughts of their own, he had realised one was missing. 'Oh, bloody hell,' he shouted as he sprinted down the hill and back into the water, 'the abbot.'

He found the community leader, still sitting on his cot with the water now round his chest. The man looked resigned to going down with his monastery. Either that or he was completely unaware of what would happen when his head went under. Egbert grabbed an arm and pulled the abbot out of the cell, along flooded corridors and into the open. He beckoned some brothers to join him in helping hoist the old man up to the top of the dyke.

'So.' Once the abbot was safely settled, Egbert dripped over to Hermitage and his companions, his habit sopping and his face heavy with annoyance. 'What now?'

'Well,' Hermitage began.

'Now that our monastery is pretty much underwater,' Egbert added, stating the very obvious.

'Is everyone accounted for?' Wat asked.

'Yes,' Egbert seemed surprised by the question. 'I think so.'

'Could you be sure?'

Egbert checked over the crowd on top of the dyke. Most were standing watching the waters slowly take their monastery to the deep. He saw that even the most difficult of the brothers were finding this moment a poignant one. After all, this place had been their home for as long as many could remember. They may have hated it but it was still a shock to see it vanish. The more sensitive were sitting on the ground weeping and beating their fists into the ground or their own legs. He noted that they were the ones who beat themselves at every opportunity, so didn't worry too much. 'Yes, they're all here,' he confirmed.

'Are you sure?' Cwen piped up. 'No one missing at all?'

'No,' Egbert said, quite firmly. 'No one missing.' He scowled at them all, 'What's going on?'

'Nothing, nothing,' Hermitage assured him. 'We just thought that with everyone out of the monastery, the guardians of the secret might be revealed.' He shrugged in the face of Wat and Nicodemus giving him profound frowns.

'We are all guardians of the secret,' Egbert said.

'Yes,' Wat agreed, 'but you didn't all kill Ignatius.'

Egbert just raised his eyebrows.

Wat narrowed his eyes in return, 'Or did you?'

'Did we what?'

'All kill Ignatius.'

'Are you mad?'

'Perhaps the whole monastery got together and put Ignatius on the sundial to get at the secret,' Wat suggested, in a very accusatory manner.

Egbert gave a short laugh. 'And then we sent Brody to report the matter to the king instead of doing nothing, keeping our heads down and hoping no one noticed. Which they probably wouldn't, in this place. No, instead we sent to the king to come and deal with the murder that we'd all just done.'

'Hm.' Wat obviously saw that this would be a pretty stupid thing to do if you'd just killed someone.

Egbert held out his arms to take in the assembly of brothers on the dyke wall. 'Go ahead, spot your murderer.'

Hermitage looked over the collection of brothers and had to admit that they all looked alike. Of course they would, being brothers and all dressed alike, but there wasn't one who stood out from the rest. He wondered what the standing out might consist of anyway, presumably not someone with blood dripping from their hands or an evil look on their face.

There wasn't even one who was behaving any differently from the rest. They were all watching the monastery intently. None of them were skulking in an obvious manner or creeping around the back of the group, looking for the chance to slip away and vanish into the reeds. Very disappointing.

'So, what do we do now?' Egbert asked, rather pointedly. He held an arm out to direct their attention to the Monasterium Tenebrarii which was now more suitable for fishing than prayer. 'Our home didn't have quite so much water in it before you lot turned up. Perhaps you've got some suggestion where we're going to sleep tonight?'

Nobody had an immediate answer, nor the words to express apology for flooding the monastery.

'We had better make for the nearest village,' Hermitage suggested.

Egbert gave a short laugh. 'Most of these brothers haven't been outside the walls for as long as they can remember. I'm not sure they'd cope with a village. And I doubt the nearest village could cope with thirty monks turning up out of nowhere.'

Hermitage didn't like to mention the secret passage and the suggestion that the brothers might be far better informed about the world outside than Egbert suspected.

'We'll just have to send Brody,' Egbert concluded when no one else came up with any suggestions. 'He knows the paths through the marshes. We can get what rest we can out here tonight. Doesn't look like it's going to rain, but if it does we can build some shelters out of books.'

Hermitage thought better of protesting at this as they'd only blame him for causing the whole problem in the first place. People did that a lot, he had noticed.

'Brody can get some supplies and prepare the village for our arrival in the morning.' He was still cross. 'There might be some Lord who'll give a brotherhood succour. Though goodness knows who's going to want this lot.' He gestured at the books.

Again, Hermitage kept his peace while Brody was called over. He would quite happily sit on top of the dyke looking after the books until the snows of winter froze him to the parchment.

Brody appeared from the back of the Dyke, looking quite excited at the sight of the flooded monastery. The scene of the great walls being slowly consumed by the waters was going to get him many a fireside meal and flagon for free.

'God's dyke eh?' Wat arched an eyebrow at him.

'And God's flood,' Brody said with awe.

Egbert addressed him. 'You're to go to the village and bring back as much bread and ale as you can carry. Take Brother Martin with you. He doesn't believe in eating or drinking at the best of times so won't be tempted. Tell the village what's happened and see if you can find somewhere for us to reside tomorrow. The abbot and I will have to take things from there.' He looked at his leader and blew a sigh of resignation, doubting that the abbot understood anything that was going on around him.

'Right oh.' Brody was bright. He searched briefly in the crowd for Brother Martin, found him, and went off to lead the way to the village.

Egbert regarded them all with folded arms. 'Perhaps you could organise a fire between you? It's going to get cold tonight, we're all soaking wet and personally, I think it's the least you can do.'

Hermitage surveyed the land for anything capable of starting a fire. The wash of green reed that stretched out in all directions didn't look like it would burn very well at all. He looked at Egbert for any hint of where to start, saw where the brother was looking and stepped defensively in front of the nearest pile of books.

Before he could suggest that the idea of burning the books was unthinkable, a loud scream rent the air and the babble of conversation that had broken out among the monks was stunned to silence. Everyone looked around to see who had made the noise but they soon saw that everyone else was looking round as well.

'What the hell was that?' Athan demanded.

'Probably a monk being frightened by a frog,' Nicodemus scoffed.

'That was no monk,' Egbert said, his face pale and an expression of worried fear on his face. 'That was Brody.'

Caput XIX

On Top of The Dyke

'He didn't sound very happy,' Nicodemus observed.

'Didn't sound very happy?' Hermitage said, with the best outrage he could manage. 'The poor man sounded like something horrible has happened.'

Wat was looking out into the reeds where Brody had gone. 'He had that Brother with him,' he said. 'He hasn't called out. Perhaps Brody's fallen and broken a bone or something.'

'Brother Martin has sworn an oath of silence,' Egbert said, urgently. 'He didn't even cry out when he was sitting by the Michel-mass fire and a burning log rolled out and caught him right in the habit.' Egbert gave a modest nod to indicate exactly which bit of Martin's habit had taken the blow. The men in the group all gave sympathetic gasps of discomfort.

'Ooh,' Cwen said after a moment when she got the message.

'Brody!' Egbert called out into the dark reeds. 'Brody, answer me.'

The rest of the monks on top of the dyke were looking anxiously out to see if they could spot Brody or even the route he had taken.

Hermitage saw that these reeds covered all activity so effectively that there wasn't even a trail of broken stalks where Brody had gone. They just had to be pushed aside to get through, after which they sprang back to their original position. He also noticed that none of the monks were exactly leaping to the assistance of their missing companion. True, they didn't know where he'd gone but surely some random running about and shouting would help.

'What's happened?' Hermitage asked. Egbert folded his arms and stared at him.

'What's happened? What's happened down in the reeds only lit by the moon? The reeds that are so tall we can't see through them anyway?' The man seemed quite tetchy.

As Egbert shook his head in disappointment and turned to Wat, Hermitage looked to the ground and mumbled to himself, 'I only asked.'

'Sounds like we have a new problem,' Egbert noted. 'One that's hiding in the reeds. Waiting for us.'

'And one that didn't like Brody,' Wat observed.

Athan came over to join them. 'An animal?' he suggested.

'Unless it's a stoat the size of a house, there's nothing out here capable of dealing with a full-size man.'

Athan looked very puzzled indeed.

'No,' Egbert confirmed, raising his eyebrows at Athan. 'We don't have stoats the size of houses.'

'Ah,' Athan nodded, clearly irritated that stoats had been brought up in the first place if there weren't any.

Egbert was surveying the dismal scene, his eyes darting from the top of the dyke to the depths of the reedy marsh. 'We're safe enough up here I think. Whoever is down there would have to emerge from the reeds before they could climb the dyke.' He raised his arms and called out across the heads of the assembled monks, all of whom had descended into alarmed discussion, speculation and wild fabrication. 'Brothers. Be alert. Keep your eyes on the reeds and shout out if anyone emerges towards us.'

The brothers did move their attention to the land before them instead mulling over their own visions of what was in the reeds. These ranged from the dragon that had escaped from the king's door to a tribe of savage women who had only been waiting for the monks to emerge from the monastery before taking them to do their worst. Many of the monks were quite looking forward to the worst.

'There could be more than one.' Wat scanned the field of reeds for any sign of movement.

'There could,' Egbert acknowledged. 'But I don't know where they'd have come from. All the brothers are accounted for, the village is miles away and if there was a swarm of people living in the reeds we'd have noticed by now.'

Wat hesitated to make the next suggestion, it seemed highly improbable and had a strong whiff of defeat about it. 'The Trusted Brotherhood?' He was disappointed to note that Egbert did not dismiss the suggestion out of hand.

At the sound of the title, Lefric materialised at their side. He was closely followed by Cwen who seemed to have made it her mission to keep a close eye on the strange monk. She seemed convinced that if any of them was going to turn out to be a dangerous loon, it was this man.

'The Brotherhood hovers in the reeds,' Lefric explained, becoming quite misty-eyed. 'Even now they protect the secret and none of us shall leave this place alive.' He was obviously very happy at the prospect.

'Perhaps you could be the first,' Cwen said with a twist of her lip.

'Can I?' Lefric asked, full of enthusiasm. He even started to move towards the reeds before Egbert pulled him back.

'No one is going down there until we know what we're dealing with,' he instructed. 'Stay here.' He quickly pointed at each of them in turn before heading off into the press of monks.

The top of the dyke was quite a wide space, easily enough to accommodate the brothers of the monastery, but they had started to straggle out a bit. The far ends of their line were ragged and disorganised and one brother had even gone for an evening stroll along the top, taking in the marvellous sight of a horizon that was more than fifty feet away.

Egbert called everyone back to the central huddle and organised those at the extremes so that they were facing along the dyke. He instructed them to keep an eye out for anyone climbing the hill out of sight and approaching them along the top.

The inside of the dyke was very nearly up to its final level now. The walls still held their duty all around but mysterious things seemed to be happening under the water. It swirled and ran around its new containment as if being stirred by some giant spade, happily swallowing the last vestiges of the great Monasterium Tenebrarii. A few pieces of wreckage floated to the top; furniture from the chapel that must have been swept out of the door, a good-sized island of straw was starting to build in one corner and a desultory book slowly circled as if searching for its companions.

As far as any new arrival was concerned this could simply be some inland port, in which a great ship had just sunk. What all the monks were doing standing on the dock would be a bit of a mystery. Perhaps the vessel had been delivering a fresh batch of monks and they had got off just in time. Or they were about to embark and were now debating why God had just sunk their ship.

Egbert stood for a moment to take in the sight of this great disaster. Then he shrugged and turned back to the matter in hand. He'd seen so many great disasters in his time that they really didn't bother him anymore. He'd been personally involved in several on the battlefield and this one was rather tame by comparison. He usually had a lot more people trying to kill him than one who was hidden in reeds.

Back with Hermitage, Wat and the others once more, the sky had clouded a little, taking the moon away every now and again and darkening the scene. As far as those on top of the dyke could tell, they could be on an island. The sea still shone slightly but with only a dim and shaded moon to illuminate the scene, it was starting to make a few of them nervous. Speculations about the death that waited for them in the reeds started to gather pace; pace and a remarkable imagination for a brotherhood of isolated monks.

'We are going to have to have a fire,' Egbert instructed. 'We're vulnerable to an approach in the dark like this.'

Wat looked at Egbert. 'Have you done this sort of thing before?' he asked.

'Something like it.' Egbert acknowledged. 'Except it wasn't the sea, they weren't reeds and I didn't have as many monks. Apart from that, very similar.'

'Aha,' Hermitage said, which surprised them all. 'There's some wood and straw down there.' He pointed into the pool which used to be the monastery and directed them to a collection of detritus that had gathered on the new shore below their feet. This should mean no need for burning books.

Egbert directed some of the brothers to retrieve the wreckage and drag it up the slope to the top of the dyke. It was wet from the water but only on the outside. Once that had burned away the wood should go up nicely.

Brother Uttar was assigned to getting the fire going. He

liked getting fires going and did it quite often; frequently when it wasn't asked for, in places it wasn't needed. This was the first time anyone had let him get on with it. Once there was a good blaze lighting up the area, more floating bits of monastery could be seen which were collected for the night's fuel.

Egbert organised monks for watch duty and monks for sleep and once satisfied that everything was in order, returned to thoughtful examination of the situation.

The reeds nearest to them were now illuminated by a flickering glow that did nothing to encourage Hermitage's hope that everything would turn out all right in the end. His habitual question, "how on earth did I end up here?" was going to take more time to work out than one night in a flooded wilderness.

'Now what?' It was Nicodemus who asked the question they had all been thinking. Hermitage had been thinking of it as a question of general debate for them all to consider. Nicodemus seemed to be accusing Egbert.

'What do you suggest?' Egbert said as if Nicodemus actually had the answer.

'I don't know, do I? It's not my monastery.'

'No,' Egbert said with a bit more force. 'It isn't. It isn't anyone's any more. It was until you arrived. Now we've got a lake. Can't live in a lake.'

'All we can do is wait 'til morning.' Wat interrupted an argument that might give people the opportunity to express their frustrations at events by starting to hit one another. 'There's no point in going down there now,' he nodded towards the reeds. 'Unless we've got someone we want to get rid of.'

'Athan could go,' Cwen said with a smile that had no

place anywhere near a religious establishment. Even a drowned one.

Athan just pointed a finger at Cwen while some noises rumbled round inside his chest.

'No one is going anywhere,' Egbert instructed. 'Wat is right. We just have to wait here until morning and then we all leave at once. We travel out three abreast in a tight column until we reach the high ground.'

'High ground?' Nicodemus asked.

'High-er ground,' Egbert clarified.

'You have done this before,' Wat commented.

'It just makes sense. If we move that way no one will be able to pick anyone off. Everyone is watched by two other people and we'll be perfectly safe.'

His confident plan was disturbed by a strangled gurgle from down the line and the sound of a struggle of some sort.

'Someone been picked off?' Nicodemus asked, nonchalantly.

'What's happened?' Egbert called, urgently running towards the source of the commotion. When he arrived he saw Brother Godric, climbing frantically up the slope away from the reeds.

The brother crested the top of the hill and stood, getting his breath back. He put his hands on his hips, blew hard a couple of times and explained to his prior. 'I fell over,' he said.

'You..,' Egbert was lost for words. 'He raised his voice and addressed the throng. 'No one is to fall over,' he instructed, impatiently.

Egbert re-joined the others, the look on his face saying that his patience with his brothers was now in very short supply. 'No sleep tonight,' he said. 'Just in case one of them decides to go for a swim.'

Hermitage wondered why anyone would go for a swim out of choice, but detected that was not the point of the comment.

With the fire burning steadily and conversation dying as all the obvious points about the monastery and the flood and the disappearance of Brody were made, relative calm settled over the strange community atop the dyke. One of the brothers did suggest that they should get the cross, create a makeshift altar and observe the appropriate order of the day. Several other suggestions of a very intimate and painful nature followed, all of which persuaded the brother to abandon his plan.

The mutual hostility between Nicodemus and Athan and the rest of the group meant that nothing was said at all. No ideas, no proposals, no speculations, just a tense silence that Hermitage found unbearable. He had several topics that warranted discussion but on reflection concluded none of them had anything to do with their current situation. They were all fascinating, obviously, but he hazarded a guess that they would not be well received.

He was even astute enough to conclude that an exploration of the purpose of the great flood and the role of Noah in the expiation of sin would not go down well. Instead, he sat in the pool of quiet and wondered if it would be safe to get some sleep, or whether he would roll off the dyke.

The gentle murmur of the monks who were still talking and the crackling of the fire created an unwarranted atmosphere of calm and peace. The darkness hid the true perils that lay all around and Hermitage could imagine they were a simple band of brothers on some pilgrimage, stopping for the night on the sacred way.

His contemplations so absorbed him that he didn't immediately notice one voice louder than the rest. He only came to his senses when he saw that Egbert was standing and looking out across the reeds.

'What did you say?' Egbert called out.

'I said,' a voice shouted back, sounding annoyed that it hadn't been heard in the first place, 'that you shall never leave this place.'

'Oh, really,' Egbert retorted.

'Yes.' The voice in the darkness was deep now and sonorous as it filled the night. 'The secret shall be protected. It shall not leave.'

Lefric was at Egbert's side, hardly able to contain his excitement. 'It's the Trusted Brotherhood. And they're speaking.' He even clapped his hands in delight.

'Sounds like one man in the dark to me,' Egbert observed.

'Oh, there'll be more.' Lefric was confident. 'The entire Brotherhood will be out there. Just waiting to finish us off.' Another brother was with him now, proudly bearing the mark upon his head. This must be brother Gardon who had the look of someone who was surprised each time it got dark at night and freshly delighted when the sun came up the next morning.

'You really are away with the mushrooms, aren't you?' Cwen said as she joined them.

'You'll see. You'll see.' Lefric was confident and happy. Gardon nodded, which looked like one of the more complicated things he had mastered.

Egbert waved him to silence. 'How exactly are you going to stop us?' he called out to the night.

'We stopped Brody. We shall stop you all.'

'Who are these people?' Cwen asked. 'Where did they come from?'

'Good question,' Egbert said. 'If there really is some secret community within the monastery it's pretty small. All the brothers I know are up here with us. It's possible one or two have kept out of sight, but no more than that. The monastery is a big place.' He glanced over his shoulder. 'Was a big place. And we know there were secret passages and chambers dotted around. If a brother wanted to hide and others wanted to hide him it is conceivable that he wouldn't be seen. But a whole brotherhood? I don't believe it.'

'You shall all perish,' the voice from the reeds boomed out. This time it seemed to come from a slightly different position and had certainly practised its booming.

'I think we'll just march out of here in the morning and trample you into the reeds,' Egbert called back.

'Ha, ha,' the voice from the reeds laughed in the way that only a voice in reeds at night could laugh; completely mad. 'You have all sworn to guard the secret, yet now you try to leave.' The voice sounded triumphant that its argument was unanswerable.

'I think you'll find the secret is now ten feet underwater,' Egbert called back. 'Whatever it was.' He looked around him, asking the silent question; had any of them actually got any more clue what this secret was? The one they had all spent their lives protecting?

Hermitage gave a shrug of defeat.

'But you know it,' the voice called out into the night, starting to sound more like a startled bird than a human being. 'And all those who know the secret must die.'

Nicodemus stepped forward and gestured to Egbert that

he could take it from here. He had a look on his face that said he was entirely comfortable arguing with madmen in reeds in the middle of the night. 'Not going to be much use to future generations if no one knows this secret,' he cried out into the darkness. 'Unless, of course, you know it.' He paused. 'But if that was the case, you'd have to die yourself.'

There was a long pause from the direction of the reeds. 'What?' the voice eventually answered, sounding a bit less confident and bit more puzzled now.

'This secret,' Nicodemus said wearily as if explaining to a child playing in the fields why it was time to come in. 'If everyone who knows it has to die, that must include you.'

Another pause. 'Obviously it can't include me,' the voice shouted back. 'That would be stupid.'

'There you are then.'

'There I am, what?' The voice sounded quite annoyed now.

'If it can't include you, then not everyone who knows it has to die.'

Hermitage thought this reasoning was fascinating but wasn't sure where it was getting them. Apart from annoying the one person in the vicinity who was intent on killing them. He rapidly concluded that annoying people who want to kill you is not a good idea at all.

The monks, who had hitherto been content gathered around the fire, now came to listen to the very loud discussion, which was hard to ignore. Hermitage noticed that they looked enthralled at hearing how this developed. After all, they had devoted much of their lives to protecting this knowledge, about which most of them had not the first idea. To have the meaning of their existence explained in an argument between a man on top of a dyke and one hiding in the reeds in the dark was bound to be of interest.

'Look,' the voice seemed intent on getting this sorted out. 'If there's a secret, what's the point in everyone knowing it? It wouldn't be secret then, would it? The whole point of the monastery was to keep it from prying eyes and ears.'

'Ah, but you said no one could know it.' Nicodemus seemed equally intent on provoking the killer in the dark. Which, as a principle, Hermitage was now firmly against.

'No, I didn't.'

'Yes, you did. You said everyone who knew it had to die.'

'Yes, but I didn't mean absolutely everyone.'

'Aha,' Nicodemus drawled in victory. 'So we don't all have to die.'

'All right,' the voice snapped with irritation. '*We* don't all have to die. *You* all have to die. How's that, mister know-it-all?'

A rumble from the monastic community indicated that they weren't keen on this outcome.

'But we don't know the secret,' Nicodemus replied.

'Er,' the voice said, clearly thinking quite hard. 'Yes you do.'

'No, we don't,' Nicodemus confirmed, quickly. 'Never found it. Haven't got the first idea.'

'You opened the king's door.'

'That's true.' Wat looked in disappointment to Cwen who shrugged back.

'Wasn't any secret in there,' Nicodemus called back to the reeds. 'Just some old altar.'

'Just some old altar,' the voice cried out, in great offence. 'The altar of the tangled bones is not just some old altar.'

A wave of "aha's", and "oho's", flittered among the monks of the Monasterium as they took in this information.

'Oh damn,' the voice spat as it realised that no one was even supposed to know about the altar.

'You know what's in the king's chamber eh?' Nicodemus drove home his advantage. 'The one sealed for judgement day.'

'We are the Trusted Brotherhood. Naturally we know.'

'And now you've told all of us.'

'Which means you really all have to die now!' The Trusted Brother was very pleased about that.

'And that's the secret?' Nicodemus was dismissive. 'The altar?'

'No, of course it's not just the altar. That's not much of a secret is it? An altar.'

'In which case we have no idea what this wretched secret of yours is.' Nicodemus threw his hands in the air.

'The monk does,' the voice called back.

'What monk?' Nicodemus asked. 'There's quite a few up here you know.'

'The king's monk. He knows. He followed the trail from the chamber.'

Everyone turned rather slowly and looked at Hermitage. He rather slowly realised everyone was looking at him and gave a very weak smile. Noticing the inquisitive looking faces he gave a haven't-got-the-first-idea-what's-going-on look.

'No, he doesn't.' Nicodemus interpreted Hermitage's face correctly.

'He may not realise he knows it, but he does.' The voice was confident. 'And so he's the reason you all have to die.'

Caput XX

The Trusted Brotherhood

Hermitage sat on the ground and stared in dumb shock at the reeds. He didn't at all relish the idea of being the reason everyone was going to die. He thought it might make them quite cross. It could also inspire those of a more physical disposition, like Athan, to take matters into their own hands. Hermitage knew very well what happened when Athan took things into his own hands; they got broken. He offered a smile to the group which, even from his side, he could tell was rather hopeless.

'So.' It had to be Athan. 'You know the secret then.'

'I don't,' Hermitage replied, promptly, looking up at the figure of Athan looming over him. If anything could generate inspiration it was a looming Athan. 'I don't know what he's talking about. Others have seen what I've seen. The altar, the library, the drain, the Sacerdos's door. We didn't find any secret.'

'But the man in the reeds says you don't know that you know.'

'Well, what good is that?' Hermitage protested at such nonsense. 'How is not knowing I know something any different from not knowing it in the first place?' It was a very good question but seemed to cause Athan no end of trouble.

'Stop babbling,' he snapped.

'And if I do know it, but don't know that, how could I tell anyone?'

Athan just looked at him and then seemed to feel the need to walk away, clenching his fists and talking to himself as he did so.

Wat tried next. 'Perhaps it's something we haven't spotted? In all the running about and nearly getting drowned we could have seen something but not realised at the time what it was.'

It was a reasonable suggestion and Hermitage cast his mind back over the complete collection of bizarre experiences that had forced themselves upon him. Nothing came to mind. 'We have no idea what this great secret is even about,' he said. 'Is it an object, a piece of information, a name, a location?'

'I give up,' Wat said.

'So do I,' Hermitage complained.

'Oh, right, I see. I thought you knew. Sorry.'

'How would I know? Even the man in the reeds says that I don't know that I know.'

Wat shrugged. 'You're clever. You work these things out. We all stumble about making it up as we go along and then you say "aha" at some point, and explain it all.'

While Hermitage was grateful for the compliment, he didn't feel like any "aha's" at the moment. If he had seen this secret during their travails he didn't know it so comprehensively that it wasn't even a tickle at the back of his head. Putting everything together didn't add up to anything at all. There was only one thing for it. If he really was the reason everyone was going to die only one course of action lay open. He stood and adopted a pose he thought might look decisive.

'Are you all right?' Cwen asked, sympathetically. 'Have you got cramp?'

He ignored her. 'There is only one thing for it,' he announced. 'This figure in the reeds thinks that I know the secret and for that reason the rest of you must die.'

'That's what he said,' Nicodemus confirmed, helpfully.

Hermitage spoke bravely but there was a crack in his voice. 'Then I will go into the reeds and he can do with me what he will. That way the rest of you will be spared.'

This brought a general hubbub to the whole gathering. Wat and Cwen protested loudly that this was a very stupid idea and they would let him do no such thing.

They were drowned out by the lead of Nicodemus and Athan who thought it was an excellent plan and offered to help Hermitage down the slope. Many of the monks gathered round the fire seemed in favour.

Egbert barked an order for them all to shut up. 'No one is going anywhere,' he shouted. 'As far as we can tell there is one man in the reeds threatening about thirty of us up here. No one is sacrificing themselves. We wait until morning, march down there, find the idiot who is causing all this trouble and deal with them. If they've killed Brody and Brother Martin we'll take the appropriate course of action.' It sounded like Egbert had experience with appropriate courses of action.

'You shall all die.' The voice from the reeds wailed into the night as it had clearly been listening.

Cwen stooped to the fire, picked out a flaming chair leg and hurled it out into the reeds, hopefully in the general direction of the taunting voice.

'Who threw that?' the taunting voice cried out in some alarm.

'Good shot,' Wat said. Cwen grinned.

Lefric leapt from the crowd and stood in front of Cwen. 'Stop that,' he ordered. 'You mustn't throw things at the Trusted Brotherhood.'

'We could set light to you and let you walk down,' Cwen suggested. She reached for another flaming weapon.

'Satisfying though it may be mistress,' Egbert laid a hand on her arm, 'I think we had best keep the fuel for the night.'

Cwen reluctantly dropped the wood back into the fire and gave Egbert one of her moderately nasty looks.

'We need to all settle down and get as much rest as we can in what's left of the night. If there's any burning wood left over in the morning, we can throw that,' the prior offered.

. . .

'This is ridiculous,' Egbert confided to Wat as they stood in the watches of the night. The top of the dyke was a cacophony of snores and grunts as the community of the Monasterium slept on what had been their rampart. Egbert and Wat stood alone, having taken the guard before dawn between them. The night had quieted and the suspicion that the figure in the reeds was just that, one figure, gave them confidence that there would be no surprise attack.

'It is pretty unique,' Wat agreed.

'A whole monastery held on top of a hill by one man skulking around in the bushes.'

'One man who appears to have already killed two of your number.'

'I suppose so.'

'And who does seem to be comprehensively mad.'

Egbert gave a hollow laugh at this.

'And you don't even recognise his voice?'

'Not a clue. No idea where he's come from. I do object to being threatened with death by a complete stranger.'

'Much better people you know, eh?' Wat looked to the

eastern sky which was just starting to be disturbed by a timid dawn that seemed reluctant to illuminate this peculiar scene. 'We'll sort him out once we have the light.' He nodded towards the coming morning.

Egbert glanced over at the fire, which was still burning well. 'And we'll have plenty of flaming brands to root him out with. I always find a flaming brand does wonders to coax one's enemies into abject surrender.' There was something very un-monk-like about Egbert's comment. He seemed to be contemplating sinful ideas about revenge and violence.

'He may have simply run away,' Wat suggested. They hadn't heard a peep from the reeds for hours now.

'I doubt that,' Egbert speculated. 'It would be the sensible thing to do, but as you say, he seems pretty mad.'

'What happens when we find him?' Wat asked. 'If we do, and he doesn't scuttle off when the whole band marches down the hill.'

'We get to the bottom of it.'

'What, exactly?'

'Everything.' Egbert was sombre and serious. 'I haven't been here for as long as most but the whole place reeks of stagnation. The brothers have been too isolated for too long. They chatter and mutter and now we find they've started their own secret societies. I imagine that when the millennium was just around the corner they had something to concentrate on. When that passed without incident someone says they've got another thousand years to wait? You'd go a bit peculiar, wouldn't you?'

Wat nodded. He knew that monks shut in monasteries tended to be odd bunches of people at the best of times. Anyone closed up in the Monasterium Tenebrarii for any length of time would have every excuse in the world to start having conversations with their own toes. 'Are they ready for it?' Wat nodded towards the sleeping figures.

'They've got nowhere to go now. All this secrecy has done their heads no good at all. Best get it out.'

'The great secret waiting for the second coming?' Wat asked. 'Are you sure it's real?'

'Not sure of anything anymore. Perhaps this is God's will. Maybe even He doesn't want to wait any longer.'

'The abbot?' Wat suggested. 'Perhaps the leader of the place has something to say about it.'

Egbert looked around and saw the abbot's habit laying by the fire. He started as he realised the abbot wasn't in it. 'Where's he gone?'

Wat scanned the top of the dyke and could see no one.

'Good God,' Egbert let the expletive burst out of him. 'If he's out there wearing nothing but what's under his habit.'

'And what is under his habit?'

'Nothing.'

Wat shivered at the thought.

'It's warm enough that he won't die of cold but if he's mad enough to take his clothes off, he's probably mad enough to walk into the sea.'

'Perhaps he's gone after our attacker?'

Egbert had no answer to that suggestion. 'Up brothers, up,' he called loudly. Kicking the monk nearest to him to start the process of waking the community. The light of the new day was creeping through the reeds, perhaps hoping that it wouldn't be spotted and could head straight for the following night without having to deal with all the nonsense it was about to expose; including the abbot, who would be more exposed than most.

'We have more to find now,' Egbert cried. 'Your abbot has gone.'

There was much muttering and the sounds of shock and surprise ran around the group.

'And he has left his habit behind.'

The sounds rapidly change to disgust and revulsion. One brother was even heard to say that if the abbot was down there with no clothes on, he would stay up here and wait for Judgement Day on his own.

Ignoring the protests and grumbles, Egbert gathered the monks into a coherent group by the side of the fire. Hermitage, Cwen, Nicodemus and Athan joined Wat and surveyed the rescue force. Or was it an escape? Egbert instructed the brothers to gather what remains of the fire were still safe to carry.

'Keep close,' Egbert instructed. 'Lines of three together and no one wanders off. Always keep the line in front of you in sight. I will take the front line with master Wat here and Brother Athan.'

Wat didn't look too pleased about that. Athan looked delighted.

'Mistress Cwen will go in the middle.'

'I will not.' Cwen hefted a very solid flaming chunk of furniture she'd selected.

'Mistress Cwen will protect us in the rear line.'

'Better,' Cwen said.

'Brother Hermitage will go in the middle as he may be the main target of our attacker.'

The main target of the attacker eh? It was all Hermitage should have expected but it was still pretty disheartening when it was said out loud. 'What about the books?' was all he could think of in the middle of this military campaign.

'We'll send a cart back for the books,' Egbert huffed. 'I don't think they'll wander off.'

Hermitage worried that they might get wet, or be taken by birds for their nests. He surmised that no one else would share these concerns so he kept them to himself.

'And master Nicodemus will walk with Hermitage.' Egbert looked at Nicodemus with disappointment as the man dropped a small stick he had been holding back into the fire and brushed his hands clean of ash with distaste at all the mess.

Egbert addressed the whole band. 'Even if you see anything. If you spot the abbot or our attacker, you call out and we all go together. Anyone going off on their own will either get completely lost or get completely dead.' The brothers seemed to see the sense in this. 'And if we see no one we simply keep going until we emerge from the reeds. Is everyone clear?'

Nods and mumbles indicated that everyone was clear.

'Right,' Egbert ordered. 'We go.'

Checking that his band was with him, Egbert stepped off the top of the dyke and took cautious steps down the slope, being careful not to slip. With Athan to his left and Wat to his right, he led his phalanx into the reeds.

Taking no care where they walked, the assembly trampled the reeds into the soggy ground. Occasionally the marshy land was so soft that a foot would sink and there was a hesitation while the owner freed themselves. The pace was slow but steady and the dyke was moving slowly to the rear with no hint of interference. And no sign of a naked old abbot popping out of the greenery.

Most of the monks expressed a strong preference for dealing face to face with a mad man who chopped people up rather than having to see what their abbot looked like with no clothes on.

After fifty or sixty uninterrupted paces there was a shout off to their left. 'Where are you going?' the voice from the reeds called out once more. It was a heartfelt protest, sounding like the man had just woken up and noticed that his prey was escaping.

'We are either leaving undisturbed, or we are leaving with you face down in the bog,' Egbert called back.

'No, no, no. You can't.' The voice sounded frantic and the sound of reeds being thrown aside drew closer and closer.

Egbert signalled the column to come to a halt and they turned to face the direction of the noise. Cwen moved from the back to the front, blowing on her burning weapon to bring the flames back to life.

Egbert nodded to Wat and Athan to move slightly out to the flanks, ready to cover whatever emerged from the reeds and protect against an attack from the side.

Although the noise of the approach had sounded close, the landscape must be deceiving. The entire group had held their breath, waiting for whatever was coming for them. Then they had to breathe again as nothing appeared. The crashing of reeds continued and it was difficult to tell exactly which direction it was coming from.

Egbert looked alarmed. Could there be more than one person out there after all? Were they surrounded and a great force was about to emerge all around them? Had he been tricked by a clever tactician who had lured them down to this place where they would meet their deaths? He quickly directed the monks to turn and face outwards. With their numbers they could at least face in all directions and so see the attack the moment it arrived.

The thrashing of the reeds grew louder until the tension was almost unbearable. Surely their adversary must be upon them by now. Then as if to raise their alarm to breaking point, the noise suddenly stopped.

'My God,' Egbert muttered, loud enough for Wat and Athan to hear. 'Whoever this is they are clever. They are not emerging from the reeds but probably have a clear view of us. Perhaps they even have bows and will pick us off without us ever seeing the faces of those who take our lives.'

Wat crouched down, partly to see if he could discern anything through the reeds, but partly to make himself a smaller target. Athan stood tall as if daring anyone to shoot him.

The voice from the reeds called out once more. He was not letting anyone else speak, ensuring that information about the strength of his force remained unknown.

'Where've you gone?' it asked, in annoyed puzzlement.

'What?' Egbert replied, not at all sure what was going on now.

'Stop moving about,' the voice instructed. 'How can I find you if you keep moving?'

Egbert looked askance at Wat and Athan. 'We're not moving,' he shouted back to the reeds. 'You are.'

'Stay there,' the voice demanded. 'Bloody reeds,' it talked to itself. 'Can't see a bloody thing.' There was more crashing about, this time it sounded that it was receding. 'Who built a monastery in a place like this for God's sake?'

'You're moving away now,' Egbert called out, relaxing and letting his confidence build that the voice was about as much threat as a light beating with one of the reeds.

'Keep talking,' the voice called back. 'I'll be there in a moment.'

'Glad to help.' Egbert raised his eyebrows at the others. 'Do let us know if there's anything else we can do.' He paused briefly. 'Shall we send someone to find you?' He offered this as he would offer to pick up a walking stick for an old crone with a bad back.

'I can do it myself,' the voice snapped.

'Not having much luck so far.' Egbert was mocking. 'How did you manage to find Brody and Brother Martin at all? Or did they tread on you?'

Now the noise of the reeds was getting closer again, and some movement of their tops could be seen straight ahead.

'That's it,' Egbert encouraged. 'Keep coming. Nearly there.'

At last, with the brothers of the Monasterium Tenebrarii having comprehensively lost interest in what was going to appear, a lone figure stepped from the reeds.

'Aha,' it said, in dramatic fashion.

Egbert appraised the monk who had stepped from the cover. He was a rotund little fellow. Of middling years and dressed in the simple garb shared by them all. Unlike the rest of them, he had the look about him of a life lived well. His ruddy cheeks and a habit that was straining to contain his girth told of someone who fed and drank better than most. The fact that he also had his hands on his knees and was panting for breath after all that running around in the reeds said he was not a man used to vigorous exercise.

'Who the devil are you?' Egbert demanded.

'I,' the monk adopted a dramatic pose, albeit a rather panting one, to go with his delivery, 'am the Trusted Brotherhood.'

Lefric and Gardon pushed their way through the throng of their brothers and prostrated themselves at the feet of the new arrival.

'Just you?' Egbert asked, folding his arms. 'I hate to criticise, but a brotherhood usually requires at least one more brother.'

The Trusted one frowned at the disrespect. 'There was another,' he explained, defensively. 'But he went off,' he mumbled.

'Went off?'

'Yes,' the new arrival snapped his irritation. 'Some nonsense about not wasting his life any more. But as long as the Monasterium has been in existence there has been a Trusted Brotherhood. I am but the latest in a long line stretching back into the distant past.'

'Well, sixty-eight years.' Hermitage felt he had to point out.

The monk ignored the impertinent interruption. 'Just as I joined the Trusted Brotherhood others will replace my companion and I will be replaced in my turn.'

Lefric and Gardon leapt up at this news.

'You see,' the fat monk said. 'Already our numbers swell.'

'You're welcome to them,' Egbert snorted. He stared hard at the monk. 'How come I've never seen you?'

'I have been protected.' The monk indicated Lefric and Gardon. 'The monastery was a convoluted place. It was easy to hide and be given supplies by my supporters.'

Lefric spoke up with pride. 'We left food and drink in special places, and when we came back, it was gone.' He still sounded in complete awe about how this had happened.

Egbert gave a wry smile and indicated the size of the Trusted brother. 'I rather think you left too much.' He shook his head slowly at the situation they had got themselves in over one strange monk who hid in the walls and ate too much. 'And now you're going to deal with us are you.'

'That's right,' the monk confirmed.

'All of us.'

'You are all sworn to protect the secret and so I only have to give the order and you will be silenced.'

'Go ahead,' Egbert offered. 'Have a try.' He judged that the mood of the other monks would leave this Trusted Brother in serious trouble. 'And what have you done with Brody and Brother Martin?'

'They are safe. The monk says nothing, so he is no threat. And Brody won't shut up, but it's all nonsense.'

'So why did Brody cry out?' Hermitage asked.

'He was startled when I emerged from the reeds.'

'I bet he was,' Egbert barked a short laughed. 'Well.' He clapped his hands. 'Let's get on with it then. Let's get this great secret made safe. The one we know nothing about and couldn't reveal if we wanted to. How exactly do you propose to deal with us all?'

'Brothers,' the monk held his arms up and called them all to attention. 'The secret of the Monasterium Tenebrarii must be made safe and..,' He came to a juddering, embarrassed halt as the first of the monastic community pushed past him and headed off in the direction of the village. 'Where are you going?' he cried after them. 'Come back. The secret must be protected.'

Egbert's careful ranks of monks broke up into a gaggle of disinterested individuals who were not going to be stopped by one fat monk with his arms in the air.

'Your sacred duty brothers,' the Trusted Brother cried in despair. 'Now is the moment. The time has come for which destiny has been preparing you. All your years of careful study and preparation have come to this day. And this is the day in which you shall stand against the forces of evil.' He rose to a crescendo of passion, 'You must protect the great secret.' He shouted these last words to the air and held his arms aloft.

One passing brother bothered to pause as he walked by. 'Don't know it, don't care,' he said. 'Fifteen years in this place. Fifteen years!' The man sounded like he was on the edge of doing something rash. 'And for what? To see the whole place and everything in it disappear underwater. I assume you did that?' he glared at the brother.

'I had to,' the rotund one replied, defiantly. 'I had to protect the secret.'

'Well, now you have,' the brother concluded before walking off. 'And now we've got nowhere to live,' he called back over his shoulder. 'And you ate all the pies,' the voice drifted over the reeds.

The Trusted Brotherhood seemed completely nonplussed by this turn of events and plainly couldn't comprehend why no one was obeying him. 'The secret,' he whimpered pathetically as the last of the monks brushed him aside with contemptuous glances. Only Lefric and Gardon remained attentive to his wishes.

'So.' Egbert looked at the man with some sympathy. Mainly contempt but a bit of sympathy. 'All this for nothing.' He held his arms out to take in the destruction of the entire monastery and the chaos that had ensued.

The monk at the centre of his attention was still looking round, hoping that someone was going to take him seriously.

'At least your precious secret is safe under the water,' Egbert said. 'No one's going to know what it was now.'

'He knows,' the monk pointed at Hermitage. 'I've been watching him. He's followed the trail, he visited the sacred places and seen the signs. He knows.'

Hermitage looked to Egbert and indicated with an expression as blank as a freshly scraped parchment that he still had not a clue what the man was talking about.

'You can't fool me,' the monk went on. 'You have seen. You know what the great treasure is. The one secret that we have guarded all this time and which must never be told.'

They all looked at Hermitage now, which he always found disturbing. 'There was nothing, really,' He explained. 'I didn't see anything that would give me the slightest hint what this great secret might be.' He stopped. And he thought. And he considered once more all the places they had gone and all the things they had seen. And he slowly, tentatively came to an awful conclusion. The only one that was possible in the circumstances but surely it couldn't be true. Was that really it?

Had he been thinking along the wrong track all along? It was somehow satisfying that he managed to get his mind to jump from the path it had been following to come to this completely different conclusion. It was a whole new way of thinking.

He felt that he was inside his own head, looking at himself contemplating this development. On the one hand he was congratulating himself on this fine piece of reasoning and on the other berating himself for coming up with such a ludicrous idea. As he watched, the pieces darting around his head like swallows on a summer evening, swooped under the eaves of his mind and settled.

'Aha,' he said.

'There you are,' Wat said. 'Told you so.'

Caput XXI

Secrets Revealed

Cwen was impatient. 'What is it then?'

'Don't tell them,' the monk instructed. 'You can't tell them.'

Hermitage gave this some thought. 'I think I have to. After all, it is an important matter. And if I am right, then I think it has to be said.'

'It'll be the worse for you.' The Trusted Brother's tone was very serious. He cut a rather ludicrous figure; a fat monk in a marsh threatening a larger number with death, but there was something about his tone that set off another thought in Hermitage's head.

'Aha,' he said.

'Again?' Wat sounded very impressed.

'Ignatius,' Hermitage said the name with quiet surety that he had now answered two puzzles in a very short space of time.

'What about him?' the Trusted brother asked, in an irritated tone, waving the name away.

'I think I need to sit down.' Hermitage did so. He felt quite faint at all the answers he had come up with at once. He sat in the small clearing of reeds that had been made by the tramping of many monks. The floor was a bit damp and started to soak the bottom of his habit but that was a minor distraction. After a few moments watching and seeing that he wasn't going to get up, the others joined him. Except for Athan who stood glaring at this indulgence.

'Well?' Cwen demanded again when Hermitage didn't immediately say anything.

He looked around the circle and considered the best order in which to explain things. The ideas were starting to fight one another in an effort to be the first out of his mouth, but if they weren't organised they wouldn't make any sense at all. He battered them into some sort of queue and took a deep breath.

As everyone was gathered here he thought it was safe to explain the whole story. If they all knew everything there would be no misunderstandings, disagreements or wrong conclusion leapt to. He wasn't entirely confident about that last one but what they did with the information wasn't really his problem. Once they had the truth, what could they do but repeat it honestly?

He did wonder about exposing all the details in front of the group. It felt more like an entertainment than a serious exposition that involved a death. Surely this wasn't the appropriate method for revealing a killer? Gather everyone together and explain all the personal details in public? But then he was in the middle of a marsh miles from anywhere and if it wasn't explained soon, the audience would get restless.

He gave the best serious look he could to each in turn. Wat's response was an encouraging sort of get-on-with-it look. Cwen's was an impatient get-on-with-it look. Nicodemus was paying rapt attention, the sort of attention a very greedy man gives when he is about to be told where great treasure is buried. Egbert had the worn-out look of someone who just wanted this over with and Athan was glaring. Of course. The Trusted Brother's face was set as if daring Hermitage to speak. Lefric and Gardon plainly had not a clue what was going on.

Hermitage closed his eyes to blot them all out. 'One of us

here is a killer.' There. He had said it. Terrible words, he knew. A great accusation made with only the evidence of his thoughts to go on. He cautiously opened his eyes to gauge the response.

'Well, yes,' Egbert said as if it was obvious. 'It's him.' He pointed at the Trusted Brother.

No one else was showing any surprise at this at all. In fact, one or two looked rather disappointed that this was all Hermitage had to say. 'He killed Ignatius,' he specified the murder in question.

'I think we'd figured that out for ourselves.' Wat sounded very disappointed. 'Ignatius being the dead body and this being the only monk who's threatening to kill people.'

'Erm.' This had knocked Hermitage off his carefully assembled train of thought.

'It couldn't be one of us, could it?' Cwen explained. 'We only got here after Ignatius was dead. Hardly likely to be the prior. And I don't think either of these two,' she gestured at Lefric and Gardon, 'could tell the time if the sun came down and read out its own shadow. Sticking a priest on the spikey bit? I don't think so.'

'Ah.' Hermitage tried to sound pleased that they had worked this out for themselves.

'And this so-called Trusted Brother has been hiding in the monastery for goodness knows how long.' Egbert gave his own hard look at the monk. 'Doesn't sound very trustworthy to me. Just the sort of man to go round killing people.'

Hermitage could see that while their conclusion was sound, their reasoning was all over the place. He recovered his satisfaction that he had worked this out in the proper manner. 'Just because a monk hides, or happens to be the only one in this group who says he'll kill people does not make him a killer.'

'What?' Athan snapped. 'Make your mind up. First you say he did it, now you say he didn't.'

'Oh no,' Hermitage corrected, 'he definitely did it. The question is why did he do it?'

'Is it?' Athan didn't seem at all interested in why.

'Of course. It's all connected. The great secret treasure of the church, the death of Ignatius and the Trusted Brother. All connected.'

'Lovely,' Athan said; a word which sat ill upon his lips. 'Well, now we all know who did it let's get out of this place and hand him over to the local lord.'

Nicodemus raised a hand. 'I think we need to know about these connections.'

Athan growled.

'Particularly the one to do with the great treasure,' he said, very pointedly. 'Do go on Brother.' He signed that Hermitage could continue.

'Oh, er, thank you.' Hermitage was getting confused. 'Right. Yes. So. The Trusted Brother Killed Ignatius because he knew the details of the secret.'

'Who, the brother?' Athan asked.

'No, not the brother,' Hermitage replied, impatiently. Weren't these people paying any attention? 'Ignatius knew all about the secret.'

'Well, of course he did,' Egbert looked puzzled. 'He was the Sacerdos. He was supposed to know about it.'

'No, he wasn't,' Hermitage said. 'It was the Sacerdos's job to guard the knowledge of the rites and processes around the opening of the king's door and the revelation of the secret. Once revealed he would probably have the knowledge from his books about what came next. I don't think he was supposed to know what the secret treasure actually was.'

The way the Trusted Brother was grinding his teeth indicated that Hermitage had hit the thumb on the nail.

'But,' Hermitage went on, 'we know that the padlock to the back door of the king's chamber was well used, indicating that it had been opened recently.'

'With the abbot's key,' Egbert pointed out.

'The key the abbot was holding for Ignatius. It is possible that Ignatius had the key and could not resist the temptation to see what was behind the door. Mayhap he did so, could not bear the knowledge or the temptation that he found and so gave the key to the abbot for safekeeping.'

'We're sure it's not the abbot who went in?' Egbert asked.

'That poor man's mind seems addled,' Hermitage said. 'If troubles such as we have gone through did that to him, I cannot imagine him being able to kill Ignatius. And why would he do so anyway? And of course, he sent Brody for the king. He would hardly do that if the blame was to fall on him.'

'Ignatius knows the secret so this one kills him for it.' Cwen summed up the revelations so far with a contemptuous wave at the Trusted Bother.

'Not entirely,' Hermitage went on. 'If it was a simple case of knowing about the great secret treasure, Ignatius could be admitted to the Trusted Brotherhood to guard it. He was the Sacerdos after all. He was privy to the most secret rites and ceremonies. He was one man who could surely be trusted to protect the knowledge.'

'Then what is going on?' Egbert said in some exasperation. 'This whole thing is just ridiculous. I said to Harold when he sent me here that I didn't believe the place existed. Then I find it did and it's full of monks guarding some treasure they don't know about.

'Then I find there's a priest who's supposed to know what's going but it turns out he doesn't. Or maybe he does. On top of that, there's a secret organisation of one, the Trusted Brotherhood, skulking around the place keeping secrets from the secret keepers. You couldn't make it up.'

'Exactly.' Hermitage thought that Egbert had summed the place up quite neatly. 'Why would the Trusted Brotherhood kill Ignatius?' He waited. Surely someone would work it out. 'Why would the Trusted Brotherhood kill anyone?' he prompted.

The group looked nonplussed and deep in thought. Except for Nicodemus who was regarding them all with his customary contempt. 'They'd kill anyone who was going to give away the secret of the treasure.'

'There you have it,' Hermitage said amidst the hums of the assembly as they understood.

Cwen put her hand up.

'Yes, Cwen?' Hermitage asked, please to see they were taking some interest at last.

'If Ignatius was the Sacerdos and all. And he was supposed to be guarding the treasure, why would he want to give it away?'

'Aha,' Hermitage said, and he thought it came out the best of all his recent "ahas". 'That is the great secret at the heart of the treasure and its secret.'

'Eh?' Cwen looked quite lost.

'And what exactly is this secret about the secret about the treasure?' Nicodemus asked. 'If you could get to the point eventually we'd all be terribly grateful. You are dragging it out a bit.'

Hermitage took one last glance at the Trusted Brother, who was still looking daggers. He drew his breath and held it in what he thought was quite a dramatic manner. Cwen looked at him as if he was having a fit. He let his breath out.

'There isn't one,' he announced, to very little reaction at all, which was quite disappointing.

'Isn't one what?' Egbert asked. 'I thought I was confused before but I'm completely lost now.'

'There's isn't a secret,' Hermitage explained.

'What?" Wat asked, looking as lost as Egbert. 'You mean we all know it. But we don't know we know it? Like you didn't?' He tailed off as he fell into the gaps between his own words.

'No,' Hermitage repeated himself, carefully. 'There is no secret.'

'Is that no secret about the secret or are we talking about the secret now?' Cwen was starting to look quite cross.

'Both,' Hermitage said, which didn't calm her down at all.

'And the treasure?' Nicodemus asked.

Hermitage shrugged. 'None of that either, I'm afraid.'

Nicodemus let out a long, slow sigh of disappointment with a strong hint of I-should-have-known.

'No treasure?' Wat understood that bit.

'That's right,' Hermitage confirmed. 'No treasure so no secret about the treasure. And the secret about that was that there was no secret. That's what the Trusted Brotherhood was guarding and what Ignatius found out.'

'They were keeping the secret that there was no secret?' Egbert shook his head. 'And thirty of us have spent years protecting something that didn't exist.' He looked around the group. 'I've only been here a while but I suspect some of the others aren't going to be very happy about that.'

'But there must be something,' Nicodemus had recovered himself and had thought things through. 'Who would go to the trouble of building this whole place all those years ago if there was nothing to protect? The millennium was real. People thought judgement day was coming. The church put something here.'

'They probably put a lot of things here,' Hermitage nodded. 'And then came and took it all away again when judgement day didn't appear. It would be an awful waste to leave the great treasures of the church in some monastery in a bog if the Lord wasn't going to turn up asking for them after all. I imagine that is when they set up the Trusted Brotherhood. Trusted to guard the secret that everything had been removed.'

'And of course, the senior figures of the church could take everything without anyone else knowing it had gone,' Wat said with resignation at the venal nature of mankind; including the mankind in positions of religious authority. 'They created a whole Brotherhood to keep their secret.'

Hermitage looked at the Trusted Brother, who was now looking quite puzzled himself. 'That's not it at all,' he explained, in some annoyance.

'Oh, yes?' Wat asked. 'Where's it all gone then?'

'The Lord took it,' the Trusted Brother said, trying to sound confident but failing.

'Really?' Wat pressed. 'Although it wasn't actually judgement day, God came down to a bog on the outskirts of Spalding and took away just the valuables? Who told you that?' Wat's suggestion was clearly that the Trusted Brother had heard this in a tavern somewhere.

'My predecessor,' the monk explained. 'And he had it

from his, who had it from his, all the way back to the first Trusted Brother.'

'So there isn't anything here,' Cwen confirmed. 'And that's your secret. I think Egbert's right. When the others find out about this they're going to want a long talk with you.'

'We still protect the church,' the Brother protested. 'If knowledge of this got out, confidence would be lost.'

'And you killed Ignatius for that?' Cwen's disgust was clear.

'He was going to reveal everything.'

'Ignatius could not resist the temptation of the king's door,' Hermitage speculated. 'And so he used the key to let himself in.'

'He should never have done that.' The Trusted Brother clearly thought this was the first betrayal.

'And when he did get in he found the altar of the twisted bones and that was that. He probably thought the Holy Grail was going to be in there. Or at the very least a really significant relic. Like us, he must have thought that the hiding would be more obscure and complex than just a door. He worked it out and followed the trail to the library and then to the drain and then to the abbot's chamber only to find the abbot knew nothing.'

'He went mad,' the Trusted Brother reported, shivering slightly at the recollection. 'He kept going on about how many years he'd been here. How he'd been a young man when he arrived and now look at him. He said he'd had dreams about serving the Lord, perhaps even in Rome but instead had devoted his life to the Monasterium; which now turned out to be completely pointless. His life had been wasted, his youth thrown away and his plans were as dust cast upon the waters.' He took a breath. 'Talk about selfish.'

'Did you finish him there and then?' Hermitage asked, trying to make it sound very accusatory.

'No, of course not. I talked him through the Trusted Brotherhood. I explained that if we worked together we could maintain the secret of the Monasterium for the next generation. With his knowledge of the books and the ritual and mine of the fact that there wasn't anything to know about, we would make an impregnable bulwark.'

'And what did he say to that?'

'It was very rude. And blasphemous. And he said that he was going to leave the Monasterium that very night and spread word to the land that the whole place was a fraud.'

'Which it is,' Wat noted.

'No it isn't,' the Brother protested. 'It's a place that's supposed to hold a great secret, and it does.'

'But it's not the right secret.'

'Now you're just being picky.'

'I hardly think it's picky to push a priest onto a sundial,' Hermitage said, trying to get back to the point.

'Ah.' The Brother at least had the grace to look at the ground. 'That was an accident.'

'An accident!' Hermitage could not believe this. 'How does a priest end up on a sundial by accident?'

'Well.' The Trusted Brother had lost a lot of his confidence as he explained the death of the Sacerdos. 'He said he was going, and I said he couldn't. And he said he could, so I said he couldn't. And he said who was going to stop him, and I said I was. And he said I could try and I said I would.'

'If we could get to the sundial?' Nicodemus queried, wearily. 'The sun will be going down again in nine or ten hours.'

The Brother took a deep breath and plunged on. 'He pushed me first,' he got his defence in early. 'Then I pushed back and so on. Then I pushed hard one time and he fell backwards onto the sundial.'

'It must have been a very hard push,' Egbert said, knowing how this had all ended up.

'It was,' the Brother mumbled. 'And the spike went into him.'

'And killed him?' Hermitage found this hard to believe.

'Not at first,' the Brother confessed sheepishly. 'I might have pushed him a bit more after that.'

'You pushed him onto the sundial, which stabbed him. Then you pushed him some more?'

'And then I got a bit carried away.'

'Brother!' Hermitage reprimanded.

'I think he was dead by then,' the Brother explained as if that made it all right.

'When we found him he was completely impaled,' Egbert painted the gruesome picture.

The Trusted Brother whispered something unintelligible and rubbed the ground with his foot.

'What was that?' Athan stood over him.

The Brother snapped back, like a child caught in the act of lying. 'I might have jumped up and down on him. A bit.'

There was nothing but stunned silence at this piece of information.

'I was very angry,' the Brother justified his actions.

'You're very mad,' Cwen concluded. 'I think the best thing we can do is pop you back in the monastery and be on our way.'

'But, it's full of water,' the Brother protested.

'Exactly.'

'Adding another death will not make things any better,' Hermitage smoothed the conflict. 'I think all we can do is take the Trusted Brother with us and hand him over to someone in authority.'

'More like put him in a fool's tower and lock the door,' Cwen suggested.

'At least we know the end of the tale now.' Hermitage offered.

'Long, dangerous and pointless though it was,' Wat sighed his disappointment. 'No secret, no great artefact and no treasure. What a waste of a week this has been.'

Egbert added his poignant comment to the sad scene. 'It is a pity we had to leave the rest of the gold behind.'

The silence at this was even more profound than the one about the priest stamped to death on a sundial.

'What gold?' Wat asked very carefully and slowly.

'The gold in the treasury,' Egbert explained. 'Just ordinary gold that belongs to the monastery. Did we not show you that?'

'No, you did not.' Wat was barely maintaining control. 'Why did we not bring the gold with us?'

Egbert shrugged and pointed at Hermitage. 'He told us to bring the books first.'

Caput XXII

Treasure After All

The journey out of the reeds was not a comfortable one for Hermitage. Not only was his backside wet from sitting on the ground too long, but his feet were now wet from tramping through the bogs and ditches. If it were possible, they could have been quickly dried out by the looks he was getting from the others.

The large gold cross was strapped firmly to Egbert's back, which seemed to make the mood of Wat and Nicodemus even worse.

He tried a few humble smiles but they got him nowhere.

'We do know where the gold is,' he pointed out when one of Wat's glares got bright enough to tell the time by.

'At the bottom of the underwater monastery,' Wat explained.

'Well, yes.'

'Unless you have a way of breathing at the bottom of the sea, it's going to stay there.'

'This is a time of marvellous advances. There may be some great mind working on that problem right now.'

'We could tie some rocks to his feet and throw him in until he works it out,' Athan suggested.

Hermitage had quite a speech ready about greed and the love of gold and how there was more to man's existence than the pursuit of worldly possessions. He glanced around the group and thought he'd keep it for another day.

On the way, they collected Brody and Brother Martin from their place of concealment. They hadn't actually been tied up or restrained in any way. Brody had been given a large sack of the monastery's best preserved beef and a huge skin of wine and had to be woken by his rescuers.

Brother Martin explained, by the use of hand signals and some contemptuous leg movements, that Brody was useless and he had felt obliged to protect the young man from falling face down in the bog, he was so drunk. Naturally, he could not cry out or reveal his situation as that would break his vow.

Egbert looked quite ready to break something.

As they walked on in silence, Hermitage reflected that surely these events had been a great success. They had uncovered the murderer of Ignatius, they had revealed the false secrets of the Monasterium Tenebrarii and had all come out of it alive. Yes, there was no gold to show for it, but that hadn't been the point. If they had to, they would be able to report back to the king that the door he probably didn't know about had contained a secret that didn't exist. What more could you ask?

And, of course, they had found the great treasure of the library and rescued the books from the advancing waters. The world of learning would be delighted by that discovery. He couldn't immediately think who was in the world of learning just at the moment to be delighted, but something would come to him. Perhaps Wat would let him bring the books home himself. Of course, he'd have to build a bigger house to put them all in.

It was going to be quite a long journey before they got back to Derby, he just hoped that Wat would have calmed down by then.

. . .

As the group trampled through the reeds, sighing with

relief as they started to thin and the ground began to rise, two pairs of eyes watched them from between the stalks.

A wizened and grizzled shape, looking like a giant, shaved mole, shivered and gibbered in the chill shadow of the reeds.

'We must find you some clothes,' the other said. 'Wandering around naked in a place like this? I don't know what you're thinking.' If this second figure had more of a whiff of sanity about him, the other whiff was pure fish. 'And then we'll have some fresh eels. That'll set you right. You see.'

The eel man led his new companion away by secret paths known only to him, into an area where the reeds were thickest, the water slowest and the wildlife quite peculiar. An aura hung around this place as if it was the centre of the world and everything else rolled around it. The stillness and calm were palpable as if the wind and waves originated here and disturbed it not at all.

It was slightly warmer in this spot, and the abbot's fretfulness and confusion seemed to fall away to a simple contentment with his surroundings and acceptance of whatever was to come.

The eel man invited his guest into a simple dwelling of living reeds, woven into walls and a roof that would shelter from any gentle rain. There was nothing here but a plain table made from more woven reeds and a gathering of straw for sleeping. It was all there was and it was all there needed to be.

'Here we are.' The eel man had gone to one corner of his green and breathing house and produced a monk's habit. It was obviously one from the Monasterium and the abbot slipped it on, calmly.

'I'll get some eels,' the eel man said. He stepped from the

shelter and knelt at a hidden bank where a pool of water slumbered. He dipped his hand in and brought it out again. In his palm nestled four fat and healthy eels. They lay quiet and still, though plainly alive. 'I don't know why they do that,' the eel man said, shrugging at his good fortune as he held his catch out for the abbot's appraisal.

They sat, cross-legged at the table and the abbot bowed his quiet thanks to God for the gift of their meal.

'Ah,' the eel man remembered, 'we must drink.'

He went to the corner and took up his cup; the one he had rescued from the Monasterium when all those church men had been running about the place taking things away. Had that been yesterday or last summer? It was always difficult to keep track of time in this place.

Whatever the reason, he considered the cup to be his only worldly possession but it gave him the most comfort. He could spend what seemed hours just looking at it. It was a simple thing, not made of the gold the churchmen had seemed so concerned about. They'd been glad to get rid of it.

He reached out of the door and dipped the cup in the water. He handed it to the abbot first, as was only right and proper. The abbot drank, cautiously to begin with, but then with surprise and pleasure at the sweet drink that surely had not come from the ground. Was that a hint of wine in the taste?

The eel man refilled the cup and drank himself. As usual he started to feel at least ten years younger and was filled with a contentment that inspired him to simply sit still for the rest of his life. He knew he had a reputation for madness but he didn't care.

Nobody believed him when he told them he had a

marvellous home in the reeds and that they should come
and drink from his wonderful cup. They brushed him aside
and called him all sorts of rude names. Even those two new
people he'd met. They were obviously looking for the great
secret treasure, but then they went off to the monastery
instead. Never mind.

Finis.

Brother Hermitage returns in ***The Case of the Curious
Corpse.*** Read the opening chapter below:

The Case of the Curious Corpse

yet more

Chronicles
of Brother Hermitage

by

Howard of Warwick

The Case of the Curious Corpse

Caput I

𝕿he attack by the force of Normans was unexpected. But then, Brother Hermitage reasoned, could an attack that was expected still be called an attack? Everyone talked about surprise attacks and he had naturally assumed that all attacks were surprises. He had been attacked himself, who hadn't in these difficult times? And he was still only a young man of, what was it now, twenty-three? Something like that. Every one of those attacks had come as a complete surprise.

He couldn't imagine that people sent word of an attack, or made arrangements for a time that suited everyone. Surely the attacker would not want their opponent to be prepared. He couldn't imagine anyone arriving for an attack and then having to rearrange the whole thing because it wasn't convenient.

But presumably, if something had to be called a surprise attack there must be attacks that were not surprises, otherwise what was the point of the nomenclature?

'Pay attention,' Cwen snapped as she smacked him lightly on the back of the head.

He came back to the real world in which the real attack was making a lot of noise outside Wat the Weaver's workshop.

'What do they want?' he bleated, observing the organisation of horsemen taking place to the front of the building.

'What do the Normans always want?' Cwen sneered. 'They've only just arrived in the country and here they are throwing their weight around.'

Hermitage's appraisal of Cwen comprised the usual contradictory evidence. An excellent weaver in her own right but no more than a young girl really, elfin thin, small and, when it appeared, with a smile that could light the darkest chamber; and a temper like the same dark chamber set on fire with a pack of mad dogs inside. And a scowl that could clean rusty metal. Her willingness to take on the entire band of Norman attackers on her own was absolutely clear. And she wouldn't be worried about whether it was a surprise or not.

'How many?' Wat's voice called as he scrambled the stairs to this upper chamber.

'At least a dozen,' Cwen called back from her place at the window overlooking the front of the workshop; the window from which Hermitage's immediate response to the sight of a dozen well-armed Norman soldiers had been to consider the linguistic proprieties.

Wat joined them at the window. His wild smudge of black hair perhaps presenting an unintended target if the Normans had brought archers. He straightened his very well made jerkin, brushed the dust from his exquisite leggings and flicked a smudge from the toe of his well-fitting left boot.

He was the oldest of them by a small margin, and the richest by a whole collection of very large margins laid end to end. He didn't get to have his own workshop by being a humble weaver of cloth. No, he got to be a very rich weaver by making tapestries with images the like of which Hermitage had only seen in a book of something called anatomy. And in the anatomy book at least the bodies had the decency to be dead. There was no decency in Wat's tapestries at all. And people paid ridiculous sums for them. Very bad people and very bad tapestries, as Hermitage frequently pointed out as he persuaded Wat to stick to more wholesome works.

In the face of the oncoming Norman onslaught, Wat would make sure he looked his best, Hermitage would check that everyone addressed one another properly and Cwen would do any actual fighting.

'What do they want?' Wat asked with some exasperation.

'That's what I wondered,' Hermitage put in. 'Perhaps they've come to buy some tapestry?'

Wat looked over the band trampling around outside and took account of their rough appearance, their grizzled and careworn faces and their use of language that would make a pig blush.

'They don't look the tapestry buying type,' he concluded.

'Tapestry stealing, probably,' Cwen huffed.

Wat faced Hermitage with an explicit look. 'Could they want you?' he asked.

'I hardly think so.' Hermitage was shocked at hearing the idea out loud, having come to roughly the same conclusion about their uninvited guests.

'You are the King's Investigator,' Wat made the title sound very grand.

'Don't remind me,' Hermitage replied. And he meant it. Being made King's Investigator had been awful. First King Harold, and then, when he was dead and Hermitage thought it was all over, King William went and renewed the appointment. Doing the investigations was terrible and constantly living in fear of being summoned to yet another scene of violence and sin kept him awake at night. 'The king is hardly going to send a whole band of horsemen just to fetch me. He's just sent a messenger in the past. Or even a simple threat on its own. I'm hardly likely to put up a fight, am I?'

Wat shrugged that this did seem out of keeping with King William's usual ways.

'Pillage, violence, robbery,' Cwen determined, with a grunt. 'The usual. Just a gaggle of Normans out for what they can get. Although why it takes quite so many of them to do anything, I have no idea. Probably because they wouldn't be safe if they went out on their own.' She made it quite clear that she would be one of the main causes of harm to a lone Norman.

'Perhaps they're just passing and are going to make us provide hospitality,' Hermitage speculated, hopefully.

'We could always get Mrs Grod to poison them,' Cwen said, suggesting that Wat's cook could do what she did best.

'I don't think they'd line up like that and draw their swords to get an invitation to a meal.' Wat nodded out of the window where the Normans appeared to be making themselves ready for a significant fight.

'What were you doing downstairs?' Cwen asked. 'Barring the door?'

'No,' Wat replied, 'opening it. Don't want that lot knocking the thing down when there's no need.'

Cwen snorted her contempt.

'Be reasonable,' Wat went on. 'There's no way we can keep them out. You, me, Hermitage, Mrs Grod and old Hartle with the apprentices at his back? That meal would be us on a plate. If they find the door's shut it'll only make them angry, and they'll probably just burn the rest of the place down so they don't have to use it.'

'Why don't you just go down and invite them in?' Cwen's

opinion of Wat's strategy was clear. It was lower than a very low thing.

'Because I suspect the first person to speak to them could end up with the bits of their body a lot less joined up than is usual. You know the Norman approach, chop first and ask questions later. In fact, why bother with the questions at all?'

Hermitage studied the visitors again. They had arrived in a flurry of dust and noise having thundered up the road from nearby Derby. Goodness knew what state they'd left that place in, but they were clearly prepared for a major confrontation.

Even now, the one who appeared to be in charge was ordering the others about, moving them into the right position and checking their equipment. He was clearly unhappy with something as he was shouting orders and deprecations in language which, apart from being quite revolting, occasionally slipped into some local dialect akin to Norman French; the sort of kin the rest of the family doesn't talk about any more.

Hermitage knew an order and deprecation when he heard one though. That raised fascinating questions about the role of tone and expression in language.

Cwen hit him again.

'Will you keep your mind on the problem at hand,' she ordered and deprecated all at once. 'What was it this time? The Norman approach to the care of horses?'

'Not at all,' Hermitage protested, having very little interest in horses. Nasty, bad-tempered animals, just like the people riding them, in his experience. Which gave him another thought. And quite a good one this time. 'Who do they think they're going to fight?' he asked.

'Does it matter?' Cwen indicated that the three of them would not make for a very long battle.

'Well, of course it does. Look at them.'

They all looked.

The leader now seemed relatively satisfied with his troop's turn out. All the horses were lined up side by side, the men on top had swords in hand and reins were at the ready. The leader turned his attention to the building in front of them and seemed to be waiting for something.

'They've obviously prepared for a major confrontation. It's as if they've come to this place specifically for quite a significant battle.'

This did give Wat and Cwen pause for thought. Despite Cwen's protestations, it was quite common for a single Norman to cause an awful lot of trouble on his own. Everyone knew that if you provoked a Norman sufficiently, another thirty would turn up within a day or so to make sure that you, your family, your village and probably several of the neighbours never provoked anyone again.

A dozen Normans were quite a force. Twelve professional soldiers on horseback could take most small towns unaided. It was only when the object to be defeated was a lord or a king that serious forces were required.

A Norman child on a dog could probably conquer Wat's workshop. And not a very healthy dog at that.

Wat slapped his hands to his thighs in anger and frustration. 'Don't say they've arranged to have a fight in my front yard.'

Hermitage didn't like to answer, as he couldn't immediately think of anything else these men would be good for.

'Why me?' Wat howled his protest. 'If they want to take

over the country and defeat all the local forces, why don't they do it in a field, like a proper army?'

Now Hermitage was lost. He looked to Cwen and Wat for some explanation.

Cwen sighed at the impracticality of monks, and of this one in particular. 'If some local lord has refused to submit to the new king, there's going to be a fight.'

Hermitage could follow that. It still seemed to be a very poor way to organise a country, but it was tradition.

'So,' Cwen went on. 'Said lord and king agree where and when they're going to sort it all out.'

Ah, thought Hermitage. So attacks could be organised and not surprises at all. How fascinating. 'But, why here?'

'Exactly.' Wat protested.

'No point in ruining the lord's manor,' Cwen explained. 'The king will want that.'

'But,' Hermitage held his finger up as some scintilla of information about battles wandered into his mind. 'Doesn't the lord stock up with provisions, raise his drawbridge and fight from behind his walls?'

'If he has any,' Cwen gave a short laugh. 'Castles are for the very rich. You don't send a dozen disorganised Normans to fight someone with a castle. No. This is most likely some petty landowner who is either mad or an idiot.'

'An idiot?' Hermitage raised an eyebrow.

'King William?' Cwen asked Hermitage to recall who they were talking about. 'The one who has just conquered the country and defeated Harold sends word that he'd like you to swear fealty, and you say no thank you? You'd better have a thousand Vikings at your back.'

This was a whole new world to Hermitage, and he hadn't really got the hang of the first one yet.

'Perhaps the local lord has changed his mind?' Hermitage suggested, looking out of the window again and seeing no sign of any opposition turning up for the Normans, who had clearly gone to a lot of trouble.

'Very sensible,' Wat said as they cast their eyes over the Norman force, which was starting to look a bit impatient.

Hermitage considered that as armed Norman warriors were bad, impatient armed Norman warriors were probably worse.

'Pah,' Cwen dismissed such defeatism.

'I thought you said they were either mad or stupid to fight in the first place,' Wat pointed out.

'At least they should see it through,' Cwen said. 'You can't put your defiance down when it gets difficult.'

'Die with honour, eh?' Wat said as if it was an invitation.

'Perhaps we should go and ask,' Hermitage interrupted what might become one of Wat and Cwen's loud and awkward arguments, or "discussions" as they called them.

'After you,' Cwen beckoned towards the stairs. 'I'm sure they won't stab a monk. Not straight away.'

They gathered and looked out of the window some more.

It was inevitable that they should be spotted really. You can't sit at your window staring at the soldiers in the garden without one of them noticing. It was too late to duck out of sight, so Hermitage just raised a timid and half-hearted hand. 'Hello,' he mouthed.

'Hello?' Cwen turned to Hermitage, aghast. 'Hello, indeed.'

'Maybe they'll realise they've come to the wrong place,' Hermitage suggested. 'If they're expecting this defiant lord and all they get is a monk, they may go away.'

'Normans don't do going away,' Wat said.

They chanced another look out of the window. Now that he had their attention, the leader raised his sword and pointed it at their vantage point.

'Well done, Hermitage,' Wat sighed.

They all raised their hands to acknowledge that they had only just noticed a force of armed men had appeared at the front door.

'You,' the Norman leader barked up at the window. 'Bring out your forces.'

Hermitage turned back to the others. 'Bring out our what?'

'Forces, Hermitage, forces,' Cwen said, sounding rather annoyed. 'When a force wants a battle they usually have another force to do it with?'

'We haven't got any forces.'

'We know that,' Wat said. 'Not sure they're quite so up to date.'

'Why do they think we've got forces?'

'Normans think everyone's got forces.' Cwen was grim. 'I suppose we're going to have to go out there.'

'Really?' Hermitage could see quite well from where he was.

'If we don't send out our forces they'll think we're insulting them,' Wat explained. 'And there are better people to insult than a dozen armed Norman horsemen. Come on. There's only one tactic that will work in a situation like this.'

'And that is?'

'Abject surrender.'

Hermitage was in a bit of a daze as he realised that he was walking down the stairs and towards the door, outside of which a band of mounted warriors was waiting for him.

He'd never been a force before.

'Aha,'   Wat said, in a loud, friendly greeting, holding his arms wide as if he could embrace his new best friends who had turned up on their horses.

'Who are you?' the leader barked.

'Wat the Weaver,' Wat announced, bowing low. 'Pleased to make your acquaintance.'

'You won't be,' the Norman grumbled with a nasty smile.

Cwen and Hermitage strode bravely forward. Hermitage stopped just behind Cwen.

'Wait a minute,' the Norman commanded. 'Is that a monk?' He pointed his sword at Hermitage.

'This monk?' Wat asked, turning and indicating Hermitage. 'Yes. This monk here is a monk.'

'Hm.' Perhaps the Norman had second thoughts about doing battle with a monk. Hermitage certainly hoped so.

'Right,' the man on the horse came to some sort of conclusion. 'Let's get on with it then. Where's the rest of you?'

'Rest of us?' Wat looked and sounded clueless. 'This is it.' He shrugged his apology.

'Three?' the armed man clearly thought this was either an insult or a joke.

'And one a monk,' Wat explained.

'We can't do battle with you lot.'

'Oh, that is a shame,' Wat sympathised.

'We were sent to do battle.' There was a definite complaining whine in the voice.

'You do look ready for it. Perhaps it's somewhere else? Can we give you directions?'

'This is the right place,' the man insisted, looking around from atop his beast.

'Not sure I can help,' Wat tried meek.

'This is really not good enough.' The man on the horse turned to his companions and through various noises and gestures indicated what the position was and how unsatisfactory the whole business was turning out to be. The grunts and sighs that were returned indicated that they shared his opinion.

'Do you know how far we've come?' the man asked in complaint.

'Er, no,' Wat confessed.

'A long way, I can tell you. And for this?' He took in Hermitage, Wat and Cwen with a sweeping and dismissive gesture. 'Isn't there anyone else you can go and get? Round up the village, something like that?'

'To come and do battle with you?' Wat made it sound as ridiculous as it was.

'That's right.' The Norman didn't think it was ridiculous at all.

'I think they're probably a bit busy at the moment. This time of day and all.' He turned and gave Hermitage and Cwen a look that said he thought these particular Normans were one shaft short of a quiver. 'Was it anyone in particular you were expecting?' he asked.

'A bit of decent opposition,' the horseman moaned. He dismounted his animal and wandered over towards the three of them in a desultory manner, his weapons clanking as he walked. 'What did you say you did?' he asked.

'Weaver,' Wat explained the name. 'Wat the Weaver.'

'Well, Wat the Weaver. Just think what it would be like if you travelled the length of the country to do some weaving and when you arrived, there wasn't any, what-do-you-call-it in your stupid language?'

'What do you call it?'

'You know.' The man made waving gestures with his arms and fiddly movements with his fingers that indicated nothing at all.

Wat shook his head with a blank expression.

'Sheep's covering.'

'Wool,' Wat suggested.

'That's the stuff. Think of that.'

'Sound awful,' Wat tried to look sombre.

'Too right. So we do battles. We're sent to do battle and there's no battle. What are we supposed to do?'

'Go home without killing anyone,' Cwen suggested, quite strongly.

'We could do that,' the man mused. 'But it doesn't look very good, you know.'

'Doesn't look very good?' Hermitage queried. Now that the man was on the ground he just seemed like an ordinary fellow. Still carrying more weapons than most villages possessed, but at least human.

'That's right. We can't go back and say there wasn't any battle. Not after we set off with such thunder. What will the others say? We'll have no tales of great fights, no wounds to display, none of us will be dead.'

Hermitage thought that sounded like a good thing, but then what did he know? He heard Cwen whisper in his ear. At least her hatred of the Normans was being tempered by plain common sense in the face of this many of them. 'We could kill one of them if it would help,' she hissed.

'You could say we ran away,' Hermitage offered, managing to ignore Cwen's outrageous offer.

'What?' the Norman seemed to think that was even worse.

'Yes. You could say that in the face of your overwhelming strength the enemy turned and ran.' He tried to make it sound as exciting as possible.

'Hm,' the man gave it some thought.

'Perhaps you shot several of them in the back while they were running,' Cwen suggested, brightly. 'Probably the women and children who couldn't run fast enough,' she added in a much quieter tone.

'There's nothing for you here anyway,' Wat pointed out, gesturing to his not very humble dwelling. 'It's only a weaver's workshop. Who sent you to have a battle here?'

'Le Pedvin.' The man said calmly.

Hermitage's insides stopped being calm straight away. The bits of him that were in charge of keeping his legs firm and solid were the first to leave. 'Le Pedvin,' he croaked, his breath having skipped off as well.

'That's right,' the man confirmed as if that were sufficient explanation.

Wat had a resigned and despondent look about him. 'Le Pedvin sent you,' he confirmed. 'William's right-hand man, who knows us well, too well, sent all of you to come and have a battle here. Right here.' He pointed out the space in front of his workshop, which was nothing like the size needed for any sort of battle.

'Yes.' The man was firm in his belief and his disappointment at what was on offer.

'You're sure he didn't just tell you to come and fetch the monk?'

Hermitage watched as a fleeting expression wandered onto the face of the Norman before being sent on its way. It was the sort of expression that said its owner may have just got something horribly wrong but has almost immediately worked out how he's going to get away with it.

'That's right,' the man said confidently. 'And he said not to let anyone get in our way.'

'I assume that means us,' Cwen said, who only really came half-way up the side of one of the horses. 'Did Le Pedvin actually say there would be a battle?' she asked, through narrowed eyes.

'Well,' the man drawled, obviously thinking how he could say yes when the answer was no. 'It was King William's instruction.'

'And did King William say there would be a battle?'

'King William doesn't give details like that,' the Norman scoffed at Cwen for not understanding the ways of the king. 'He just asked who would fetch him this troublesome monk.'

'Troublesome?' Hermitage was offended. He'd never been troublesome in his life.

'So, Le Pedvin gathers us and dispatches us to fetch the monk.'

'So,' Cwen retorted, folding her arms as she presented her conclusion. 'No one told you there would be a battle. No one told you to come prepared for a battle. No one even told that the monk would be any trouble at all, let alone that there would be a force resisting you.'

'Might have been more,' the man mumbled his protest.

'More monks, perhaps,' Wat offered.

The man was shaking his head slowly from side to side with a look of despairing sympathy. 'It's not a very good show is it?'

Wat looked at him askance. 'This is our fault?'

'Of course. You might have put up a decent bit of resistance, instead of giving in like this. It's typical, that's what it is.'

'Well, I do beg your pardon,' Wat laid it on thick. 'Deepest apologies for not throwing ourselves in front of the horses and being dead before you could say good morning.'

The Norman gave a great, heavy and growling sigh and turned back to his men. 'Bloody Saxons,' he said loud enough for everyone to hear.

'There could be a surprise attack on the way back,' one of his men sounded hopeful.

Ah, thought Hermitage. If that were the case he would be able to see what the difference was.

'Tell you what,' the Norman turned back to Hermitage, Wat and Cwen with a rather determined look on his face.

'What?' Cwen asked, very cautiously.

The Norman smiled a Norman smile: full of threat, built on a foundation of truly horrible thoughts. He gestured his men forward. 'You three can put up a bit of a fight before we carry you off.'

Get the rest of the pages from Thefunnybookcompany.com

Printed in Great Britain
by Amazon

68447985R00175